True Freedom: A Novel

How America came to fight Britain
for its independence

Michael Dean

Holland Park Press London

Published by Holland Park Press 2019

Copyright © Michael Dean 2019

First Edition

A CIP catalogue record for this book is
available from The British Library.

ISBN 978-1-907320-86-6

Cover designed by Reactive Graphics

Printed and bound by
CPI Group (UK) Ltd, Croydon CR0 4YY

www.hollandparkpress.co.uk

for Judith

True freedom is to share
All the chains our brothers wear
And with heart and hand to be
Earnest to make others free.
  James Russell Lowell, *Stanzas on Freedom*

Cruel is the strife of brothers
     Aristotle: Politics

Set in Boston and London over sixteen years, *True Freedom* is a panoramic account of how America came to fight Britain for its freedom in the eighteenth century.

The Boston scene is set through vignettes about the people who shaped its history. Thomas Hutchinson, sixth generation of Boston aristocracy, whose wealth is seemingly unassailable. Self-taught medical doctor Thomas Young, an idealist, meeting his hero Samuel Adams, who is determined to have his revolution. Their Sons of Liberty and Mohucks play a key role, all the time supported from London by the radical politician John Wilkes.

True Freedom is full of vivid period details; you can almost smell Parliament in London or hear the clerks scribbling away in the American Department. So too, in Boston, you can picture the meeting-place Faneuil Hall, experience the might of the British navy in the harbour, and feel the determination of the Boston people to defy Parliament in London.

Together they form facets of the main character: the Boston uprising. The facts are described but by focusing on personal relationships Michael Dean takes us right to the heart of identity and sovereignty.

The Seven Years War was fought between 1756 and 1763. But well before it ended, it was clear that England's coming victory over France would leave it with a much larger empire to govern. This meant more and higher administrative costs, but even more importantly, England was left with a huge debt from financing the war. Parliament would therefore require the American colonies to pay some of the costs of their administration and defence, for the first time in their history.

Chapter 1

Lieutenant Governor Thomas Hutchinson sat alone in his mansion on Garden Court Street, the loveliest dwelling in Boston. His restless pale blue eyes swept over Turkish carpets and painted hangings; over mouldings and gildings; over marble tables and St Domingo mahogany panelling with the arms of England in the recesses of swan-like arches.

There was a polite tap on the door which led from the Hall Chamber into the Great Chamber, where he sat. A footman in the Hutchinson blue-and-gold livery walked softly in, ushering a Negro slave runner, as if he were driving a sheep to market.

'A message for you, sir,' said the footman.

Hutchinson raised one eyebrow, a trick handed down to him from five generations of Bostonian aristocracy. 'From?'

'From the Assembly, sir.'

Hutchinson permitted himself a bleak smile. Sure enough, the note, when the Negro slave runner handed it over, confirmed that the petition to the Massachusetts Assembly had been received and would be discussed.

Hutchinson's smile widened. The petition was in the name of the Governor of Massachusetts, Hutchinson's superior, Thomas Pownall. It requested the Assembly to approve measures designed to reduce smuggling and so increase the tax revenue from traded goods.

'No reply,' Hutchinson said.

'Very good, sir.' The footman shepherded the Negro slave from the room, watching him closely as if he feared some unspecified crime.

Thomas Hutchinson re-read the note. 'That'll show you, you little popinjay,' he said aloud to the absent Governor. 'Now what will you do, I wonder?'

Like all his predecessors as Governor of Massachusetts, Thomas Pownall lived in the Province House on Milk Street. This place, selected by the early settlers for their governor to dwell in, lacked the grandeur of the Hutchinson mansion but it was pleasant enough, being a three-storey brick building set in finely timbered lawns.

Governor Thomas Pownall was that most gregarious of creatures, an underlyingly lonely man. No wife for Thomas Pownall, at least not yet. Not even a regular companion in his bed, much as he loved women. The two moth-eaten lions on the Pownall coat of arms, the Governor used to joke, represented himself and his brother rampant and pawing the air because they were looking for a mate.

But at this moment, as he gathered together his drawing materials in his chamber, the Governor soared above the torments of his flesh. His mind was roaming the realms of art.

His sketch of the Boston waterfront, as seen from the British garrison, out on its island at Castle William, showed promise, he told himself judiciously. He had caught both the grace and the power of the British men-of-war at anchor. It needed more work … But at the last minute he decided to improve his map of Boston instead.

A footman in red and green livery appeared. He had neither knocked at the door nor sought permission to enter. The footman carried a message.

The Governor took the message and said 'Wait, please' to the footman. The footman smiled. This may have been because the Governor was famously polite to the underlings. Or it may have been that the majority of people who encountered Thomas Pownall smiled at the sight of him.

His short, plump figure presented no threat. His artless grin aroused affection. He looked like the Lincoln Imp. This stone figure, grinning and gap-toothed, was mounted high on the east wall of Lincoln Cathedral, near the Pownall family home. It sat on a stone bench with one calf crossed over the other thigh. Whether by chance or out of impish imitation, Thomas Pownall habitually sat like that, too.

But as he read the message, the Governor's half-smile faded. Even the laughter lines round his eyes appeared to droop. Thomas Pownall knew very well he was seen as pleasant but trifling. He did not particularly mind that. Usually, the love he won from those who knew him outweighed the occasional lack of respect. But this ... THIS ...

Thomas Pownall just stopped himself from screwing the message into a ball and throwing it on the floor. He thought hard, while the footman waited, looking concerned. The message confirmed a motion before the Massachusetts Assembly. It was in the Governor's name but tabled by Lieutenant Governor Thomas Hutchinson. The motion was designed to reduce smuggling and increase revenue from customs duties.

Thomas Pownall had of course discussed this issue with the Lieutenant Governor, again and again. He had discussed it with everybody; it was vital. But Thomas Hutchinson putting it before the Assembly in the Governor's name was the most rampant mischief. Of course they would reject it. It would arouse the utmost irritation – even fury. And he, Governor Thomas Pownall, would look crass and clumsy for such an inept attempt at root-and-branch reform.

Lieutenant Governor Thomas Hutchinson wished to wreck Governor Pownall's policy once and for all. And he had been fiendishly clever about it. As he calmed, to a degree, and felt some of the colour come back into his face, Pownall could not help but admire Hutchinson's political skill – or low cunning. It was worthy of Machiavelli himself.

Thomas Pownall sighed. His only course of action, the only one Hutchinson had left him, was to get this wrecking motion withdrawn from the Assembly. Then Pownall could go on pressing for what was clearly best for Boston – proper payment of customs duties – in the subtle manner he had always employed, working with the grain.

But Hutchinson and his faction dominated the Assembly. The only way to get the motion withdrawn was to go on bended knee to the Lieutenant Governor. Oh, how Hutchinson would enjoy that!

Pownall addressed the footman, speaking absently, mind elsewhere. 'Make ready the landau and the greys.'

'Not the chaise?'

'No! Not the chaise.'

Should he have insisted the footman address him as sir, or as Governor? He did not know how to treat the servants and they knew it. They sensed it. A man carries his past like a sack on his back.

When he first arrived as Governor, some three years ago, the staff at the Province House assumed Pownall had been brought up in a house with footmen. And Thomas Pownall did not disabuse them. Nobody in Boston knew how far below the salt the Pownalls were. Thomas Pownall had hardly seen a footman, a servant or a secretary before he came to Boston.

His father, William, was a poor country squire and soldier who died young. With the family plunged into poverty by William's death, they lived in the shadow of the Poor House, forever listening out for the heavy tread of the bailiffs. His mother, Sara, had to rent out part of the house in humble Saltfleet, Lincolnshire. In the nick of time, the industrious Sara Pownall had wangled a connection to Lord North. Otherwise they would have starved.

While waiting for the carriage to be made ready, Thomas Pownall changed his clothes. He habitually dressed informally – a short frock coat, no ruffled shirt, no powdered wig, as often as not no sword. But not this time. Lieutenant Governor Thomas Hutchinson was about to be impressed by the full majesty of Governor Thomas Pownall.

He would wear the yellow silk waistcoat. Oh yes! Hutchinson would not know what it meant, but he, Thomas

Pownall, would. And that was all that mattered.

Thomas Pownall was shown into the Great Chamber, where Lieutenant Governor Hutchinson sat enthroned in a floral-pattern walnut chair.

'Governor Pownall,' drawled Hutchinson, with little enthusiasm.

He had heard the horses as they drove up to the house, guessing from their number that it must be Pownall. How vain to visit in the gubernatorial phaeton with the greys he was so proud of, rather than just take a one-horse chaise.

And why for heaven's sake was Pownall wearing that ridiculous waistcoat? Oh yes! Lincoln yellow. Pownall was a Yellerbelly, a Lincoln man.

Thomas Hutchinson was the most notable historian in the American colonies. He fondly pictured in his mind his magisterial *History of Massachusetts*, ten years in the writing, presently lying as a nearly completed manuscript on his desk in the library.

So he had naturally traced his own lineage back through generations of Hutchinsons until he reached William and Anne Hutchinson, who had made their way from Boston, Lincolnshire, to Boston, Massachusetts 125 years ago.

What piqued Hutchinson was the parvenu Pownall not realising that he, Hutchinson, would understand the reference implied in the yellow waistcoat. You underestimate Thomas Hutchinson at your peril, little man, thought Hutchinson.

Hutchinson respected Pownall as a governor, he admitted to himself grudgingly. One simply could not respect him as a man. He was not serious.

The main importance of Governor Pownall was his younger brother, John. John Pownall was an undersecretary at the American Department in London. He was the most influential authority on the American colonies in the government, deferred to on American matters even by his superiors. Hutchinson made sure that whatever

Governor Pownall reported back to John Pownall was exactly what Hutchinson wanted him to know.

There was a pause, a heavy silence between the two of them. Hutchinson noted that the Governor was standing with his tricorn hat facing inwards, not outwards. No gentleman would do that. 'No *ton*,' Hutchinson thought to himself. 'No breeding.'

'Pray sit down, sir,' Hutchinson drawled, but with the force of a command.

Governor Pownall hastened to sit down, crossing one plump stockinged calf high over the other thigh. Hutchinson gave a patrician wince of disdain.

It was as if nature itself had illustrated the difference in social standing between the two men: the aristocratic Hutchinson, tall, gracious of form with fine aquiline features; then the man of the middling sort, Thomas Pownall, like a plump little robin but with a yellow, not a red, breast.

Pownall knew very well what Hutchinson thought of him. He touched his Yellerbelly waistcoat, defiantly. 'I'm as pleased as a dog wi' two tails,' he thought to himself in Lincolnshire dialect. 'You won't get me!'

Pownall broached the subject which had brought him here. 'Mr Hutchinson, I understand you have put a measure before the Assembly, in my name, seeking to reduce smuggling and increase tax revenue.'

'That is your policy, is it not? Those are your views?'

Pownall fought down a flash of anger. 'As you know very well, those are my views but the route to seeing those views carried through into policy does not lie in the Assembly, where, as you also know perfectly well, they have absolutely no chance of success.'

'That remains to be seen.'

'No, it does not,' Thomas Pownall ground out through clenched teeth. 'Lieutenant Governor Hutchinson, your co-operation with the government's policy of achieving customs payments by gradual persuasion has been noted.

18

Should you depart from that policy, such a departure will also be noted.'

The patrician Hutchinson eyebrow went up. 'I see.'

Thomas Pownall saw John's sardonic face before him. 'I'll tell my brother of you,' he heard John say, in his mocking way. And of course that was exactly what Thomas was saying.

And it worked. Even the tacit invocation of John Pownall's name was enough.

'Leave it with me,' Hutchinson said. 'The measure will be withdrawn from the Assembly. I shall explain that I misunderstood the Governor's intentions. Please accept my apologies for the misjudgement, Governor Pownall.'

The two men shook hands. 'Thank you, Mr Hutchinson. That is good of you.' Pownall meant it. He spoke softly now – this was important. It was vital to Boston's future. 'The war is as good as won, you know? After Quebec there is no doubt. We will soon drive out the French and the Indian tribes that backed them.'

'Yes.'

'Parliament is going to pursue the colonies, very much including the American colonies, for payments in the form of taxation.'

Hutchinson waved a languid, blue silk-sheathed arm, but respectful now, if not actually humble. 'You know the situation in London far better than I. Is that the prevailing view?'

'Yes. We must *persuade* the merchants of Massachusetts to pay more – pay something, for God's sake – in revenue. If we can *persuade* the biggest merchants, Rowe and above all John Hancock, the others will follow. In this way we shall mollify Parliament and blunt the heaviest of its demands regarding taxation, even before they fall on us.'

'And we persuade Mr Hancock to pay his dues how, exactly?'

'I have no idea.'

'Neither have I.'

With that, Thomas Pownall returned to the Province House to find a letter awaiting him from London. The letter bore the stamp and crest of Lord Hillsborough, whose many responsibilities included the headship of the American Department, though his offices were in the Board of Trade.

The letter was characteristically harsh, even brutal. It informed Thomas Pownall that he had been recalled from his post as Governor of Massachusetts. Thomas Pownall, it seemed, had become too close to the citizens, merchants and institutions of Boston.

Thomas read with growing dread and disbelief that he had 'gone native'. He even repeated the phrase out loud, white in the face with shock. The phrase was not of itself unusual – although it was unusual in a formal letter, perhaps. It was more often used of East India Company employees who had – in another colonial phrase – been out in the Indian sun too long and forgotten their responsibilities to home.

'Gone native.' Thomas said it again, out loud. 'Gone native'; John accused him of that in letter after letter. It was one of John's set phrases. John – being John – wanted a harder line taken with Boston than Thomas was prepared to agree to.

John, Thomas's own younger brother, was behind this terrible blow to his life and work. Thomas was sure of it.

CHAPTER 2

Boston's farewell to its beloved Governor was to be at the British Coffee House. Belying its cosy name, this was a huge granite slab of a place on State Street. For this special occasion, four of the trestle tables had been placed end to end facing all the others, as a 'top table'. The cream of Boston society, about 300 of them, sat on benches in no particular order at the remaining twenty or so trestle tables.

Thomas was determined to travel to his farewell dinner in the landau, pulled by the six greys. It would be the very last time he could avail himself of this, his one luxury, his one vanity.

A roar from the assembled citizenry greeted him as he made his typically diffident entrance, dressed in his usual modest garb. To his amazement, his hand was taken by a young girl of around ten years of age, dressed in her very best green satin party dress with red slippers and a red bow in her hair. This was Peggy Hutchinson, Lieutenant Governor Thomas Hutchinson's adored daughter.

Since his wife had died in childbirth, Thomas Hutchinson had doted on Peggy, pouring all his love into her. Tears came to Pownall's eyes that Hutchinson had honoured his old adversary, for such Pownall was, by allocating his daughter to lead him to the place of honour in the middle of the top table.

A band struck up the 'Yankee Doodle' song. The celebrants stood at their tables and cheered and stamped. Thomas solemnly thanked little Peggy for seeing him safely to his seat. The blushing, thrilled child rejoined her father, who was standing alone at the back of the room, and took his hand. She was to be allowed to stay for the entire ceremony, or 'party' as her daddy called it. She was in a state of bliss and as he beamed down at her, Hutchinson's heart soared to see it.

The tributes to the departing Governor were to be led by the merchant, John Hancock. Hancock remained as much a paradox to Thomas Pownall as he was when he first met him, three years ago. John Hancock could be almost puppyish in his eagerness to please; but at other times he could be stubborn. Some put these vacillations down to his troubled childhood, when he had been confined to bed for years with critical fevers. This had left him strange, as an adult – unstable, unknowable.

Hancock was the richest man in Massachusetts, let alone Boston. Some said a thousand Boston families depended on him for their daily bread. His fleet of ships was huge; he owned more wharf space than the next two biggest merchants in Boston combined and more shops than the next three. But he had inherited most of his money from his uncle, not earned it. In Boston they respected earned money more.

The paradoxes went on. On the one hand, he was generous with his money, especially for public projects and celebrations for the people of Boston. On the other, he was notorious for not paying bills on time and sometimes not at all. Some of the other merchants, John Rowe especially, detested him for this.

Hancock earned respect, sometimes grudging, as a dashing, almost reckless trader who travelled with his cargoes more than any other merchant. But the corners he cut over payments, dues and other matters could make life difficult for other traders, especially the small traders and shopkeepers. There was a rumour that two of the vessels which sank at Hancock's Wharf in a recent storm had been holed deliberately, for the insurance money. Nobody would have been surprised.

As a man, Hancock cut an imposing figure, except when he was hobbling, bent over with a gout attack. He stood nearly six feet tall, lean, with blond hair and a jauntily pointy nose and chin. At the moment, he was wearing a scarlet, richly embroidered coat with ruffles of the finest linen – and this was his day-to-day dress, nothing special or fancy.

But there remained something of the provincial about him, even of the country bumpkin, despite being born in Braintree, just thirteen miles south of Boston. There was nothing of Lieutenant Governor Hutchinson's natural aristocracy in his bearing, demeanour or nature. It was as if Boston, the big city, was too grand for him, not he for it, the impression Hutchinson sometimes gave.

As ever, Hancock was flanked by his factotum and shadow, George Hayley, who travelled with all Hancock's cargoes, arranging everything. Hayley's wife, Anne, sat next to him. Both George and Anne had listened to John Hancock rehearsing his speech for hours, up at his luxurious house atop Beacon Hill. They had both criticised where they thought criticism was warranted – Hancock did not welcome sycophants.

Hancock addressed the packed room.

'I will begin with a tribute to the work of our Governor, Thomas Pownall, in the recent fire which ravaged our city.' That got an expectant buzz of approval, all faces tilted upward to John Hancock.

'As we all know,' Hancock went on, 'this latest terrible affliction of fire was started by an evil north-west wind sent by the devil himself. It quickly demolished over a hundred homes and the Quaker Meeting House on Congress Street, as well as warehouses, business, shops and wharves, all the way to Fort Hill, threatening Long Wharf itself.'

Some of the shareholders in Long Wharf, the vital artery of Boston's trade, nodded solemnly. All of them were sitting at the top table.

'It was Governor Pownall personally who ordered the factories and the wharves doused with water *before* the flames reached them, which I have no doubt is what saved Long Wharf from destruction.'

There was a murmur of approval. Hancock waited for silence. 'And after the fire? What did Governor Pownall do in this, Boston's hour of greatest need? Let me remind you folks. He opened his office as a centre of relief work for the needy. He worked there, tending the injured and homeless with his own hands, sleeves rolled up. THAT is our Governor. A man to be proud of!'

There was a roar of cheering and applause. Tears sprang to Pownall's eyes, two of them rolled down his chubby cheeks. He mouthed 'Thank you' at the multitude.

Thomas Hutchinson joined in the applause sincerely enough, letting go Peggy's hand to do so, as they stood unobtrusively at the back of the room. But he was wryly aware of the disparity in recognition for Pownall's work and his own. Thomas Hutchinson had ordered and personally paid for the Newsham Engine, the firefighting device which had saved dozens, even hundreds of lives on the day of the Great Fire.

Not only that: as the fire started, Hutchinson had run to the gunpowder store, the Battery, in the centre of town, seized the barrels nearest the flames, run with them one by one to the harbour and dumped them in the water. It was an amazing feat of physical strength and raw bravery for which he had never received a word of acknowledgement, let alone thanks. Not that he sought it. After the fire, he had the munitions store moved out of the centre of town, to Concord, twenty miles away.

Hancock had hit his stride. 'I wonder, did Governor Pownall think when he was on his way to us from Lincolnshire that he would have to deal with an invasion of giant bears?'

Everybody bellowed with laughter, Pownall included. He drained yet another tankard of beer, whereupon it was refilled as miraculously as in a child's fairy story.

Hancock did not elaborate on the bears; he did not have to. A gang of giant brown bears had terrified Boston for weeks. They were starving, but the Bostonians were too hungry themselves to have enough food over to feed bears. In the end, the bears had been beaten by the well-honed

24

organisation the colonists had bred into themselves since the first settlers fought off the first Indians. Captain John Parker and his militia, armed with muskets, had ambushed enough of them for the others to take the hint.

'Governor, you have learned our ways,' Hancock continued. 'You know more about navigation than I do.'

'Not difficult,' George Hayley called out.

Roar of laughter. Nobody would have guessed they had rehearsed that, too.

Then John Hancock spoke to Pownall directly. 'Thomas, you have earned our gratitude and respect by your kindest care toward us. You have protected us from the army embargoing our ships and shielded us from the wickedness of naval impress.'

They fell silent at that. Many in the room had had loved ones seized by the British navy and never seen them again. Some entire crews of fishing smacks had been overpowered by British men-of-war and taken nobody knew where.

'Yes,' Hancock said into the silence. 'It is a serious subject. But I make no apology for mentioning our oppressors tonight. And here is another serious subject for you.' There was total silence in the room. 'Four days after this man arrived, ladies and gentlemen, just four days into his governorship, the French and Indians attacked at Lake Champlain and Castle William Henry. Our new Governor called out the militia and wanted to lead the troops himself.'

Hutchinson smothered a snort of derision, but the entire room stood and applauded. Pownall was crying. Hancock went on, shouting now, furious that the wicked British had removed their one good man from among them.

'Thomas Pownall learned Indian languages,' Hancock yelled. 'He frequently visited frontier areas. And as we all know, he as good as built Fort Pownall on Cape Jellison to stop the attacks on us. As good as built it with his own hands and his own leadership.' That got a further roar of applause, which Hancock silenced with a raised hand, as the listeners sat down. 'And so, Governor, we have a little gift for you.'

Hancock remained standing, but John Rowe, further along the table, got to his feet. From under the table, the merchant took a framed drawing and walked round the top table, to present it to Thomas Pownall.

'Thomas,' said John Rowe. 'Thomas, my dear friend, as I am proud to call you, this drawing is for you.'

He handed it over. The drawing was by the painter Samuel Gore, sitting at a nearby table. It showed a front elevation of Fort Pownall, a blockhouse with two chimneys and a roof tower, surrounded by a strong stockade.

As Thomas Pownall clutched his drawing, John Rowe embraced him. 'Thomas, I shall miss the fishing with the best and truest companion I ever had. May God go with you, all the days of your life.'

John Rowe returned to his seat as they drank yet another toast to the departing Governor.

John Hancock waved for quiet to indicate he was not yet finished. 'We all know the odds,' Hancock said softly, to a newly hushed room. 'Even now, the latest battle, eleven thousand French Canadians and Indians faced by twenty-seven hundred of our boys, led by own brave Captain John Parker.'

All eyes turned to Parker, who stood and took a brief bow. He was working day and night, training and drilling the Boston militia on the Common and elsewhere, so they could one day fight the British.

'And now the war is as good as won,' Hancock went on, 'we must not forget the achievements that won it. Like Governor Pownall building a barracks for the soldiers, to solve the quartering problem.' Hutchinson, whose influence in the Assembly had been vital to getting the barracks built, resignedly joined in the applause.

'The Governor instigated food depots and money for Boston men returning from their time in the British army, who otherwise might have starved.'

Hutchinson shut his eyes for a second. Pownall, with

his warm heart, had indeed had the original idea. But Hutchinson, a far better administrator, had been 100 per cent responsible for the implementation. He had worked on the scheme for hours every day over two years.

'Governor Pownall, you leave us with peace coming to Boston. A peace hard won, by defeating the French and making terms with the Indians. A peace won by winning the war, in which you played a great and courageous part. And so our final gift to you tonight, Thomas, is this. And I call on Peggy Hutchinson to present it.'

The child walked confidently to the front and recited what she had learned: 'Governor Pownall,' she sang out in a clear, high, bell-like voice. 'On behalf of the people of Boston I wish to present you with this certificate, which makes you a Freeman of the City of Boston for all your life.'

Thomas Pownall stood. 'Boston's salt water runs in my veins and it always will,' said the Governor.

Then he again burst into tears, before he was carried shoulder-high from the room and back to his waiting carriage.

CHAPTER 3

The long-distance stagecoach came to a halt in Brattle Square. Thomas Young eased his massive frame out with some difficulty. He stood unsteadily, wobbly from the journey all the way from Albany, New York, with the wind whipping through his clothes.

He wore a black frock coat, black worsted breeches and a white muslin shirt, every stitch of it lovingly crafted by his wife, Mary. He carried a cane with a ball on the top filled with vinegar, such as doctors carry. This had originally belonged to Dr John Kitterman. Mary had insisted he take it with him: 'So you look the part, Thomas. Look like a doctor, behave like a doctor and people will see you as a doctor.'

Over a solitary drink in Wilde's Tavern, just across Brattle Square from where the post-chaise pulled up, Thomas Young reviewed the wild events that had driven him to Boston. He thought of Dr John Kitterman, floating ethereally above him like a newly dead soul, still attached to someone else's body by a cord.

Dr Kitterman had been fifteen years older than Thomas Young. At Young's earnest request, he taught his acolyte everything he knew about medicine, back in Albany. The doctor took the disciple with him on visits to patients. He let him try his hand at bleeding, blistering, cupping. The patients didn't mind, Young was good at it.

Dr Kitterman gave him books to read, especially *A Short Discourse Concerning Pestilential Contagion, and the Methods to be Used to Prevent It* by the mighty Richard Mead. But he also gave him Locke's *Treatises of Civil Government*, telling him Chapter 16 contained everything a revolutionary could possibly need.

Young started the deep study of the medicinal properties of flowers and herbs on his own. He was soon telling Kitterman about it, things the doctor didn't know.

He also read every word John Locke had ever written. And Rousseau. Again, the pupil quickly outstripped his tutor in philosophical thought.

Being the man he was, Thomas Young was looking for an Answer from the books – an Answer as big as he was. And not only an Answer, there had to be a Solution. A Solution to Everything. This Solution had to encompass both the human body and the body politic, because the body politic was nothing more than the aggregate of human bodies.

The solution to a poison in the body was purgation. The solution to the British occupation of the American colonies was also purgation. The poison must leave the body. The British must leave America.

John Kitterman was a Bostonian himself. He had come to New York, to the Albany area, to woo and then marry a local girl. New York was patriot territory, and they wanted an end to British rule. But it had nothing on Boston, in that respect. Boston was to patriotism what Bethlehem was to Christianity, as Young himself put it, in a typically blasphemous analogy. Not that Kitterman minded, far from it. Kitterman was a patriot in his blood and bones and paid only lip-service to religion.

At this point, Young's ever-present hero-worship kicked in again. Kitterman had known the patriot leader, Samuel Adams, before he left Boston. He knew him well. Young, however, knew Adams only by reputation and was mightily impressed that Kitterman had known this biblical figure; had conversed with him, broken bread with him, read the scripture of his articles. And now it appeared that Kitterman had kept these articles, sent by mail from the *Boston Gazette*, written under the name of 'Junius' by Samuel Adams.

Young took the articles home, hugging them to his bosom. Excitedly, he read them aloud to Mary, who was equally exalted by them and needed no second bidding to become a disciple too, a follower in step with her husband.

Samuel Adams's articles illuminated the true way, setting out the path to a better life free of the colonial master.

Mary and Thomas Young, revelling in their new calling, determined to go to Boston and be part of the great work of revolution. Dr Kitterman happily wrote a letter of introduction to Samuel Adams.

The move to Boston with Mary and the children was to have taken place next spring, when enough money was scraped together. But then a series of explosions occurred in their lives.

First, John Kitterman died. He caught smallpox from a patient who had not had the inoculation and in days he was gone. He had time to make a will, leaving his medicines and medical equipment, his doctor's cane and all his books to Thomas Young.

Then, on the day of Kitterman's funeral, while he and Mary were standing over the freshly dug earth of the doctor's grave, came word that the sheriff had a warrant for Young's arrest for blasphemy.

'Oh, you goddamn fool,' Mary had said. As Mary knew, Thomas Young had never been too partial to the illogicality of divine revelation. This had led him into a heated tavern discussion with half the luminaries of Albany, during which he said that Jesus Christ, the main exponent of divine revelation, was a knave and a fool.

This blurted-out statement, and perhaps the reaction to it, shocked even Young into some semblance of sense. At Mary's behest, he wrote a renunciation of what he had said. But it was not enough. They were going to hang him. Young had gathered his possessions and what little money they had and took the first post-chaise out of Albany, to Boston.

A few days after his arrival, with the wild Irish blood of his ancestors pulsing in his head, Thomas Young strode through the slush and mud to Samuel Adams's house on Purchase Street. He was expected. A splintering wooden door was pulled open quickly at Young's knuckle-rapped knock.

'Don't tell me, you must be Dr Young?' The speaker had a thin voice with a strong, reedy Boston accent.

'That I am, sir.' Thomas offered a polite bow.

'I'm Sam Adams.'

Samuel Adams was well below medium height, with a prominent belly, parchment-pallor skin and grey hair. Young noticed his stubby arms, which were so short they were near deformed. The skin and the arms together, and even the belly, gave him a reptilian aspect, like a lizard. An old and tired lizard; a basking, feeding lizard.

Adams sneezed, then extended a hand in welcome. The hand shook. Young looked at it with interest. Palsy! Not a lot to be done about that.

Young grasped the shaking hand. 'I'm honoured to meet you, sir.'

'And I'm intrigued to meet you.'

This was nearer the truth than Young knew. In Kitterman's letter of introduction, he had written that Young was a self-taught genius, a force of nature. He had taught himself Latin and Greek to read the classics and French to read Rousseau. He had taught himself the violin and the fife. And he was the most passionate revolutionary Kitterman had ever met.

'Where have you come from today, Dr Young?' Adams said, as he led the way up some broken wooden stairs. As they climbed, Young caught glimpses of an orchard through a filthy window, presumably an orchard belonging to Adams, then distant hills.

'I managed to rent a house on Wing's Lane, sir. I was lucky to find it so quickly. It will be big enough for my entire family when they arrive. And please call me Thomas. Only my patients call me Dr Young.'

'Thomas it is then,' Adams said, as he opened a door at the top of the stairs. 'And this is my observatory,' he added, waving a shaking hand round it. 'I can see the stars from here. That's my hobby, astronomy. Do you have a hobby, Thomas?'

'Now, that's a good question, sir. As I have to think about it, I guess I don't. Unless seeking the truth is a hobby. More a way of life ...'

Samuel Adams's whole body shook with what Young thought was unaccustomed laughter. 'Oh, you and I are going to get on just fine!'

They sat down in a couple of battered armchairs. Adams proffered no refreshment. That pleased Young, who disliked such fripperies and just wanted to get down to the business of revolution.

'You knew John Kitterman, I hear,' Adams said. 'Such a loss. What did he tell you about me?'

'That you were a pillar of the patriot struggle against the British, sir. He told me you correspond with John Wilkes, freedom's champion, in England.'

Adams smiled, increasing the lizard-like effect. 'That I do, Thomas. That I do. Did you know John Wilkes is in Parliament now? The Member for Aylesbury?'

'I had heard tell of that, yes, sir.'

'And do you know the essence of Wilkes's credo?'

Young shook his head. 'No ...'

He was the devoted supplicant again, hardly breathing, eyes wide, awaiting enlightenment.

'John Wilkes said, "My only patron is the PUBLIC, to which I will ever make my appeal and hold it sacred. *Provoco ad populum*, like an old Roman." It means ...'

'It means "I appeal to the people". It's from Livy. It's a direct appeal to the people over the heads of the Senate or any other institution. It makes public opinion supreme.'

'Yes, indeed!'

'Have you ever met him?'

'No, I haven't. But I know John Hancock's agent, George Hayley, well, along with his wife, Anne. Anne Hayley is John Wilkes's sister. She and George have a house in Boston as well as one in London. So I hope to meet Mr Wilkes himself one day. I hope he will come to Boston, perhaps sailing here on one of John Hancock's trading ships.'

There was a moment's silence between them. Adams was thinking, calculating rapidly. He knew himself to be a polemicist of vast power – in newspaper articles. He could not carry this gift over into speaking. He was an average public speaker, at best, and not that much better even in the small group caucuses so suited to his wiles.

The minute Thomas Young opened his mouth, speaking out of that imposing frame, Adams knew he had found a man who could inspire the multitude and lead a tumult.

'Thomas, you have the appearance of one promising great and spectacular deeds,' Adams said.

Young inclined his head in a mock bow. 'Thank you for the compliment.'

'I have something of the greatest secrecy to show you. Can I count on your discretion?'

'Totally.'

'Then let's go, Thomas. Let's go.'

CHAPTER 4

Until now, Thomas Young had walked everywhere in Boston, enjoying every minute of it. You could walk from the tip of the North End to the tip of the South End in under an hour. But to Young's surprise, Samuel Adams drove them in his one-horse chaise, wearing a red cloak, with a filthy grey tie-wig balanced on his head. And he drove like the devil after a rich sinner, flicking his whip incessantly at the poor spavined horse, yelling at passers-by to get out of the way.

This behaviour intrigued Thomas Young. The way a man drove his carriage shone a light on the state of his soul, Young believed. If that was right, the state of Samuel Adams's soul, beneath the placid basking-lizard exterior, was wild and turbulent. Just like his own.

Their first stop was Thomas Hutchinson's mansion on Garden Court Street. They stopped in sight of it. Adams was silent for a while, a deep silence. Young knew better than to break his reverie. Then Samuel Adams spoke in a dry, cracked voice. 'That is the home of the most evil man on God's earth,' he said, flatly.

Thomas Young thought it politic to maintain his silence. He gave the faintest inclination of his head, to show he had heard.

Adams spoke on in the same flat monotone, not looking at Young, staring straight ahead. 'Between them, a group of families I call "the Medici" control the Assembly, the judiciary and all aspects of trade in this town.'

'I see.'

'When you deal with Hutchinson, you do not get only the Hutchinsons. You get all the other Boston clans: you get the Olivers, the Clarkes, the Copleys. All intermarried, interrelated, trading with each other on favourable terms. Offend one, you offend them all. Hutchinson is the head, people call him Sir Thomas Graspall, but they are all arms of the same Graspall octopus, which has its tentacles everywhere, strangling Boston.'

There was silence for a while in the tiny chaise. When Adams spoke again he unburdened his soul in a way he had never done in his life before. He did it just that once and neither he nor Thomas Young ever referred to it again.

The creation of Samuel Adams started back in his father's time. The father, known to everybody in Boston as Deacon Adams, loomed large in young Samuel's life.

At a time of hardship, a near-permanent condition in Boston, the Deacon hit on the idea of a Land Bank. The Land Bank's assets, so-called, were pie-in-the-sky dreams of sales of land in the west. It had no government backing but still issued its own money. With the support of the artisan class it became a kind of Bank of the People.

The rich merchants felt threatened by the Land Bank. The merchants had as currency Bills of Exchange based on the pound sterling in London. The Land Bank's soft currency challenged that.

Enter the young Thomas Hutchinson. Hutchinson's opposition to the Land Bank was social as much as economic. The needy part of Boston favoured the scheme – the artisan class: the shipyard workers, cordwainers, coopers and tavern keepers. Thomas Hutchinson sniffed at them. He and a cousin came up with a scheme that was an alternative to the currency issued by the Land Bank. It was to use money from various Medici businesses to guarantee the colony's existing currency, so boosting the value of all their Bills of Exchange.

Thomas Hutchinson used his contacts to push this scheme through the Assembly, and it was carried. The Land Bank folded as a direct result. Deacon Adams was ruined. Thomas Hutchinson had ruined him.

The young impressionable boy, Samuel Adams, came upon the Deacon, a broken man, sobbing on the bosom of his wife like a baby. It was an image he never forgot, etched in acid for ever in his heart. As he sobbed, the Deacon ground out the single word 'Hutchinson'.

Worse was to follow; the nightmare became a way of life. The Deacon had assumed, on no evidence, that he could be held liable only for his initial investment in the Land Bank. This turned out to be wrong. Bank directors could be held personally responsible for all debts incurred by their banks, without limit.

So for the next twenty years the Deacon and his family lived with the threat of their home on Purchase Street being seized and the house and every single item of their possessions sold to pay off the debt. Public notices would appear, many times, in the Boston newspapers announcing that the Land Bank Commissioners intended to sell the Adams' house from under them. Sheriff Stephen Greenleaf would appear at the door with an official notification.

With the Deacon now a husk of a man, it fell to his only son to try to save the family from destitution. Young Samuel took to threatening Sheriff Stephen Greenleaf, until he realised the Sheriff, like most of the artisan class, was actually on his side.

He then put advertisements in friendly newspapers warning off possible purchasers of the family home. The newspaper owners let him place the advertisements for nothing – feeling was running high against Hutchinson and for Adams in Boston.

But even so, again and again, young Samuel had to attend a Board of Arbitration for Bankruptcy hearing, to plead for their judgment, knowing the consequences if he failed: homelessness. Penury. Destitution. Some of these hearings were held at the British Coffee House, which was owned by the Medici. So it was enemy territory, where he had to appear as a supplicant, pleading for the shirt on his back.

This loss of all dignity gave Samuel Adams the curse of sleeplessness for the rest of his life. He slept two or three hours a night, sometimes less. His habit of walking the deserted streets of Boston in the small hours of the morning with his red cloak wrapped around him started at this time. Thomas Hutchinson was the spectre on those early morning walks and appeared as a demon haunting his dreams in what little sleep he ever had.

Incredibly, Samuel Adams single-handedly saved the family from bankruptcy and destitution, but not from poverty: his attempt to take over and run the family malt business was a disaster. Adams was a clever man, a shrewd man, an intelligent man, but he had limitations as great as his strengths. One of these was number blindness – he could hardly add up. This made his failure at business inevitable, although it did not inhibit him, in later life, from wangling a job as a tax-gatherer, a *publicanus*, for the access it gave him to all classes of society. The people of Boston called him Sam the Publican after that, out of fellow feeling and some affection.

Just before the Land Bank failure, Samuel Adams had enrolled as a student at Harvard, as did all the young intelligentsia of Boston, Harvard being just a short horse-ride away.

When the Land Bank crash came, Adams stayed on at Harvard but to make enough money to live on, he had to wait at tables at the refectory, serving his fellow students their food and drink. As luck would have it, these fellow students included Thomas Hutchinson, Andrew and Peter Oliver, Richard Clarke and other aristocratic young bloods, scions of the Medici.

The Medici's belief in their superiority over Samuel Adams was set hard. They knew Adams was on his uppers. They saw him as a funny-looking fellow, like a comic little lizard with a pointed snout and short stubby arms. He became the butt of their mockery; at the sharp end of their torment.

The Hutchinson group of aristocrats did not eat in the

main refectory; they had a panelled side-room permanently reserved for their sole use. At first, they would merely jeer at their waiter, Samuel Adams, telling him to get a move on, hurry up, quicky-quicky little man. There was sometimes a kick up his backside, to great merriment.

But as time went on they hit on more sophisticated forms of torment: they would swear blind they had not ordered the food Adams brought them, even though they had. They insisted Adams brought them the fictional original order.

After a while, with this happening nearly every day, Samuel Adams was summoned to the Bursar and threatened with being charged for the wrongly ordered meals if he made any more mistakes. Adams went to Hutchinson, pleading with him to stop the torment or he would lose this humble job, incur even more debts, maybe even lose his family house.

He chose the wrong time to ask. Young Hutchinson was drunk on Madeira and the adulation of his cronies. He made Adams beg. He made him kneel before them all and beg. Then they stripped him and made him beg some more.

CHAPTER 5

After his confession to Dr Young, Samuel Adams whipped the chaise away from Thomas Hutchinson's house, his face frozen stiff. Neither of them said a word.

When they arrived at Dock Square, Young guessed they were going to Faneuil Hall. He felt a twinge of disappointment, assuming Faneuil Hall meant some sort of meeting. He did not want to share Samuel Adams with anybody, right now. The realisation embarrassed him, even shocked him a little.

Adams jumped out of the chaise, his ripped brown boots squelching in the mud and slush. He sneezed and wiped his nose on his sleeve. Young followed. He had brought no cloak or hat with him from Albany, so he shivered in the knife-edge Boston November cold.

He had seen Faneuil Hall before, on his first perambulations round Boston. It was a solid block structure broken by big windows set into the façade on the first storey and smaller ones on the second storey. It had a tower atop the roof, with a grasshopper weather-vane.

Adams saw the direction of his gaze.

'The grasshopper is on the crest of the Faneuil family,' he said, laconically. 'But it suits us patriots just fine. You ever tried to step on a grasshopper?'

Young laughed.

'The Faneuils are a Huguenot family,' Adams continued. 'French. We like that. We like the French.'

Young nodded, taking on Adams's attitudes, willingly becoming a Boston patriot.

Adams sniffed. 'Benjamin Faneuil runs it all now. Old Peter Faneuil who built this place is long dead.'

As he spoke, Adams selected a large key from the belt round his waist and unlocked the door. Young followed his mentor into Faneuil Hall. The word 'mentor' came into his head as he walked; it made him smile. The original Mentor

39

had been a friend of Odysseus the voyager, his advisor and guide. Adams would be this voyager's mentor, not against the Trojans but against the British.

And like Odysseus and Mentor they would eventually prevail.

Adams was walking briskly, stubby flippers of arms swinging, along the side of the huge hall with chairs set out in rows. Empty now. He headed up a wooden staircase with Young in his wake. Up three flights of stairs they went, finally entering an attic.

'Here we are,' Adams said. 'Look at this.'

He pulled aside a large ornate mahogany fire-screen. Behind it, not especially well concealed, were about twenty muskets, some powder, a few spare ramrods and some ball.

'There,' Adams said, in the manner of a conjuror on the London stage. 'What do you think of that?'

Young cleared his throat. 'It's … a start, I guess. So … You add to these from time to time, no doubt. I … er …'

Young stopped. Adams had his hands on his hips, pushing out his round belly, bunching up his red cloak. He was shaking from head to foot with laughter.

'I'm sorry, Thomas,' he finally said, getting a grip on his mirth, wiping his nose on his forearm. 'I couldn't resist it. Those muskets are for the British to find, if we are betrayed. Only a couple of them work and the powder is old and dry.'

Young did not mind the laughter. He felt relief that his hopes were not so soon to be shattered. But he was bewildered. Again. This sorcerer Samuel Adams seemed privy to worlds of magic beyond his ken.

'Betrayed?' Young said. 'Who would …?'

'Oh, the British have spies among the patriots. There are always those ready to take the thirty pieces of silver. We have allies over there, of course, but they tend to be more open and honest.'

'I see.' Young did not often feel stupid. He felt stupid now.

'Come with me,' Adams said, gently.

He led Young back down the stairs to the main hall, then further down by another flight of stairs. Down and down.

The air in the cavernous cellar was surprisingly fresh. Huge wheels of Cheshire and Gloucester cheese leaned against the walls. Large trestle tables and spare chairs were lined up down the middle.

Samuel Adams, with the air of a man carrying out a much-practised action, rolled aside two of the massive cheeses. Then he pulled aside two already loosened stones. A small ante-chamber was revealed. It was stacked with muskets. There were also barrels of powder, ramrods and wooden chests full of lead ball.

Young whistled, pleased to be impressed. 'How many …?'

'About four hundred muskets. Gathered throughout the war.'

'But how? Don't the British know they're gone?'

'Nope. They're so arrogant it does not occur to them that we might not do as we are told.'

'So the militia men …?'

'At the end of the hundred days of service in the British army, our boys simply keep their musket. Or they say it is broken. We encourage our people to enlist under false names, so if the British want their Brown Bess back they don't know where to start.'

'This is wonderful,' Young blurted out. 'Let me play my part. When do we start?'

Adams shook his head; the movement brought the palsied twitching back.

'You'll play your part all right, my boy, but not with a musket. I want you to rally the troops with your words, not lead them in battle.'

'Fine! Be proud to. Just as a matter of interest, who

does lead them? You?'

They both burst out laughing, the clearest sign of their friendship yet.

'No, the Boston militia are led by a fine man called John Parker. Captain John Parker. He was the hero who took Louisburg for the British, spilling much of our boys' blood, before the perfidious British gave it back to the French.'

'And he will lead us in battle?'

'One day, yes. The militia is the lever of our freedom. But we need cannon, not only muskets.'

Young nodded, unconvinced, wondering if he should speak out. He dragged the words out of himself. 'But against the British army? The most fearsome fighting force in the world. Not to mention their navy. What chance do we ever stand of beating them?'

'None whatsoever.'

'Oh. Right. Well, that's honest anyway.'

'We don't have to beat the British. We just have to hold them off until the French come in.'

CHAPTER 6

As Young and Adams left Faneuil Hall, now bound as allies and confreres by the secrets they shared, light powder snow began to fall in an even and dignified fashion. Even though it was still only mid-afternoon, the sky was heavy and portentous, as if it, too, shared some of the burden of the secrets buried in the past lives of Samuel Adams and Thomas Young.

'Does Pope's Day mean anything to you?'

Young shrugged. 'Heard of it. Every November 5th. A protest against the Catholics from ancient times, isn't it?'

Then he blushed, cursing himself for a fool. He remembered today *was* November 5th.

'Something like that,' Sam Adams said, absently. 'Listen, Thomas. A revolution needs unity. And we do not have even a semblance of unity. Which is why I need you.'

Adams drove the chaise out of Dock Square, then turned right along Ann Street over one of the bridges that separated Boston's North End from the South End. The events of Pope's Day, Adams explained, were due to take place at Mill Creek, which was on the border between the North and South Ends.

As they drove, Samuel Adams filled Young in on the background of this, to Young, bizarre event, which was unknown in Albany. All Young had gathered so far was that some sort of fight was about to take place, confirming Boston's reputation as a mob town.

'All through the day, the two sides, the North End and the South End, parade through the streets,' Adams explained. 'They both make effigies of the Pope, who masterminded the Catholic conspiracy to blow up Parliament, led by Guy Fawkes. There's also an effigy of the devil, whispering in the Pope's ear. In the late afternoon, early evening, they fight – the North End against the South End. They try to

43

capture each other's effigies.'

'Why?' Young asked, genuinely perplexed.

'Good question. A lot of people think it is stupid. The merchants will increasingly have nothing to do with it. And that certainly includes giving either side money.'

'So why?'

'What matters is not why it happens but how we stop it. We must unify our people. No unity, no revolution. It's that important.'

'Do these two Ends of Boston hate each other, or what?'

'Not hate exactly. The North End is where the shipyards are, the wharves, the chandleries. So it's easier for the North Enders to get jobs and the South Enders resent that. At the South End you get lowly jobs, say in the ropewalks. They are the poorest of the poor. Like Ebenezer Mackintosh. He's the Captain of the South End Pope's Day Company. You come across him yet?'

'Nope.'

'You'll see him in action soon enough. His father, Moses, was warned out of Boston many times, but always came back. Finally, he joined the British army. So did Ebenezer. He's a trained soldier, or he was. Now he tries to scrape a living as a cordwainer and just about stays out of jail. If we are ever to get unity among our people we need him. He can bring the whole South End over to us.'

Young nodded. 'Fair enough. Anything else I should know?'

'Yes. Before this farrago starts I have to make a speech attacking Catholics.'

'Eh? What for? Where's the nearest Catholic? Quebec?'

Adams smiled his thin-lipped smile. 'My sentiments exactly. But our people are traditionalists. They do what they did before, until we can wean them off it. If I didn't make the speech, someone else would. And it is vital to maintain influence. Anything else?'

By now they had reached Mill Creek and got out of the chaise. Groups of mechanics, as the manual labourers were known, and artisans were streaming past them, on the way to the civil war that was Pope's Day.

'No,' Young said. 'Nothing else.'

Mill Creek was a strip of grassland running from the watermill at Mill Pond at one end, to Boston harbour at the other.

The Creek was beginning to fill with artisans. They were indeed gathering in two opposing groups but it all looked peaceable enough at the moment. Over in one corner a sack race was going on. It even stopped snowing.

Young noticed a strange sort of carriage, stationary at the side of the Creek.

'What the hell is that?' he asked his mentor, pointing at it.

Young went over to it, and Adams followed. On closer examination, the thing appeared to be a mechanical device. It had four wagon wheels, a long wooden body carrying a pump with long cross-handles and a cistern full of water.

'It's a Newsham Engine, imported from England,' Adams explained. 'A Deluge Number 1, they call it. One of the Fire Companies probably arrived on it.'

'It looks like a device to drive sinners to hell.'

Adams laughed. 'Far from it. There was a big fire at the North End not long ago. It was as well we had ordered the old Newsham to help out.'

Adams implied some participation in the ordering of the fire engine. He knew perfectly well that Boston owed everything to Hutchinson for the Newsham, but he did not share that information with Thomas Young.

Adams was looking nervous and unsettled. 'I've got to make this speech now,' he muttered to himself. Young understood that this was the sort of task he wished Young himself to handle, in future. And indeed it would not have worried him in the slightest. A public speech? He would relish it.

Adams's fears turned out to be well founded. He spoke poorly, both in delivery and content. His reedy voice did not carry. He spoke without authority or clarity, his diatribe poorly organised. As he started, quite a few of the mechanics and artisans from both sides gathered round to listen, but many more did not bother.

'My aversion to Popery,' Adams croaked out, 'is grounded not only on its paganism and idolatry, but on its being calculated for the support of despotic power and inconsistent with the genius of free government. It introduces into politics that solecism *imperium in imperio*, a government within a government.'

As Young understood, Adams meant this as a dig at the British Parliament, coming between the people and the King. But nobody else in the rapidly thinning crowd around Adams understood the over-subtle point.

Young left Adams to it and went to look at the effigies. The North End effigy had the Pope tarred and feathered. There was also a British flag, ready to be burned. As well as the Pope, the South End cart also had a recognisable effigy of Thomas Hutchinson, with the Lieutenant Governor represented as looking both ways; that is, two-faced.

By the time he finished his inspection and walked back to Adams, Sam the Publican had lost most of his audience and was grinding to a somewhat lame anti-Papist conclusion.

'I need some water,' he croaked to Young. 'I've got a cold.' His hands were shaking badly.

Young mutely indicated the Newsham Engine, with its water supply. As they walked over to it, the two sides were clearly organising on military lines: some men were carrying barrel staves, some a supply of stones. Young reckoned that by now there were maybe a hundred of them, evenly divided into two makeshift gangs.

As Adams found a tin cup from somewhere and scooped water from the mechanical device, they were joined by one of the strangest men Young had ever met. He stood there, grinning wildly, until Adams introduced them.

'Dr Thomas Young, this is Ebenezer Mackintosh, commander of the South End forces.'

Mackintosh cut a strange figure. He was tiny, coming maybe halfway up Young's chest. His thin, lank hair was sandy, with the freckles that go with that colouring. He had a black leather cap on, with a pewter blaze with the number nine set into it.

Mackintosh noticed Young looking at the pewter blaze. He touched it. 'Fire Company Number Nine, sir. That's what that means. I have the honour to be its commander. I always command. I was a captain in the army, you know.'

Young nodded, having no idea how to respond.

'It was the proudest moment of my life when Sheriff Stephen Greenleaf sponsored me to be in Fire Company Number Nine.'

'Congratulations.'

'Oh yes, indeedy.'

Young took in the rest of Ebenezer Mackintosh's outfit. He wore a grimy green army jacket with mouldering epaulettes, maybe taken from a Hessian soldier in some long-ago battle. Below the jacket, a fascinated Young saw ripped and torn canvas trousers through which Mackintosh's skinny legs peeped. They were caked with mud.

Young noticed that his leather shoes were in a better state than anything else – almost presentable. Then he remembered Adams saying that Mackintosh had learned the shoe trade, and was now a cordwainer.

But what struck Young most was his smell. Ebenezer Mackintosh stank worse than a hog in muck. Mackintosh noticed Young wrinkling his nose and grinned, giving a glimpse of brown and black teeth with many gaps between them.

'Are you in charge of the North End this year?' Ebenezer Mackintosh asked Young.

'No sir, I am not,' Young said, trying to keep the disdain

from his voice.

'Then who is?'

Adams told him: 'William Molineux.'

'Oh him!' said Mackintosh. 'London-born!' he added with scorn.

Adams ignored him, speaking to Young. 'If the South End wins, the North's effigy will be taken to the Common and burned. If the North wins, the South's effigy will be burned on Copp's Hill.'

Young spoke without thinking, as he so often did: 'It's goddam medieval.'

'Oh, is it now? And just who the hell are you?'

Ebenezer Mackintosh wound his wiry frame into a longbow shape and uncoiled with great speed and force. His punch caught Thomas Young on the point of his jaw and he went down, poleaxed.

'Welcome to Boston.'

Young was unconscious for two or three minutes. He came round as Sam Adams dabbed water from the Newsham Engine onto his face with a piece of rag. He staggered to his feet. There was blood on his mouth and his jaw ached but he could tell all his teeth had survived the blow. His pride had maybe taken a dent.

'You all right?' Adams sounded amused.

'Yeah. I'll live.'

'Glad you've met Ebenezer Mackintosh,' Adams continued, straight-faced. 'He's a respected figure, believe it or not. Even the merchants and the Medici take him seriously.'

Young fingered his jaw gingerly. 'I'm not surprised.'

By now it was early evening and the numbers had swollen to what looked like close on 200 for each side. The two captains, Ebenezer Mackintosh for the South End and William Molineux for the North, were rallying their troops by bellowing through speaking trumpets, yelling last-minute tactical instructions. They had trouble making themselves heard, as they were not the only ones with speaking trumpets and some of the mechanics and artisans were also blowing into conch shells.

Then the fighting began in earnest, confirming Young's impression of the high degree of organisation in everything the Bostonians did. The men armed with stones fought like cavalry, attacking round the flanks. The barrel-stave bearers and club wielders were like infantry, walking forward in formation until they engaged.

'Come on, let's go,' Adams said. 'You've seen all you need to see.'

They set off in the chaise back the way they had come, all the way to Adams's house on Purchase Street. Adams talked as he drove: 'It is essential we stop these pitched battles and the animosity they create so we can come together against the British. To that end I have called a meeting with Ebenezer Mackintosh and William Molineux. I intend to make them make peace, so we can all unify. I want you to come with me and assist me.'

'I would be happy to.'

CHAPTER 7

The meeting with Mackintosh and Molineux was at the Green Dragon, on Union Street. It was to the patriots what the British Coffee House was to those loyal to the British cause, a kind of unofficial headquarters.

Adams and Young were early. The landlord, Richard Silvester, brought them a pot of ale each on the house and sat chatting with them about the chances of success.

'Molineux will come over to you,' Richard Silvester forecast, 'especially if you can offer him a fight. You will need to bribe Ebenezer Mackintosh.'

'I know,' Adams said.

Richard Silvester, a big red-faced fellow in a leather apron who looked more like a blacksmith than a landlord, burst out laughing. It was common knowledge that Samuel Adams dipped into the funds he amassed as a tax-gatherer when he needed money for the patriot cause, but he always paid it back.

William Molineux arrived first, filling the place with his broad build. His muscles bulged out of his worn linen shirt. But there was something of the dandy about Molineux. Obviously aware of his swarthy good looks, he dressed with care, though not richly, making a sleek impression from his well-oiled hair, pulled back into a pony-tail, to his fancy, buckled shoes. He reeked of cheap pomade.

Adams introduced him to Young. 'William Molineux, this is our illustrious new recruit, Dr Thomas Young. Mr Molineux owns a warehouse on Hancock's Wharf. Dr Young hails from Albany, New York.'

Molineux extended a meaty hand. 'New York, eh? I'll call you Dutch, then.'

'I prefer to be called Thomas.'

'Do you, now?'

He spoke in a surprisingly soft voice, with an accent

Young had not heard before, but realised must be London.

'When do we start?' Molineux asked Adams.

'When I've settled Mackintosh,' Adams said.

From that, it was obvious to Young that Sam Adams had already squared Molineux before the meeting. The North End leader was ready to stop the fights with the South End and put himself under Adams's command, as a patriot. It was Young's first experience of how Adams managed small meetings and caucuses – get as much as possible done behind the scenes before the meeting even started.

At that moment, Ebenezer Mackintosh appeared, wearing the same grimy green army jacket and the torn filthy canvas trousers he had worn at the Pope's Day fight.

He greeted Adams and Molineux cordially enough, then shook Young's hand with a tough grip.

'I'm sorry I hit you,' he said.

'Forget it,' Young replied. 'I have.'

Young thought he was drunk but holding it well. Adams bought him an ale, as he obviously expected, and came straight to the point.

'We need to end the animosity between the South End and the North so we can all pull together against the British.'

'Why would I want to stop hitting people from North End? What would I do instead?' Ebenezer Mackintosh turned his head slowly, treating the others to a wolfish grin, one by one, making sure they all got the point.

'Why don't we have a parade?' Young said. 'We used to have them in Albany all the time. North End and South, marching together. Then you burn the Pope's effigy. And Hutchinson's effigy, if you want. But together.'

Adams shot Young a respectful look. For one thing it was clear Mackintosh was warming to him.

'That's good,' Mackintosh said. 'I would enjoy that. All I need now is a reason to do it.'

51

Young and Adams glanced at each other. The hint was broad enough. 'I can arrange for you to become a sealer of leather,' Adams said, quietly.

Mackintosh whistled appreciatively. He quickly calculated the benefits of being one of only four sealers of leather allowed in Boston. No tanner or currier could sell leather without the city's seal on it. The cordwainer's eyes gleamed; such a sinecure could transform his fortunes.

'Anything else?' Mackintosh's nonchalance was poorly assumed.

'What else do you want?'

'A uniform.'

'A what?'

'You want me to join your army, don't you? Fight the British. Very well. But I want a uniform. A general's uniform. But I'll take the rank of captain.'

Adams sighed. 'All right. Any specifications? Or will you leave it to me?'

'I'll leave it to you. Except epaulettes. I want gold epaulettes.'

'Shoemaker, stick to thy last,' said Molineux, mockingly.

If Mackintosh heard that he ignored it. Adams had the money, Molineux didn't. So Molineux didn't matter.

'Soldiers get paid.' Ebenezer Mackintosh drained his ale and rattled his tankard on the table until Richard Silvester, hovering nearby, brought him another.

Adams was silent for a moment. 'I have powers of abatement,' he said, in a flat monotone.

'You have what?'

'Like the other tax gatherers, I have powers of abatement. I can pause the collection of taxes. I am prepared to pause yours indefinitely.'

'Only me?'

Adams looked set to lose his temper. His battle with himself lasted nearly a minute. Mackintosh's fresh pot of ale arrived. Molineux took the opportunity to order another, indicating to Richard Silvester that Adams was paying.

Finally Adams spoke. 'I can't let the whole South End off taxes. There's nearly two hundred of you.'

'My brother-in-law, Samuel Maverick. He's a good man.'

'All right. Samuel Maverick.'

'And Edward Proctor of Orange Street. He's a good man, too.'

'Yes!' Adams was getting rattled. 'Look, we cannot do this piecemeal. Plus the city has to have *someone* paying taxes.'

'Say twenty abatements, for the leading fighters of the South End. Eh?'

'I cannot ... I can do ten at most.'

'Fifteen.'

'All right. All right. Fifteen abatements and a general's uniform with the rank of captain. Plus sealer of leather. And that is all, Ebenezer Mackintosh.'

'How long before I get my uniform? I'd like it quickly. Procrastination is the thief of time, you know.'

'There will be a meeting in ... let us say three days' time. You will have your uniform by then. I will send word of the venue, the day and time and the password you are both to use.'

That seemed to sober the diminutive South Ender.

'Password?' said Molineux. 'Like the Masons?'

Molineux and Adams glanced at the table in the corner of the Green Dragon where the Masons had their regular meetings. It was empty now.

'Yes, a password. No, not like the Masons,' Adams said. 'This is a deadly serious business we are embarking upon, gentlemen. I demand from you loyalty. I demand from you secrecy. I demand that you declare yourselves willing to die for our cause. I demand that you do not rest or cease your efforts until the last British soldier has gone from our territory.'

Mackintosh saluted, without apparent irony. Molineux nodded vigorously.

When they had gone, Young ordered more beer. 'Good work,' he said.

'Yes, it worked,' Adams said. He looked grey and exhausted; the twitch from the palsy started in his cheek and one hand. 'I am well over a thousand pounds in arrears on tax gathering anyway. I have no idea exactly how much, in fact. So a little more will not make too much difference. I doubt they will notice.'

'Let's hope not.'

CHAPTER 8

Three days after their meeting with Mackintosh and Molineux, Samuel Adams and Thomas Young presided over another meeting. This was held at the most secret place the patriots had at their disposal – the Long Room Club above the printing presses of the *Boston Gazette*, in Court Street. The *Gazette* was owned by Benjamin Edes, a long-time patriot.

The premises were currently guarded by none other than Sheriff Stephen Greenleaf, who demanded the password from anyone seeking to go up to the meeting. The florid, heavily built sheriff had been a secret patriot sympathiser since boyhood.

The word that had to be whispered into the bulky sheriff's ear as a password was 'Revere', after the town's leading silversmith. Paul Revere himself was at the meeting, as was Benjamin Edes, on his home turf, and Benjamin Hallowell, a customs agent.

William Molineux and Ebenezer Mackintosh sat together, to symbolise their unity. Next to Molineux, on the other side from Mackintosh, were Henry Bass and Elisha Brown, both London-born, both originally shopkeepers. Then Samuel Gore, Boston-born, military man and painter. Then Edward Proctor, also Boston-born, dock worker.

When they were all assembled in the Long Room, Sheriff Greenleaf looked around to make sure he was unobserved, then made a quiet departure. It was thought unwise for him to attend the meeting; his allegiance must be kept secret from the likes of Hutchinson and even from the merchants.

Samuel Adams had asked Thomas Young to officiate at the meeting, leaving him – Adams – freer to influence events.

When all the men had settled at the long oak table that gave the Long Room its name, beer was served by

Benjamin Edes, as host. There was a relaxed, cheerful buzz of conversation.

Ebenezer Mackintosh sported his new general's uniform, as promised at the earlier meeting with Adams and Young. It consisted of a green frock coat with epaulettes, a red shag waistcoat and blue buckskin breeches. The accoutrements included a tie-wig – designed to stay on during fighting – a tricorn hat, a short sword and a gold cane. Mackintosh was delighted with it all.

By now, Thomas Young knew some of the men round the table, but Adams introduced him anyway.

'Our Chairman today is Dr Thomas Young. Dr Young has ever been an unwearied assertor of the rights of his countrymen, acting tirelessly in the cause of American freedom. For this, he has had to flee the persecution of his native town and finds himself among us today, to our great benefit.'

Adams flapped one stubby flipper of an arm, inviting applause. He got it.

'Dr Young, the floor is yours.'

'Thank you, Samuel.'

Thomas Young brought the meeting to order. He required the men round the table one by one to swear a solemn oath of secrecy devised by Adams. It required absolute loyalty to the patriot cause and a solemn promise never to betray the revolution to the British by word or deed. One by one, all the men swore the oath.

Young then called on Samuel Adams to explain the reason for their coming together. As Young now knew, the meeting today was to plan controlled violence. Only Adams himself and Young would be at another meeting, to be held a day later. This second meeting would develop peaceful protest.

These two necessary aspects of revolution were to be kept apart, watertight in their secrecy. The two groups would have different names. Nobody except Adams and Young would belong to both groups. The peaceful protest group would, where necessary, deny and even decry the actions of the controlled violence group. That, as Adams had explained to Young, was how to organise a revolution.

Adams began quietly, both in volume and tone. 'Good evening, gentlemen. Thank you for your presence here this evening. I believe most firmly that our British occupiers are in the wrong by even being here, so they must always be put in the wrong by anything we do.'

Ebenezer Mackintosh called out 'Hear, hear.' Like Adams, he blamed the British for the deaths of Massachusetts comrades fallen in the war fighting for the British army, not the French or Indians who had actually killed them. In his view, and in Adams's, they had died for nothing. Mackintosh, like Adams, wanted revenge.

Adams nodded at Mackintosh and continued. 'Mob violence will harm our cause because it will be perceived as putting us in the wrong. Random violence, similarly, will give the British a moral bonus. But we are here today to explore the possibilities of targeted violence. And we have much to learn in that respect from the way things have been done in England, especially in London.'

Adams paused, looking at each man in turn, gauging the mood of the meeting. They were with him. He was sure of that. His longest stare was for the brutally handsome, piratical William Molineux. Molineux stared back. By now, Young had learned of the power of Molineux's blasphemy-ridden harangues and his reputation for extreme violence. He was more and more impressed.

'I will hand you over now to Mr William Molineux, who will outline the work of the Mohocks in London, and what they have achieved. Mr Molineux.'

Molineux treated the company to a hard-eyed grin, flashing pearly-white, slightly pointy teeth. 'When I led the Mohucks,' he began, 'along with Elisha Brown and Henry Bass here …' he indicated Brown and the compact figure of Bass, who acknowledged the company, '… we 'ad the whole of London shitting itself with fear.'

Molineux paused, then went on. 'Let me see, now, what did we do? We used to beat the watch about the head and the privates, but that was just for our own pleasure. Just a bit of fun. We used to relieve strollers in the street of their valuables. If they objected to that in any way they got their noses slit, did they not, Mr Bass?'

'They did indeed, Mr Molineux. They did indeed.'

Molineux, Bass and Elisha Brown spoke with flat London accents, swallowing consonants like the cockneys they were. Those who were Boston-born sounded very different, nasal and twangy. But they were not saying anything at the moment.

'Let me see, now, what else did we get up to, back in that corrupt shit-pile of a city?' Elisha Brown drew breath to speak, but Molineux silenced him with a look. 'I seem to recall rolling a few women down the street in barrels, after we'd finished with them. They were the better sort, usually. We threw acid on the finery of the better sort, too. That was fun.' The room was completely silent, spellbound.

Molineux went on. 'We stopped a few coaches. Sometimes we took valuables. Sometimes we were paid to play a few games with the occupants, eh Mr Bass?' Bass grinned but knew better than to try and speak while Molineux held the floor.

Molineux scratched his chin, thoughtfully. 'We used to 'ave the occasional Skimmington.'

Young was amused. 'The occasional what?'

Molineux smoothed his slicked hair back, enjoying the audience appreciation. 'A Skimmington. Don't you know that term, Dutch?'

Young smiled at him, holding his gaze. 'Call me Thomas. Not Dutch. No, it's new to me.'

'And you an educated man, too. Not a poor gutter-rat like me. A Skimmington, Dutch, is when we Mohucks take someone what has been naughty for a little ride.'

'All through the town,' Henry Bass added.

'Yes, 'Enry. All through the town as you rightly say,

dragged on a sledge or similar. As often as not covered in some substance or other. And you have a bit of fun with them on the way. Until they understand why you are a bit cross. The error of their ways, you might say. Or the nature of their sins against God and William Molineux.'

There was complete silence in the room. Molineux continued: 'Another thing we used to do, me and the Mohucks under my command, is we used to demolish the houses of anybody what wasn't too popular. We got well paid for that, on occasion.'

Young looked surprised. 'What, set fire to them?'

'No, Dutch. Not that. That's a new boy's question if ever there was one. Fires are about as dangerous in London as they are here. And that is very dangerous. No, we used to just take them apart, pull them down until nothing was left. It's a skilled job and we were good at it. We helped ourselves to all their possessions first, of course.' Molineux flashed his blank grin.

'We could use that,' Sam Adams said. 'The Skimmington and the destruction of houses. That is what I mean by targeted violence, if you accept the discipline of acting only on behalf of the patriots.'

'Meaning we do what you tell us?'

'Exactly.'

'All right. Except for tipping the lion. I say when we tip the lion.'

Young laughed. 'All right, I'll be the one to ask. What is tipping the lion, Mr Molineux?'

Molineux was relishing the meeting's attention. Young liked him and he knew it. 'Oh call me William, Dutch. Do. So ... You lot don't know tipping the lion, eh? My my, what a backwater this dump is. The arsehole of the known world, if you ask me. Come here, 'Enry. We'll give them a demonstration.'

Henry Bass hesitated, but decided not to disobey. He went and stood meekly behind Molineux's chair.

'In tipping the lion, you put the gentleman's nose

59

against the palm of your hand and press hard while at the same time, simultaneously as you might say, you gouge out his eyes with two fingers.'

This was demonstrated on Henry Bass until he squealed for mercy, then sat down, rubbing his nose.

'As that is a London custom, Sammy boy, I and nobody else will decide when we do it.'

'We have to have a unified command,' Adams said, calmly. 'We have to have discipline. The prize of discipline is our eventual freedom from the British. This is not a joke, Mr Molineux.'

'I stand corrected, Sammy boy. I stand corrected. But I have to say, speaking more in sorrow than in anger, as the Bard said, what's in it for me? Rumour has it that my esteemed colleague, Mr Mackintosh 'ere, has been let off paying taxes. Can't think where I 'eard that.'

Molineux shook his head in mock sadness. Mackintosh grinned and swelled inside his comic opera uniform.

'It's Captain Mackintosh to you,' he said, but in a friendly, jokey tone.

Molineux sipped at his ale. 'I stand corrected *again*,' he said in mock horror, wiping his mouth with his sleeve.

There was laughter round the table. Only Paul Revere and Benjamin Edes looked serious. The meeting was close to disintegration. Molineux had bided his time and was now asking for a bribe in public, in front of witnesses. Adams thought Young should have been firmer with him. His open admiration had encouraged the cockney. Adams felt he had no choice. He was so near success. Promise anything.

'All right, all right. I can extend my powers of abatement to you. No taxes.'

Henry Bass made exaggerated throat-clearing noises. The laughter round the table grew louder. Samuel Adams feared laughter. He shot a furious look at Young, who was laughing with them.

'Molineux and Bass, no taxes.' Adams ground it out

through gritted teeth.

'What about Elisha Brown, 'ere?' He indicated the affronted Elisha Brown.

'Just you two!' Adams screamed. 'That is all that is possible! I have to … That is all that is possible. Take it or leave it.'

'All right, Sammy boy, don't piss your drawers.'

'Stop calling me that.'

'All right, Mr Adams, you unruly little fellow. You 'ave my full support.'

'Thank you. In that case we are united. The call to action will come through your Fire Companies. If anybody is not a member of a Fire Company, see Sheriff Greenleaf, who will enrol you. You will respond immediately. From now on, in tribute to Mr Molineux here, this branch of the patriots will be known as the Mohucks.'

Molineux was delighted, beaming all over his swarthy face. 'To the Mohucks,' he said, raising his tankard.

'To the Mohucks,' they cried, as one.

And drank to their success.

CHAPTER 9

Samuel Adams saw the patriot cause as an archery target. At the centre was Adams himself, but now Young was included with him. In the next ring out were the Mohucks, ready to unleash controlled mayhem when called upon to do so. One ring further out would be the Sons of Liberty, bringing about revolution by persuasion and peaceful protest. After that came a ring of Boston citizens who were potentially swayable converts to the cause, people like the merchant, John Rowe. The next ring was the loyalists, the enemy. And the very outer ring was Hutchinson and the Medici, enemies that Adams wanted either dead or out of Boston.

The meeting to set up the Sons of Liberty was held in a private room of the Green Dragon. There were no passwords; anybody who was invited was told they could bring like-minded friends. Adams wanted the Sons of Liberty to win over the merchant classes to support patriot aims; the more who came along the better.

So the turnout for the inaugural meeting of the Sons of Liberty was a big disappointment to Adams and Young. There were maybe fifteen men round the table in the Green Dragon's biggest private room, hired at some expense – paid for by the richest patriot supporter, John Hancock.

It was the first time Thomas Young had seen Hancock, that towering figure whose money and power seemed to hang over Boston. Sitting next to Hancock was the factotum, George Hayley. Young had to fight down the irrational feeling that the brother-in-law of the Godlike John Wilkes should be more imposing than this swarthy, chunky man of below average height, whose very bearing, even seated at a table, expressed dogged devotion to John Hancock.

Also among the gathering were a few of Boston's

doctors, led by Sam Whitworth, and a scattering of the merchants – John Rowe was the most prominent of them. And among the small traders there was Theophilus Lillie, shopkeeper, and John Newell, the cooper, the man who had rented Young the house in Wing's Lane where he would soon bring his family.

To Adams's great pleasure, Justice Richard Dana was there – the most prominent patriot supporter in the judiciary. Captain John Parker, who trained the Boston militia, lent his strong and silent presence, too.

The main item of discussion, when Young had called the meeting to order, was getting the newly formed Sons of Liberty members onto important positions in the Assembly.

They also needed to work towards a patriot majority in the Assembly. This could be crucial. Adams reiterated, though most of them already knew, that only the Assembly could call out British troops from the garrison at Castle William, or from anywhere else.

Thomas Pownall's replacement as Governor, when he arrived, and the detested Hutchinson, his deputy, had no direct power over the troops. The prize for the nascent Sons of Liberty, distant though it was, was control of British troops via control of the Assembly. Adams's eyes, as he addressed the small group, shone with fervour as he dreamed of that prize.

Then Young, at the head of the long table, took over. He had been well briefed by Adams. 'There are twenty places on the Assembly,' he said, looking round pleasantly at the seated gathering, so much more subdued than the Mohuck meeting. 'We realistically believe we can nominate candidates for the following, as I will call them out: who will stand for the post of Secretary to the Assembly?'

'I will,' Adams said, his short arm in the air.

'Any others? Very well, Samuel Adams,' Young confirmed.

He had wanted to write down who was standing for

what, but Adams had vehemently vetoed any written records, to preserve secrecy.

'Justice, on the Superior Court. Who will stand?'

'I will stand.' That was Justice Richard Dana.

Young confirmed the name. 'As Sheriff we have Stephen Greenleaf,' he said. Greenleaf was already in post and not due for re-election. His presence at the meeting today was thought counter-productive, too openly betraying his allegiance to them.

'Commissioner of Impost and Excise?'

John Hancock smiled at that one. He had mischievously wanted to stand, thus putting Boston's most inveterate smuggler and customs dues evader in charge of catching smugglers and collecting customs dues, but Adams had forbidden it, as part of his extensive rigging of the meeting before it started.

'I'll do it,' said Sam Whitworth.

This, for once, had not been set up in advance. Adams did not feel he could object, though he did not trust the shifty doctor. For one thing, Whitworth obviously resented Thomas Young, whose fame was spreading: there had been the case of a North End tailor who had not worked for months because of a pulled sartorius muscle so he couldn't sit cross-legged to sew. Young had made up a poultice which gave him sufficient ease to get back to work. The story was all over Boston's labyrinthine grapevine in hours.

And so the meeting rambled on. The Governor and Lieutenant Governor were appointed from London, but of the elected posts the Sons of Liberty proposed to contest another three: Young for the post of Attorney General, John Rowe for the post of Solicitor General, and Captain John Parker for Speaker of the House.

Captain Parker had agreed to stand for office only after pressure from Adams, behind the scenes, in Adams's usual secretive hand-covering-the-mouth manner. To finally persuade Parker, Adams had shrewdly chosen a post where any patriot candidate had little chance of success. The Sons of Liberty, Adams reasoned, needed to make a noise, at this early stage – get themselves noticed. Any post they actually won would be a bonus.

After all that was agreed, Young, speaking Adams's words, asked for volunteers to write articles pleading the patriot cause in the pro-patriot newspapers, especially the *Boston Gazette* and the *Massachusetts Spy*. As they all knew, articles in the Boston press were always written under a pseudonym.

Adams's heart was not in this appeal. He was the greatest polemicist in writing of his age. He did not feel, at this time, that more polemicists were needed, but he wanted the group involved and tied to the patriot cause as closely as possible.

'I'll do it,' Young said.

'That's wonderful, Thomas,' said Samuel Adams through gritted teeth. Young had not mentioned this in advance, so Adams had not authorised it. 'Anybody else?'

Dr Sam Whitworth raised his hand. He looked at Adams as he did so, pointedly ignoring Young and his position in the chair. His antipathy to Young was palpable.

'Thank you, Dr Whitworth,' said Young evenly. 'Your interest has been noted.'

Adams and Young counted the meeting a success, excepting the low turnout. It was only later that Young felt a vague feeling of disquiet. It was some time before he realised what he felt uneasy about.

Richard Silvester, landlord of the Green Dragon, had asked how many were coming to the meeting, a reasonable enough request. But why had he asked, casually enough, for a list of names? Adams had politely refused to provide one, but why the request? Something was wrong, here.

CHAPTER 10

As soon as his ship reached England, Thomas Pownall took the first coach to London, then the Edinburgh fly as far as Lincoln. He found his mother much aged, grey-haired now and delicate as porcelain, but in good spirits. She was clearly managing the upkeep of the family home in Saltfleet. His brother, she told him, wrote regularly from London and visited when he could. As far as Thomas could judge, all was well.

He therefore broached the subject of the ambition which burned in his soul: he sought to become a Member of Parliament, there to use his influence to help the good people of Massachusetts, from whose lives he had been so cruelly torn.

Mrs Pownall shook her grey head, rocking gently in her rocking-chair in the parlour as sun streamed in squares through the leaded window. 'We have petitioned Lord North before. I may be able to get you an introduction to him, if the Earl of Chester is still alive and acknowledges his connection to us.'

'Thank you, Mother.'

'And money. You will need money.'

'No, no, I couldn't possibly prevail on …'

'I can let you have a Banker's Draft for three hundred pounds.'

'Well ... If you're sure, Mama.'

'I'm sure.'

And at that the old lady fell asleep.

Back in London, Thomas found himself cheap lodgings in St James's, not far from Whitehall. He then set about arranging a meeting with his brother, to see if John could promote the introduction to Lord North his mother had mentioned. He did not think John would have any objections if he, Thomas, joined Lord North's faction in

Parliament. Why should he, after all?

However, it proved surprisingly difficult to arrange a meeting with his younger brother. He had no idea where John lived, having always sent letters from Boston to his place of work. A visit to the American Department in the Admiralty building had not taken him past the outer office of clerks, where the Chief Clerk rather humiliatingly told him that Under-Secretary Pownall was not available. He would not tell him more.

Thomas felt as though the newly inaccessible John were his superior, in some ill-defined way. As indeed he had been, briefly, when after his Cambridge days Thomas had gone to the Board of Trade where John, having started near the bottom as a clerk, had rapidly risen to Under-Secretary, before transferring to the American Department at its inception.

John had been a decent enough boss to his older brother, indeed had smoothed his path when the Lincolnshire connection to Boston opened up the chance of the Governorship of Massachusetts. But the sense that John had 'won', so to speak, in the race of life had formed in Thomas then and it was returning now.

Thomas told himself he must rise above such petty sibling jealousies. He sent a note to John at the American Department, receiving a reply at his lodgings that John would meet him at an inn, only to have the arrangement countermanded by another note, saying John was busy. He was always absorbed in his work, working twice as hard as anybody else, Thomas knew that, he had seen it with his own eyes, but even so he was somewhat put out.

Never the most patient of men, Thomas was champing at the bit until another meeting was arranged. But then his essentially sunny disposition reasserted itself. He would dedicate the rest of his life to working for Boston, indeed for all of Massachusetts, from the London end. He would begin soon. The thought filled him with deep satisfaction.

John had chosen as their meeting place the Cock, situated just behind the Royal Exchange. Thomas got lost looking for it. When he did find it, it turned out to be one of the largest eating establishments he had ever set eyes on.

It was thronged with what looked like at least 500 people. The noise was horrendous. Thomas found himself a seat at a booth from where he could see the door. He was early. Calculating that John would probably pay, he ordered a bottle of Burgundy.

John arrived, bustling in, cloak flapping, £20 suit, wig well powdered, no sword. Thomas stood to greet him, like the supplicant he was.

John Pownall did not resemble his older brother in the slightest. John was a man of straight lines; Thomas was a man of curves. John was two heads taller than his older brother; he was even leaner now, which emphasised Thomas's plumpness. His aquiline features, by common consent, were more handsome than Thomas's homely phiz.

As ever with John, he was on time to the minute, consulting an automatic fob watch as he came in the door.

He spoke absently, his mind on his work. 'Hello, Thomas.'

'Hello, John.'

A glance at the opened bottle. 'That is the third most expensive Burgundy they have in this place. I see you have not changed.'

'We can split the cost.'

'Damn right. Do you want some food? I'm starving. They are famed for turtle soup here. Should remind you of Boston. It's quite good value.'

Thomas grinned, deep familiarity with John's ways making him feel suddenly warm towards his younger brother. 'Turtle soup it is, then.'

John clicked his fingers imperiously and ordered, brusquely. 'Two turtle soups and a tankard of small beer.' He turned Thomas, explaining the small beer. 'I have a full evening's work ahead of me. I'll leave the wine to you. I take it you have seen Mama?'

'Yes, she sends her love to you.'

'Very good of her. You didn't try and borrow money from her, did you?'

'No, John. I didn't *axe* her.' Thomas said the dialect word for 'ask' in broad Linkisheer – the Lincolnshire dialect.

John smiled at the dialect, but shot his older brother a sharp look. He detected that shiftiness in Thomas he thought so typical of him.

'You are quite sure about that, Thomas?'

'Yes!'

'Good. Well don't ask her, that's all. She's not *ayabul'* – the Lincolnshire dialect word for having plenty of money. 'In fact, she hasn't got two farthings to rub together. Not that that would stop her giving the last farthing to you. The darling boy.'

The bitterness in John's voice was clear to both of them. Not for the first or last time Thomas thought of saying 'It was not my fault there wasn't enough money to send you to Cambridge.' But, as on previous occasions, he left it unsaid.

He tried to win John over with reminiscences of their shared happy boyhood – happy to Thomas, that is. He had prepared a memory in advance and brought it into play now.

'Do you remember those last finds of ours just inside the old Roman city wall, when we were – what? Twelve and fourteen? Our findings that day were medieval, not Roman, weren't they? Do you remember those beautiful pieces of glassware? Light green, were they not? with darker green threads. You thought Venetian, thirteenth or fourteenth century ...'

'Funnily enough, I do remember that day. The digging was backbreaking. After half an hour or so, you left all of it to me and wandered off to produce one of those dreadful shaky watercolours of yours. When we got home, Mama was not remotely interested in what were indeed some remarkable Venetian finds but praised your picture to the skies and hung the bloody thing on the wall where, as I recall, it stayed for years, like a mildew stain.'

The turtle soup arrived. Thomas thought it vastly inferior to Boston turtle soup, fresh from Menotomy Pond. He remembered his last trip to the pond with his fishing friend, John Rowe. Tears sprang to his eyes at the memory.

'What do you think of the soup?' John's eyes were twinkling with mischief.

'Very tasty.'

The younger brother shot him a grin. 'Liar!'

There was silence between them while they ate and sipped their different drinks. Then John spoke again.

'I was nearly late for you, today. I've been dealing with your bloody Boston militia. They are more trouble than the rest of His Majesty's colonies put together. Mutinous pack of dogs. You know, we nearly lost Crown Point to the French because the Boston officers, led by *your* Captain Parker, refused to serve under certain British officers *they* considered amateurs.'

Thomas bit his lip, biting back a strong retort. 'They were right,' he muttered, finally.

'What?'

'Nothing.'

'And the Boston soldiers don't take service seriously. They wander off into the woods like little boys playing, shooting their muskets at flying birds. Their officers don't care. They go off and visit friends, then hire carriages at our expense to catch up with their men.'

Was John deliberately baiting him? Hard to tell with John. And how did he know the names of individual Boston officers like John Parker? He was impressively well informed about Boston, which made his evident bile all the more dangerous.

'Well?' John said.

'Well what?'

'Nothing to say in your people's defence?'

'When I was building Fort Pownall in the wilderness,' Thomas said, evenly, 'the Boston militia saved my life from the Indians, more than once.'

John smiled, having achieved wat he wanted. Thomas had risen to the bait. 'I see you are near to tears once more, at the memory. Very moving. I hear you want to make a figure in Parliament?'

'Where did you hear that?'

'Oh, I have my sources. Mama actually. She wrote.'

'I don't know about making a figure. I want Parliament to be my future.' Now that I have been cast out of Eden, he thought, but he did not say that aloud.

'Are you seeking my help, in this endeavour?'

'No.'

'Good. Let me give you some advice, Thomas. You won't get anywhere tearing your shirt and beating your bosom for a cause. You know the old saying? "The greatest common good is to be reached by each man pursuing his own advantage." Bear that in mind, Thomas.'

'I shall.'

When John left, somewhat abruptly, he did not ask where Thomas was lodging.

Chapter 11

Frederick, Lord North had received a letter from the Earl of Chester, asking him to promote Chester's kinsman as a candidate for Parliament. North had never heard of the Earl of Chester, but the kinsman went by the name of Thomas Pownall.

It was an unusual surname, which surely indicated that this Thomas Pownall must be related to John Pownall. Lord Hillsborough always spoke warmly of John Pownall. Indeed, John Pownall was known up and down Whitehall as Mr America, the man who knew more about the American colonies than any other man alive. Lord North therefore invited this Thomas Pownall fellow to come to his office in Whitehall.

On the day arranged for the meeting, North had been called to his wife's estate in Somerset. He was trying to contain the latest riots there. A mob of labourers had seized cartloads of butter, then raided bakery shops in search of bread and flour. Lord North supervised the capture of the ringleaders, who were subsequently deported to America in chains.

Thomas had arrived for the appointment, tense and nervous, to find North absent elsewhere. He showed his letter of invitation to a clerk. A second date was arranged. On this occasion there was a debate in the Commons so North again did not appear. A third appointment was set, which North apparently forgot completely.

A full month after the original contact, Lord North appeared an hour late for a fourth appointment. Thomas Pownall was powerfully struck by North's appearance. He thought him the ugliest man he had ever beheld. His eyes rolled about, apparently out of control; his thick lips twitched; his cheeks looked as if too much air had been blown forcibly into them with a bellows. He had the air of a blind trumpeter. The artist in Thomas found this virtual disfigurement fascinating.

North was warm and affable enough, though. Although the affability stopped short of offering any form of refreshment or hospitality.

'Now then ...' North began as Thomas settled into his chair opposite North's desk. 'Your name is Pownall. Charles Pownall ...' This was followed by a flutter of blinks from both eyes. Thomas realised North could hardly see him.

'No. My name is Thomas, my lord. Thomas Pownall.'

'Ah. Quite so. But you are a relative of John Pownall?'

'Yes, my lord. He is my younger brother.'

Clouds that had started to gather over the surface of that blubbery face quickly dispelled. Even the rapid blinks appeared to have cleared up.

'Splendid. Splendid. And you are seeking, what, a place in the Houses of Parliament? In the Commons?'

'That is so, my lord.'

'Why would you not, indeed? It is the most august of assemblies.' Lord North chuckled, his flabby cheeks shaking. There was a twinkle in his eye. One could discern his last three meals, at least, by the food stains on his bulging waistcoat and his satin breeches.

Thomas liked him. And he appeared to have taken to Thomas, as most people did.

'To tell the truth, Mr Pownall, the Commons is a very agreeable coffee house, no more, no less. Our gentlemen deign to drop in there, if they are in London at all, and not away in the country, only when they have no pressing social engagements; nobody to lay a wager with or play billiards with, and the theatre does not charm.'

North chuckled roguishly. Thomas politely laughed with him.

'But we need more people who share your brother's views on the America question,' North said, suddenly serious. 'We cannot go on as we are, everybody is in agreement on that.'

Thomas thought it politic to say nothing at this.

73

'You know that famous quip of Burke, I think it is about America?'

'No, my lord.'

'"A robbery on Hounslow Heath would make more conversation than all the disturbances in America." That is how it goes.' Lord North laughed heartily. Thomas forced as much laughter as he could muster. 'We need to change all that.' North sounded firm. 'We need more people like you and your brother, who are ready and willing to bring these rebellious fellows to book until they pay their fair share.'

Thomas swallowed hard and nodded.

North was beaming. 'That is all we are asking. Their fair share.'

'Yes, my lord.'

'Good, good. What is your station in life, sir?'

Thomas cleared his throat. 'Until recently, my lord, I was Governor of Massachusetts.'

'Were you now? You must be relieved to be back, eh? A few creature comforts, a bit of civilised conversation, eh? Where are your family from?'

'Lincolnshire, my lord.'

'What? Where? You have land there?'

'Not really, my lord, no.' Thomas shifted uncomfortably in his chair.

'No land? What then? Trade?'

'No.'

'Thank the Lord for that. The King is rather … How can I put this? His Majesty has retained some of the habits of the Hanoverian court. Excluding people of trade from his advisors is one of them.'

'I have no connections with trade, Lord North. No. None.'

'What about pedigree?'

'My family has a coat of arms. Two lions contournes in pale between two fleurs de lys.'

'Good! I think I have the picture. An independent

character is valued in Parliament as well as an independent station in life. A rise from a humble position is possible in these modern times. Social advancement through Parliament? Yes, perfectly possible.'

Thomas was wriggling with embarrassment in his chair, wishing he could cross one leg over the other knee, something he did not dare do in front of Lord North. But his lordship noticed his unease, looking kindly at him.

'You know, the going rate for a seat in Parliament is about fifteen hundred pounds? Have you got that?' Thomas was silent. 'Mmm. Yes, I see.'

Thomas saw his dreams of helping Massachusetts dashed. But North went on: 'As you are John Pownall's brother, we could help you out from the King's Fund. It is funded by His Majesty. We are known as the King's Men.'

Thomas had heard tell of the King's Men. Under North's leadership, they controlled the Commons to carry out the King's will with thirty or so mainly Tory members because the Whigs on the other side were so divided.

'You could perhaps join us. Be one of the King's Men.'

'I ... would be most grateful, my lord.'

'Not at all. Not at all. Once you are in, we'll tell you what to do.'

'Thank you, my lord.'

'Yes. Well. We can perhaps take it as read that you are grateful, so you can stop thanking me, Mr Pownall.'

Thomas nodded. 'Indeed.'

'Let me see ...' North fell to more myopic blinking. 'The borough of Sudbury is advertising for a buyer. No, I tell you what, Tregony in Cornwall. That would be ideal for you. Not too many voters to pay. Not as good as my constituency of course. In Banbury I have only eighteen.' North chortled. 'You'll need about three thousand to pay the voters, then keep them sweet, but we can handle that from the King's Fund.'

'Thank ... I really am most appreciative, my lord.'

'Did you know, Charles ...?'

'Thomas, my lord.'

'Yes, quite. There was a proposal made recently subjecting each election candidate to an oath that he had not used bribery. Lot of hot air, the lot of it. But anyway we have to get round it, so there will be a sale of trifling articles. We buy all sorts of flummery from the electors at enormous prices, you see? Then they vote for us. Don't worry, there will be an election agent who will organise all that for you. You don't have to do a thing.'

'Good!'

Lord North chortled to himself good-humouredly, shook Thomas's hand, then left the room without another word.

CHAPTER 12

At five minutes before eight in the morning, John Pownall jumped out of a sedan chair outside the lobby of the Admiralty Building, in the Cockpit, Whitehall, where the American Department was housed. He hauled his leather bag after him, grinding his teeth at losing more work-time than he had lost in months.

Seething with impatience, he paid the chair man with bad grace, proffering no tip, then ran into the building with the man's sarcastic 'Have a very good day, sir,' ringing in his ears.

He ran up the wooden stairs, taking them two at a time. The American Department was on the first floor. The outer office housed seven clerks at seven standing-desks but only two of them were in at this early hour. They were presided over by the Chief Clerk, William Pollock. He was already at his post, sitting at his imposing desk at the front of the office, facing the clerks.

William Pollock stood as John Pownall burst in. He was steeped in the ways of the Civil Service, having spent twenty years at the Northern Department. He was greying at the temples, being over a decade older than the two Under-Secretaries, John Pownall and William Knox. That and his grand house in Downing Street, while the Under-Secretaries were both still in cheap lodgings, gave him a knowing air with his superiors, though he was never less than respectful.

'Good morning, Mr Pownall, sir.'

'Morning, Mr Pollock. Anything fresh in? Anything from Boston?'

John Pownall glanced impatiently at the mahogany panelling of the outer office, covered in shelves, compartments and pigeon holes all containing myriad petitions from America, loosely tied in ribbon. Most of the petitions remained unread, if only because there were so many of them, but reports from spies were a different matter. That is what John Pownall meant by 'Anything fresh in?' Reports from spies, especially spies from Boston, were taken through to John Pownall and William Knox immediately.

'Yes, sir. There are fresh reports from our informants in Boston.'

'On my desk quick as you can, please.'

'Yes, sir.'

John Pownall walked through to the minuscule inner office. Hs face relaxed, as far as it ever did, falling into an automatic smile at the sight of Under-Secretary William Knox. He felt the familiar flush of affection, even love. Their work together, side by side at adjacent desks, elbows almost touching, had made them more like brothers than John ever felt towards his true brother, Thomas.

William Knox was an Irish descendant of the protestant radical John Knox, but he was no radical himself – he was loyalist in his blood and bones. As usual in the morning, he was reading a newspaper with his feet up on his desk, appearing to do nothing. But there was an almost finished background report on his desk, the work of many weeks.

Pownall regarded the last background report Knox had produced as the best analysis of the colonial question he had ever read. Knox's paper pointed out that the Romans treated each colony differently, according to circumstance and need. The British tried to establish the same colonial policy not only for every American colony but for all the Caribbean colonies, and for India and Ireland. It was too broad and so, warned Knox, it was doomed to failure.

Knox was the only man on the British side to look at colonial issues from the colonists' viewpoint, perhaps because he had spent some years living in Georgia as a rice planter. Pownall, deep though his factual knowledge of America was, never did that. He never saw any need to.

Having lived among its people, Knox understood

the lack of hierarchy in American society: no religious hierarchy, no class hierarchy. Pownall always shrugged that off. Americans saw themselves as subject to the King and God only. They rejected every other man put over them, be it bishop or rule-maker. And they most certainly rejected the authority of the British Parliament.

That analysis, like all the others, had made its way to Lord Hillsborough's office, where it – like all the others – lay gathering dust, unread by Hillsborough or anybody else.

William Knox lowered the newspaper as far as his nose, peering over it for comic effect. His deep blue eyes were twinkling, laughter lines creased his cheeks. The whole of his pleasant face appeared to be smiling, even the prow of his nose.

'Top o' the mornin' to you,' he said in a Drury Lane stage-Irish voice, exaggerating his natural Monaghan accent to the point of parody. 'Where have you been?' he added, speaking normally. 'Secret meeting?'

The remark was said with Knox's usual twinkle, but it had an edge to it. John Pownall habitually kept information to himself, even if it should be shared. On one occasion this had led to an eyeball-to-eyeball quarrel between the two Under-Secretaries, the only time they had ever fallen out. While Thomas Pownall was still Governor of Massachusetts, John had spoken to the Head of the American Department, Lord Hillsborough, about him. He had done this on his own initiative, without consultation. Thomas, John told Hillsborough, was too close to the Massachusetts Assembly. He had gone native; it was handicapping their work. As John knew perfectly well, William Knox took a diametrically opposite view, seeing Thomas, as many did, as the best colonial governor then in post.

Hillsborough had recalled Thomas soon afterwards. This may or may not have been what John had intended

– it probably was not, in Knox's opinion – but William Knox still did not approve, hence the row. The breach the incident had caused between the Under-Secretaries was healing, but slowly.

John Pownall shook his head, ruefully. 'No, no secret meetings, William. I've given them up for Lent. My journey was delayed. The rioting is getting worse. London is going to rack and ruin.'

Knox, quickly mollified as ever, opened his arms in jokey avuncular embrace. 'Come, come, now. Tell yer Uncle William all about it.'

Pownall threw his bag on his desk but remained tensely standing. He shut his eyes, saying nothing.

'Have you been working all night, John?'

Pownall opened his eyes. 'No. I slept for four hours. Maybe three.' He smiled. 'I nearly spent the night here at my desk but then I thought "What is the point of paying a princely three shillings and sixpence for *exquisite* rooms in Butcher Row, the envy of all who have seen them, and *so* convenient for a quick prayer at St Clements Church, if one is never in residence?" So I worked at home. Then I set off early, tried to do some work in a Hackney carriage and … bang.'

'Bang, eh? Who were they?'

'Spitalfields weavers mainly. We should deport the lot to America.'

'No doubt we will.' Knox looked concerned. Beneath the bravado, Pownall looked and sounded shaken. 'They are not happy people, I fear. Our London mobs. Not much laughter about them, or wit, or grace.'

'Footpads and scapegraces the lot of them. Every sort of scum. The Billingsgate fish men were among them, with their disgusting argot. And the Shadwell and Wapping coal heavers, judging by the black look of them.'

'Take it easy, John.'

'I will not take it easy, William! No! They were wearing Wilkesite favours, those bloody blue cockades, and shouting "Wilkes and Liberty".'

William Knox looked mock-solemn. 'They do tend to. That does not surprise me.'

'I am in no mood to jest. I fear I no longer understand the world we live in. Wilkes publishes a seditious libel against the King in that scurrilous rag of his, the *North Briton*...'

'True. An ugly piece of work, it was. Obviously illegal, whatever Wilkes says. Go on, John.'

'I shall. An arrest warrant is quite justifiably issued against all concerned, including the printers of the *North Briton*, who cannot yet be identified. To avoid delay, which would give the unknown miscreants time to flee, a General Warrant is issued for all perpetrators, known or unknown. This is a mere legal technicality, an obvious convenience. But Wilkes blows hot air into the issue until it is a vast balloon the size of London.'

Knox nodded, more serious now. 'I've been studying Wilkes, John. I've been doing some reading. He says General Warrants are "unconstitutional, illegal and absolutely void".'

'Rubbish! And you know what really piques, me William? What annoys me almost above all else? Wilkes himself had no influence on the issue of a General Warrant against him. Yet the mob sees his attempts to evade it as a valiant blow on behalf of liberty. It beggars belief.'

Knox's Irish accent was getting stronger, as it did when he was stirred. 'I'm with you there, John. Pitt issued three General Warrants during the war against the French, to imprison suspected spies. They went completely unnoticed. So why is Wilkes getting so much joy from this?'

'Yes! Yes! Yes! And Halifax issued a General Warrant against *The Monitor* a couple of years ago. Remember? Nobody said a word. General Warrants have been issued ever since the Glorious Revolution, as routine as a fart after a large meal.'

William Knox laughed. 'Go on, John. Speak, my boy.

You are a treat to listen to.'

John Pownall managed a taut smile. 'Wilkes and Liberty, my arse! If Wilkes banged his head on a low doorway, low doorways would be an infringement of liberty.'

Knox was still laughing. 'Yes. And the mob would be called out to smash every low doorway, with "low" defined by Wilkes.'

John Pownall finally squeezed himself behind his desk, sitting down hard with a small groan.

'You weren't hurt, were you, John? Outside, by the mob?'

'No! But it was close. They stopped the coach I was in, smashed the windows and three or four of them walked through the coach, in one side, out the other. They were grinning at me like monkeys. I got out and found they had chalked "Wilkes and Liberty" on the bloody coach.'

Seeing for himself that Pownall was not hurt and thoroughly enjoying his friend's invective, Knox began to twinkle, his bright blue eyes gleaming with mirth.

'Go on, John. You tell a good story, you always do. What happened next?'

'Nothing much. Having paid my shilling for the Hackney carriage, I then had to hail a sedan to continue my journey. At a shilling a mile that cost me another one shilling and sixpence. Coming to work is going to ruin me.'

'The streets are in a state of nature. Some say we are near civil war,' Knox said quietly.

There was a respectful knock at the door. The Chief Clerk brought in the reports from Boston. Pownall tore at the first of the packets like a cat with its prey. Knox waved for William Pollock to sit in the only spare chair the office possessed.

'Ah, Dr Sam Whitworth has denounced Thomas Young,' John Pownall shouted in glee. 'He says Young is peddling quack nostrums which rely on superstition. That doesn't sound like the rational Dr Young, does it?'

'Sam Whitworth wants Young prosecuted and so removed from revolutionary activity,' Knox said.

'Removed from being a better doctor than Whitworth, more like,' said Pownall. 'What else have we got? Richard Silvester. We should be getting much better reports from him than we are. I ask you. The landlord of the Green Dragon. He should be giving us a verbatim report of every seditious meeting these rebels hold. But what have we here?' Pownall read quickly, then gave a voluminous sigh. 'Nothing on the Sons of Liberty meeting we didn't know already, and the Mohuck meeting was held somewhere else so he doesn't know anything about it, so he says. Useless!'

'Anything else?' Knox said.

Pownall waved a scrap of paper. 'William Molineux. Not a bloody word about the Mohuck meeting, although he was definitely there.'

Knox looked serious, twinkling gone. 'William Molineux?'

'Yes. What's the matter, William?'

'I didn't know we were running William Molineux. Nobody told me.'

Pownall reached over and laid a hand on the Irishman's arm. 'I didn't keep that from you, William, I swear it. I thought you knew.'

'Well, I didn't.'

'William, please. So much paper comes into this office. It's just chance that …'

'Molineux has not made many reports, Mr Knox, sir,' Pollock said. 'This is perhaps the third. Come to think of it, I believe they did all go to Mr Pownall only. That was an oversight on my part. I'm sorry, sir.'

What the born diplomat William Pollock did not say was that Knox had been away from the office on all the occasions reports from Molineux had come in. That was why they had gone to Pownall only. But the concerted display of concern mollified Knox. He acknowledged to

83

himself that he was perhaps over-sensitive.

'All right, all right,' he said. 'So how long have we had Molineux fighting the good fight?'

John Pownall looked relieved. 'He was apprehended as one of around a hundred after the attack on Lord Bute's coach. Most of those apprehended were Mohucks.'

Knox's twinkle was back. 'Did he do it?'

Pownall smiled. 'Probably not. His specialism is the destruction of houses, not attacks on coaches. He was offered deportation rather than the hangman's noose, provided he reported to us when he got there. Naturally, he jumped at it. We thought it rather a feather in our caps at the time, but his material has been of a poor standard. His heart is not in it. And now Adams has let him off taxes. That will bind him to the bloody patriot cause, no doubt.'

Knox, no longer offended, was looking thoughtful. 'This tax business, now. Old Sam the Publican collecting taxes, except he is not, if he decides to let you off. How many is it, do you think? That he has let off.'

Pownall shrugged. 'Not sure. Mackintosh certainly. Some other key figures from the South End. Why?'

'Shouldn't the authorities know of this sad dereliction of duty by Sam the Publican? What about the public finances?'

'Yes, good idea, William. I'll get on to Hutchinson about it. See if we can't get Adams that way. Get him prosecuted for embezzlement of taxation money.'

CHAPTER 13

Lieutenant Governor Thomas Hutchinson's summer house out at Milton, eight miles from Boston, was no less gracious than his main home, the neo-Palladian mansion on Garden Court Street.

Known as the Monticello of Massachusetts, the Milton mansion was a three-wing building with a raised central section, high on a hilltop overlooking the Neponset River. It boasted views from the front over Boston Bay. The view from the rear was no less spectacular, over the rolling Blue Hills.

Thomas Hutchinson referred to the place as 'my little paradise', filled as it was with sons and daughters, sons-in law and daughters-in-law and their children. There were boat trips in the summer. They even went out there in the winter sometimes, for sleigh rides through the thick snow.

And yet the place sat perched on the aptly named Unquiety Hill. Unquiet is exactly what Thomas Hutchinson felt as he sat in his study, looking out over sailing boats in the bay. In fact he quickly went from unquiet to downright sad, a well-trodden downward slope.

For Thomas Hutchinson was in no doubt which of the four temperaments was his lot in life. He was a melancholic, always had been, always would be. The fact that he had to appear sanguine and phlegmatic on occasion to carry out his public duties only made his inner melancholy worse.

In his most secret soul he railed against God for taking his darling wife Peggy from him, all those years ago. Then he felt ungrateful, showered as he was with God's benison in so many other ways.

After all, he was Lieutenant Governor of Massachusetts, was he not? As well as Head of the Assembly, Commander of the Castle, Justice of Probate, Chief Justice of the Supreme Court and ... Was there anything else? He had now handed over all his business interests to his sons,

Thomas junior and Elisha, who had even increased their seeming boundless prosperity, not least by marrying into the business interests of the Olivers and the Clarkes.

Even in the spiritual domain he was, objectively viewed, not without consolation. His cherished daughter, who bore his wife's name, had taken her place in every way except physical love. Daughter Peggy now accompanied him to every formal occasion, as his partner, tender in years though she was. She was chatelaine to his two households, as completely as ever her mother had been. She was his confidante and companion, amanuensis and inspiration, privy to all but the blackest of his thoughts.

Hutchinson sighed windily, as he frequently did when alone. The boats in the Bay appeared stationary, so calm and windless was the day. He gathered himself, about to embark on the second great consolation of his life, daughter Peggy being the first. That consolation was the physical act of writing.

Often with Peggy's help, the Lieutenant Governor applied himself to his life's work, his *History of Massachusetts*, nearly every day, though the manuscript was kept at Garden Court Street, not here. He had kept a daily journal since his student days at Harvard. And of course there was letter-writing, which took up two to three hours most days, a distraction from the dull pain of being alive.

With yet more windy sighs he drew paper towards him, dipped quill in ink and dashed off a letter to Justice Richard Dana enquiring as to the proceedings against Samuel Adams for withholding most, if not all, of the taxes he was supposed to be collecting for the city of Boston.

Hutchinson wrote mechanically, without hope, as he often did. He knew perfectly well that Justice Dana was one of Adams's rabble, Sons of Liberty, as they had the effrontery to call themselves. But he could not be seen to interfere by moving the investigation to another judge. So he sanded and sealed and stamped the letter, muttering 'waste of time' to himself as he did so.

Then he turned to more important matters. He consulted letters on his desk from London. There was talk of a Stamp Bill being introduced in the London Parliament. Hutchinson could not imagine a bigger catastrophe for Massachusetts. It must be stopped at all costs. He began to write:

To Thomas Pownall, Member of Parliament for Tregony, sometime Governor of the State of Massachusetts

Dear Mr Pownall,

I am in receipt of letters from London carrying news of an impending Stamp Bill. May I summarise what they say and ask you to be so good as to comment on the accuracy of my information.

I am told of an intended Bill in Parliament to the effect that all documentation in the American colonies is to be carried on specially stamped paper issued by the British government, at a price, or on paper franked with such a stamp, that stamp also to be purchased.

I am told that the scope of this proposed Act extends to all commercial documents – land transactions, ship clearances and so on – all legal documents, all newspapers, pamphlets, almanacs, even newspaper advertisements.

There are to be Stamp Commissioners here in Boston who will effect the sale of these Stamps. All the monies so raised are to go to the exchequer, nothing to the colonies.

Furthermore, I am informed that any disputes over these stamps are to go to the Admiralty Courts, not our courts here in Boston. And that the proceeds of this Stamp Act are to be used to pay colonial governors such as myself, thus removing payment and control of payment from our own Assembly.

I need hardly tell you what a disaster these proposals would be if they were allowed to go forward.

First, every man in Boston would be worse off. The merchants and traders would be badly affected, driving them into the arms of the Adams rabble.

Second, by attempting to pay the governors from London, Parliament is usurping a function of the American Assemblies. As I'm sure you realise, their right to do this will not be recognised here.

There remains a residual affection for the King here, though for how much longer I do not know. For Parliament, however, nothing but hostility and contempt. Historically, Parliament has transferred part of its authority to colonial government. It may not arbitrarily take that authority back. We claim the esteemed privilege of English subjects: the privilege of being taxed by their own representatives.

I ask our allies in Parliament, you foremost among them, to put an end to this unwise Stamp Act legislation or I fear the consequences

They are having public meetings here now, which did not happen in your time. The rabble are making decisions once made by people qualified to make them. This newly empowered hoi polloi talk of revolting from Britain in the most familiar and shameless manner. We now have crowds here that can be wound up by any hand that touches the winch. And I hardly need tell you that the hand on the winch is that of Samuel Adams.

If this Stamp Act catastrophe is not nipped in the bud I fear riot, tumult and even revolution here.

Yours

Thomas Hutchinson

CHAPTER 14

John Pownall hurried towards Parliament for the Stamp Act debate. Not that he was late, he was never late. But he had decided at the last minute to have a haircut in the Palace of Westminster, partly because the barber was the cheapest in London, but mainly to save the time that travelling to another barber would entail.

As he arrived at the barber's, Pownall felt himself running out of time before the debate was due to start. His lean hawk-face went white. He tried to push ahead of another customer who had arrived ahead of him. A furious row ensued, with the barber taking the part of the other customer. John flatly refused to wait. The other customer had his hand on his sword pommel, but eventually gave way.

A newly shorn John Pownall raced up to the Strangers' Gallery where he found his fellow Under-Secretary, William Knox, already waiting for him.

As ever, John Pownall's face relaxed into a smile at the sight of the Irishman.

'Have they started?'

He nodded down at the Common below them; knots of members standing around in groups chatting, eating, making arrangements, playing cards, relieving themselves. It was difficult to tell if the business of the day was under way or not. Craning forward, John caught sight of his older brother on North's King's Men benches, nervously studying his papers. Thomas was due to speak against the proposed Stamp Bill.

'Started? Not quite.'

William Knox was chewing. There was a small hamper open next to him. 'Here, John, I brought you some food from the stall outside. Hot eels and baked potatoes. Eels are soothing, so I am told. They will calm you down. I

89

have no idea of the efficacy of baked potatoes but they taste most splendid. They have butter on them.'

John Pownall sat with the food spread out on a newspaper between them. He helped himself to some hot eel and a baked potato.

Knox nodded his head in the general direction of Lord North, who was asleep below them, a not uncommon occurrence with North. 'A lot of North's King's Men have stayed away. This Bill is not popular.'

John Pownall made a strange shaking motion with his head. 'Not popular? Is it not? Why? I did not realise ...'

'The London merchants don't like it,' Knox said, evenly. 'Trade is like a handshake. It takes two. Making trade difficult for the colonies will make it difficult for the English merchants, too.'

'A very generous interpretation you have there, William. If the London merchants are against it, it is because they are almost as bad as the colonists when it comes to smuggling. The Stamp Bill will codify documentation, thus making it easier to stop smuggling.'

Knox laughed. 'Right again, my cynical friend. But in any case, it's the unpopularity that has caused North to keep his head down. He's not introducing the Bill.'

'Really? So who is?'

'Charles Townshend is leading on this,' Knox said. 'The King and North want him to bear the load this time. Word is, they will make him Chancellor if he gets this through smoothly for them.'

'Townshend!' John Pownall nearly choked on his hot eel. 'He must want the Chancellorship really badly.'

'What makes you say that?'

'There were just twenty English students at Leiden when Townshend studied there. One of them was John Wilkes. Wilkes has owned Townshend body and soul ever since. Townshend goes to Wilkes's orgies over at Medmenham. He dresses up as a Cistercian monk and rogers the whores Wilkes supplies, dressed as nuns. It is

90

inconceivable that Townshend will go against Wilkes.'

'Perhaps he isn't,' Knox said. 'The colonies will be in uproar if this goes through. Wilkes wants trouble. More than trouble. Revolution. Revolution there and revolution here. And, if I may say so, technically they are not orgies that Wilkes arranges at Medmenham, John. Each monk goes off with his own nun and they do the deed in a cell, not in public.'

John Pownall smiled. 'I stand corrected, William.'

John Pownall eagerly awaited the Stamp Bill. It would finally create some revenue from the colonies. And, yes, the Stamp Bill would result in tumult in Massachusetts, especially, but the tumult would be crushed. And the revolutionaries would be crushed with it, once and for all.

One-third of the revenue from the proposed Stamp Bill was to be used to send another 10,000 troops to the colonies. The troops were ostensibly to protect the colonists from the French. John Pownall hoped they could be used against Adams and his patriot rabble.

A revolt by the patriots now would be perfect.

Below him, in the claustrophobically small chamber of the Commons, not even as long as a cricket pitch, Charles Townshend, known as Turnip Townshend, rose to speak. This had no discernible effect on the hubbub below.

John Pownall snorted with open contempt at Townshend's bulky figure and wild blond hair escaping untidily from all four corners of his wig. 'That man is a comic opera clown.'

William Knox smiled his engaging smile. 'I don't know about that. There were five Townshends at the last count. All full of the bluster and the blarney, I grant you that. But he is the brilliant one, is he not? All that learning in the Latin and the Greek?'

John Pownall snorted. 'There is no shortage of learned fools. Never was.'

Charles Townshend's voice rolled out. The din in the Commons reduced a little, but increased again when the Whig grandees on the benches opposite realised Townshend was not going to propose a Land Tax, so their estates were safe. Anything else he said was a matter of near total indifference. Most of them were drunk anyway.

'The war with the French has been lengthy …'

Pownall turned to Knox, muttering: 'Yes. At least partly because Massachusetts kept the French going by trading with them.'

'… This,' Townshend continued, 'has left us needing resources for British garrisons overseas, mainly in North America. Which are … er … expensive.'

'Whores are expensive, too,' one of the Whigs called out.

Townshend brightened. This was going well. 'Oh, I wouldn't know,' he said, his fair skin colouring.

There was a general cry of 'Yes, you bloody would.'

Townshend, grinning at his success, returned to his notes: 'And now will these Americans, children planted by our care, nourished up by our indulgence until they are grown to a degree of strength and opulence …'

'Opulence!' That was too much for William Knox. 'They are barely scratching a living in Georgia.'

'… a degree of strength and opulence, I say, and protected by our arms, will they grudge to contribute their mite …'

'I think they will begrudge it, Charlie. Yes,' William Knox said.

'… to relieve us from the heavy weight of that burden under which we lie.'

Thomas Pownall jumped to his feet, taking the floor from Townshend.

'You have lost some weight, brother of mine,' John announced to the world in general.

And it was certainly a leaner Thomas, greying just a little at the temples, now flushed with righteous fury, who spoke as loudly and angrily as John had ever heard him speak.

'The colonies planted by your care?' Thomas roared Townshend's words back to him. 'No! Your oppressions planted them in America ... Nourished by your indulgence, are they? No! They grew by your neglect of them.'

There were howls and yells of 'Sit down!' 'Give way!' 'Hold your tongue, sir!' and 'Let Townshend finish.'

Thomas Pownall abruptly sat down.

The Commons grew a little quieter while Townshend outlined the terms of the Stamp Bill, which were much as Hutchinson had written to Thomas Pownall. John Pownall had had Hutchinson's letter intercepted and had read it before his brother did. He was livid both at Hutchinson's opposition to the Stamp Bill and at his interference in writing to Thomas at all.

Thomas's successor as Governor of Massachusetts, Francis Bernard, by contrast, had just written to John Pownall expressing optimism about the Stamp Bill. 'Murmurs of dissent will die away,' Bernard had written.

Pownall did not think they would, but it was enough that Governor Bernard supported the legislation. John Pownall was well aware that Francis Bernard was an English gentleman of third-rate abilities. In fact, he was an idiot, a coward and a fool. But that made him all the more pliant. And he was from Lincolnshire, continuing that line of Lincolnshire officials in Boston that went back to the last century.

All that made him vastly preferable to Hutchinson. John Pownall made a mental note to have Hutchinson dismissed as soon as possible.

Meanwhile, Thomas was on his feet again, trying to give the speech he had prepared, with his own ideas for the governance of Massachusetts.

There were howls and groans from the Members when

his short figure bobbed up again.

Thomas Pownall was shaking from top to toe. There were tears in his eyes. He looked down for a second, rearranging his papers. Then Thomas shouted at his tormenters: 'These colonists are our own people, faithful, good and beneficial subjects and free-born *Englishmen*. They possess all the rights of freedom.'

The row was growing louder. John Pownall was shaking his head, ruefully. William Knox was listening impassively but with great concentration.

Thomas Pownall shouted on hoarsely in the mother of Parliaments. 'We should form Great Britain and its dependencies into one great marine empire and dominion extending over the Atlantic and America whose centre would be found within the British Empire.'

'Oh, that is really practical,' John muttered.

'No, wait.' William Knox laid a hand on John's arm. 'He's pleading for American representation in Parliament. That's what he means.'

'Whaat?'

Knox stood and muttered down to Thomas, below him. 'For God's sake, man. Say so clearly.' Knox turned to John Pownall. 'My, but he's the visionary, all right. That brother of yours.'

Thomas Pownall looked up at his brother and William Knox. As if he had heard Knox, which he could not have done above the furore, he abandoned his copious notes and shouted: 'They want no taxation without representation, that is their famous cry. Very well then, as we must tax them, and I accept that we must, let us give them representation. Let them elect Members in their own Assemblies to sit here in the Commons.'

'And how do we implement that, Thomas, you idiot,' John said to William Knox in the gallery. 'Do they take ship before every vote?'

'No,' Knox said. 'You forget, John, how poor the colonies are. You always do. Many there would jump at the chance of leaving the colonies for a more prosperous life here. They already do! As many leave America as go the other way. You would have no trouble finding people to stand as Members of the Commons.'

'You think this a practicable scheme, then?'

'I have no doubt of it. Your brother has just cut the Gordian knot. It is either his suggestion or revolution.'

But Thomas Pownall's plan was not put to the vote. Only a few of those present in the Commons that day even heard it. Once he had sat down, some of the Members returned for the vote. The Stamp Bill was passed into law as the Stamp Act by an overwhelming majority.

George III was too poorly to sign it. The King had had to flee the Epsom Races pursued by a baying mob chanting 'Wilkes and Liberty.' They hurled dead cats and dogs at him. He had been subject to fits of uncontrollable weeping ever since – a malady that from time to time afflicted Frederick, Lord North, too.

A group of commissioners signed the Stamp Act on George's behalf, a procedure that, as William Knox whimsically pointed out to John Pownall, arguably had no force in law.

CHAPTER 15

Adams and Young were briefing William Molineux and Ebenezer Mackintosh up in the observatory in Adams's house. Molineux and Mackintosh had been appointed crew leaders for this particular enterprise.

Molineux's handsome face was all concentration as he agreed to use the Fire Companies' well-rehearsed call-out to get his crew together. He requested Henry Bass and Elisha Brown for his crew, two of the London-born Mohucks already experienced in demolishing the houses of anybody opposed to John Wilkes.

Ebenezer Mackintosh, as he kept reminding anybody who would listen, had also destroyed houses before. Houses were destroyed in Boston if they were in the path of a fire. They were also sometimes destroyed after a fire, to be rebuilt of stone as part of a wider street.

But Mackintosh was becoming a problem for the patriots. Adams and Young were showing the strain of dealing with him. He had arrived very late to the briefing, and very drunk. The so-called uniform they had bought him was filthy and torn, hanging off him in shreds in places.

Once up in the observatory, sprawled half off his chair, he objected to using the Fire Companies' call-out plan, their trained runners. Adams patiently explained that they needed to practise for when the call-out would be a call to arms.

Mackintosh then objected to being allocated the downstairs of the house they were to pull down. The downstairs would include the servants' quarters, where pickings would be slimmer. To Young's open admiration, Adams held firm.

The Mohuck crews met up in Garden Court Street at ten in the morning the next day. The bells of the North Church were ringing as part of the general call to arms. After that, a complex system of Indian whoops and whistles told the Mohucks to assemble.

Adams was at home preparing to write his article about the day's events once they had unfolded. Young took up a post on the front lawn outside Hutchinson's mansion, at a distance from the knot of Negro slaves they had brought with them as messengers. He intended to stay there, with an overview of operations.

Young had ground-plans of the Hutchinson place. When Hutchinson's grandfather finished building the mansion, he left the drawings to Hutchinson's father, who donated them to the library at Harvard. Thomas Young regularly rode over to Harvard library to read and study. He had asked for three copies of the ground plan to be made. The librarians, patriots to a man, instantly agreed. They were glad to help.

Young called Molineux and Mackintosh over to him with an authoritative wave. He dwarfed even Molineux's bulk and was near twice Mackintosh's size. He gave one copy of the plan to Molineux, one to Mackintosh and kept the third for himself.

He looked at it again. On the ground floor, the plan showed the housekeeper's bedroom, the butler's pantry and between the two, it showed the wine cellar. Young smothered a curse. They had given the downstairs to Mackintosh's crew, so Mackintosh would find the wine cellar first.

How could they have been so stupid? He and Adams had even discussed the wine cellar as the main impediment to an orderly destruction of Hutchinson's house with no bad behaviour that would put them in the wrong. And then he and Adams had made an elementary blunder like this. They would do better. Young resolved it then and there. You don't make a revolution by making mistakes.

Molineux and Mackintosh knocked on the door of Hutchinson's house, with their crews gathering behind them. Nothing. Silence. Molineux nodded to his fellow Londoner, Henry Bass, who crowbarred the lock open. They were in.

One of Molineux's crew, the dockworker Edward Proctor, eyed the etchings in the hall. Molineux seized him by the shoulder.

'Get yer backside upstairs,' he barked out. 'Them's our orders. My crew upstairs. Now!'

Edward Proctor nodded, averting his eyes from the etchings, following Molineux obediently upstairs with the rest of the designated Molineux crew. Mackintosh, who was drunk already, took the etchings off the walls. You could get six shillings for those, easy.

Mackintosh called for a Negro slave runner from outside who loaded this first booty on a handcart, ready to wheel it back to the Mackintosh place on Pearl Street, near the ropewalks in the South End.

Mackintosh looked at the plan of the house Young had given him. The Great Chamber was to the left of the hallway. There was a drawing room to the right, kitchen to the left, then bedroom and dressing rooms. The service rooms, including the wine cellar, were below ground level. Mackintosh thought rapidly; greed overcame lust for alcohol.

'Great Chamber on the left,' he called out to his crew. 'Then we do the drawing room and the library.'

A few minutes later, Young, waiting outside, saw a procession of Mohucks carrying booty, giving it to Negro slaves who either carried it home, item by item, or loaded it onto handcarts or a couple of one-horse chaises, which had just appeared.

A floral-pattern walnut fauteuil was carried out by Benjamin Hallowell, the customs agent, and handed to a Negro slave. This was the armchair Hutchinson had sat in to receive Thomas Pownall, that time they had discussed the motion about smuggling put before the Assembly in Pownall's name. A Hepplewhite table and chairs followed

98

close behind, carried on high by triumphant Mohucks.

Then came an antique oak armoire, a chimney clock and painted hangings. Then a cane head with the Lieutenant Governor's crest, the silver bell Thomas Hutchinson used to summon a footman and the Dutch walnut marquetry table on which the bell had stood. The green Flemish patterned carpet followed when the furniture had been cleared. It was rolled up, along with an ornate Turkish rug.

From the kitchen, there were some iron pots and pans, a cheese coaster and some hams in canvas bags. From the boudoir, a rich damask bed with crimson damask curtains draped over it was dismantled and carried away.

Some of Ebenezer Mackintosh's crew had made their way through to the dining room. There they found a fine silver terrine with a laurel-leaf design on the lid and a pair of silver sugar shakers. There was also a canteen of silver cutlery. A bust of George III was smashed, not carried away. Some of the Bristol glassware was smashed accidentally as it was carried away by the wilder element of Mackintosh's crew.

Standing outside and watching, Thomas Young knew Molineux's crew had found their target when feathers started flying down out of an upstairs window. Then Molineux himself and Elisha Brown staggered out of the front door laden with women's shoes, lace gowns, petticoats and jewellery.

Molineux's handsome face broke into a wolfish grin at the sight of Young.

'Ah, the good doctor! Come and 'elp yourself, Dutch. That scoundrel Hutchinson deserves no better for his Stamp Act, making slaves of his own people.'

Young did not reply. Henry Bass appeared just behind Molineux with a haul of gauze handkerchiefs, gold snuffboxes and a satin apron flowered in gold.

There was a commotion from below ground downstairs,

the sound of barrels being broken open with axes, bottles being smashed and whooping and hollering. Young cursed under his breath. Mackintosh and his crew had found the wine cellar.

Should he intervene? Young tried to remember Adams's instructions on the subject but could not. In the end he followed the old adage that a sober man cannot manage a drunk man unless he knocks him out. And there were too many of them for yet another fight.

Meanwhile, Molineux and his crew had gone back inside for more. Molineux had a gimlet and chisel with him. Young realised they had broken open Hutchinson's bureau when a load of his papers fluttered down from an upstairs window, just as the feathers had before.

Young pursued some of the papers before they were trampled underfoot in the mud. They were from Hutchinson's *History of Massachusetts*. As he recognised the subject a smell of burning assailed his senses, closely followed by a thin trail of smoke. The fools had lit a fire to burn Hutchinson's papers. Young swore out loud. The one thing you do not do in Boston, thought the newcomer, is light a fire.

Young ran inside, past artisans from both crews carrying out Hutchinson's possessions. He ran through the hall, through the dining room and dressing room into the study. It was empty. Molineux's crew had moved on elsewhere. It was too late to save the manuscript of Hutchinson's book, burning away. Young stamped the flames out with his boots, roundly cursing Molineux for a fool.

He made his way outside again. As he took up his post outside the house he looked across at the neighbouring houses and saw Thomas Hutchinson.

Hutchinson had had warning of the Mohuck attack on his home from the merchant John Rowe and from a small group of loyalists informally led by the shopkeeper Theophilus Lillie, who had joined the Sons of Liberty only to spy on them. This group was dwindling, losing faith as the new Governor, Francis Bernard, spent most of his time at the British garrison out on the island at Castle William, in fear and trembling.

As soon as the warning came, the Lieutenant Governor had moved his beloved daughter, Peggy, his servants and slaves to his country place at Milton. He was coming back to fetch the manuscript of his *History of Massachusetts*, but he was evidently too late. Peggy had begged him not to leave Milton, but Hutchinson had been firm. He was also tranquil of spirit as it mattered less and less to him whether he lived or died.

Right now, he was standing in the garden of the Reverend Mather, his dead wife's brother-in-law. It was diagonally opposite his own house, the house where he had been born. That house was still standing at this point but with pretty much nothing portable left in it. The Lieutenant Governor had been watching while the crowd despoiled his home and stole or destroyed all his belongings

A girl of maybe thirteen years of age, moving with self-contained economy of movement, came out from the Reverend Mather's house to join him. She was wearing a plain light blue dress with smocking at the edges. He knew her. She was the Reverend Mather's daughter, Hannah.

She took his hand. 'Why are they doing that to your house?'

Hutchinson managed a grim smile. 'Because they do not like me very much, sad to say.'

Hannah nodded with perfect sympathy. 'I understand,' she said. 'There are three girls in my class at Dame School who do not like me very much, either. I don't know why.'

'Neither do I, Hannah. It's just one of those things, I guess.'

'Yes. Just one of those things.' She looked up at him, seriously. 'You put that well.'

'Thank you, Hannah.'

'Don't mention it. Are you in danger, Mr Hutchinson?'

Hannah stared unblinkingly up at him from huge brown eyes in a pinched little face.

Hutchinson pondered her question. 'Yes, Hannah. I believe I am.'

'Then I will take you to my friend's house,' she said. 'You will be safe there.'

Hutchinson laughed, a little croakily but definitely a laugh.

'Come!' Hannah added, pulling at his hand. 'It is not far.'

'All right,' said the Lieutenant Governor. 'Lead on, Hannah.'

And with that, the little girl led him away, pulling him impatiently along.

When everything that could be taken from Hutchinson's house had been taken, William Molineux took charge of demolishing the structure. The two crews came together at this point.

They began with the cupola, over the roof. It took them three hours to destroy it, working with hand axes in sub-crews of two or three, organised by Molineux. After that, the red tiles were smashed off the roof from inside. Then the plaster on the ceilings of the upper storey was broken up and the laths and the joists sawn through.

There was a representation of the British crown over every window. These got special attention. The plastered walls, adorned in places with Ionic pilasters, were smashed through; the mouldings, dado and cornices were broken off one by one. Then the orange marble Doric columns were smashed with large axes until only jagged stumps of the Portland stone exterior remained.

Finally, the little white picket fence round the lawn was kicked over and the three apple trees in the garden chopped down. And that was it. All that was left was a shell with bits of wall and some stumps of column. There was no house there any more. As a kind of envoi, the six

Corinthian pilasters at the front were destroyed, which brought the remains of the portico crashing down.

Next day, Samuel Adams, writing as Cato in the *Boston Post Boy*, condemned the violence. It was regrettable, he wrote, though also understandable as a spontaneous outpouring of emotion by provoked citizens. He also managed to suggest, in the same article, that Hutchinson had it coming, as the patriots had discovered letters in his house proving the Lieutenant Governor had colluded in the Stamp Act. Unfortunately these letters had been destroyed in a fire at the house, caused by Hutchinson's negligence.

CHAPTER 16

The day after the destruction of his house, Hutchinson appeared before the Assembly, now dominated by patriot members. He wore the clothes he had worn when he fled from his home with young Hannah Mather; these were the only clothes he now possessed, apart from a few items at Milton.

He denied he had supported the Stamp Act in any way. He was clearly not believed.

'No Lieutenant Governor since the Charter which first gave Massachusetts its existence has suffered as much as I have done,' Thomas Hutchinson told the Assembly, his voice cracking as he spoke.

The Assembly granted Hutchinson a modest compensation. But that was conditional on him accepting an amnesty for all those accused of participating in the destruction of his house. As he felt he had no alternative, Hutchinson accepted the condition, with no little bitterness.

The only man arrested for the destruction of the house was Ebenezer Mackintosh. Adams had organised that, behind the scenes, as he was trying to be rid of the cordwainer. But he misjudged the strength of the town's feeling. Mackintosh had to be quickly released for fear of a riot.

The Assembly's decision on the Hutchinson affair was signed by Governor Francis Bernard. Governor Bernard was always conscious that his salary was paid by the Assembly, something his unworldly predecessor, Thomas Pownall, never thought about and never felt he needed to think about.

And if the Assembly believed the Lieutenant Governor was complicit in the Stamp Act, which they unshakeably did, they were hardly likely to believe that the Crown's main representative in Massachusetts, the Governor, was not involved in the Act, too – even though he was not. So

Francis Bernard became even more timid and fearful in the weeks following the destruction of Hutchinson's house.

In his insecurity, the Governor asked for – actually, screamed out for – a doubling of the garrison of sixty British troops presently stationed over the causeway known as the Neck, at Castle William. The request went to General Gage, commander of British troops in America, based in New York. Gage sent another hundred men from Halifax.

While wryly acknowledging this rare success on Francis Bernard's part, Hutchinson could not see what difference the extra troops would make, as they could be called out only by the Assembly.

Thomas Hutchinson became almost unnaturally still. A heavy resigned lassitude settled on him, never to leave, as if he were permanently garbed in a massive heavy greatcoat with lead in its pockets which brought him down. He slumped in an armchair in Milton, pulling his imaginary heavy greatcoat over his head to shut out the light.

The Lieutenant Governor had been an inveterate letter writer all his life and continued to be so as middle age dragged wearily into premature old age. In sudden spasms of energy, he would leave his armchair to write letter after letter, like a mechanical letter-writing machine, as if the very motion of writing letters dulled perceptions of a life he no longer required.

He wrote from the Reverend Mather's house in Garden Court Street or from his country place in Milton. He wrote draft after draft, starting again if there was even a calligraphic slip, let alone an infelicity of expression. He preserved all the drafts. Like the born historian he was, his archive of draft letters sent and letters received was immaculately organised by time, place and sender.

After the razing of his house to the ground by the rabble, as he called them, he always referred to the rabble-leader, Samuel Adams, even in formal correspondence, as Wilkes-Adams. (Informally, especially to Peggy, he referred to the Publican as 'that little creeping Jesus'.)

Hutchinson wrote to the former Governor, Thomas Pownall, and his brother, the Under-Secretary at the American Department, John Pownall, with equal frequency. It was perhaps to be expected that letters to the Under-Secretary, who he had never met, would be the more formal, but they were not.

Hutchinson had never liked Thomas Pownall, and his woolliness of thought, as Hutchinson saw it, irritated him even more from afar than it had in Boston. John Pownall, on the other hand, he found refreshingly honest, direct, even blunt, and that was to the Lieutenant Governor's liking.

However, letters to both brothers were suddenly curtailed by a sharp worsening of Hutchinson's health. A nervous disorder kept him in a state of paralysis for days on end. The lassitude grew worse, the movement of letter-writing was no longer possible. He was subject to fits of giddiness.

He could not bring himself to consult Dr Thomas Young, even though he was universally acknowledged as the best doctor in Boston. He had seen Young grinning like a maniac outside his house while it was attacked. In fact, he had come to loathe Young almost as much as the little creeping Jesus.

Writing as Leonidas in the *Massachusetts Spy*, Young had launched a savage attack on Hutchinson. It was addressed 'To the treasonable USURPER of an *absolute* DESPOTISM over the good people of Massachusetts Bay, Thomas Hutchinson.' Hutchinson was accused of being a latter-day Julius Caesar, plotting the destruction of Republican Rome – that was the American colonies – to impose royal dictatorship via evil measures such as the Stamp Act.

Hutchinson could not lower himself to reply in kind. When his nervous illness deteriorated so badly he could no longer function, he had himself treated by Dr Samuel Whitworth, not least because Whitworth hated Young. Whitworth prescribed a total avoidance of work, attempts to divert his mind, and, when his limbs had recovered a little of their strength, long horseback rides.

However, any improvement in his well-being was entirely due, Hutchinson was convinced, to tender care from his beloved Peggy. He did not think he could be any closer to Peggy, his constant companion, but his growing frailty completed their bond, drawing their unity ever tighter.

Naturally, Peggy was bothered by suitors these days, the young men of the town. But Thomas Hutchinson brushed them all away, forbidding them her company.

CHAPTER 17

Amazing news came from London, first as shouts in the street, then as letters, then in newspaper reports. *The British have repealed the Stamp Act.* The world's mightiest nation, for so Britain was after its victory over the French, had backed down from its dastardly scheme to get money from America.

Hutchinson could hardly believe it, reading the first letters on the subject over and over again. Thomas Pownall had written that the main reason was opposition to the egregious Act by London merchants. According to Thomas, George Hayley, who he described as Wilkes's agent, had addressed 300 traders who dealt with the American colonies at the Mansion House.

Hayley had fanned the flames of revolt among the merchants over the Stamp Act damaging their trade. Simultaneously, John Wilkes and the pro-American faction, including Thomas Pownall himself, had moved for repeal in the Commons.

Actually, Hutchinson knew these developments were afoot from Anne Hayley, who he had encountered at a dinner at John Rowe's house while her husband was in London. She had told him proudly of her husband's talk to the merchants and her brother's speech in the Commons, so he knew the former Governor's account was accurate, for once.

But as usual the younger brother's analysis was closer to reality. John Pownall wrote to Hutchinson that the Stamp Act was unenforceable because there was nobody in Boston capable of enforcing it against increasingly well-organised opposition. The few Customs Officers Boston had were too weak and feeble for the daunting task.

Boston went crazy with celebration. The Liberty Tree was festooned with lights; the battered old elm had never looked so gaudy and gay. A Liberty Pole was put through the tree, as a further sign of the people's coming freedom from slavery.

A crowd of thousands gathered round Liberty Hall, the open grass area around the Liberty Tree. They wore clothes in Wilkes's colour, blue, some imported by John Hancock and given away to anybody who asked for them, some spun by the likes of Mary Young, working from the Young home in Wing's Lane, then sold.

An obelisk was erected at Liberty Hall as a permanent monument to the great victory. The obelisk was of stone with patterns and lines of poetry celebrating freedom carved into it.

Mary Young, happily clutching her husband's arm tight to her, among the celebrants, said 'Those lines are nearly as bad as yours, Thomas.' But she was only joshing. Thomas Young, aware how bad his attempts at verse were, put his huge head back and bellowed with happy laughter. He read the freedom lines aloud:

Our faith approved, our Liberty restored
Our hearts bend grateful to our sovereign Lord

The hats just coming into fashion were tricorns, but of soft felt material. They could be folded, so two Wilkes cockades could be pinned to them, one on either side of a fold. The cockades thus appeared like two eyes in a face. They were Wilkes's eyes. It was as if John Wilkes himself were looking over from England on their great victory, which many attributed to him anyway.

The good folk of Boston held onto their hats as they tilted their heads back to watch fireworks – paid for by John Hancock – soaring into the sky.

The people felt, rather than thought, that Boston would never be the same again. It was not the same town any more. It was *their* town. It was America, not a British colony. And they, as citizens, were not the same people.

They were not Britons subject to the British King any more, and certainly not subject to the British Parliament. Then, when the fireworks were finished, exhausted with happiness, the people of Boston sang the Liberty Song.

Come, join hand in hand, brave Americans all,
And rouse your bold hearts at fair Liberty's call;
No tyrannous acts shall suppress your just claim,
Or stain with dishonour America's name.

Sam Adams stood on the dais at the front of Liberty Hall. With the Liberty Tree behind him and the Liberty Pole rearing up above him, he gave an address to the crowd.

'We have been enslaved by the most powerful and haughty nation on earth,' Adams shouted into the multitude. 'The British have all the insolence of power. But of all the peoples of this earth we Americans deserve the most to be free.' Adams was already hoarse from shouting above the roars of support. 'And so I tell you for now and into the future for all time: *vox populi est vox dei* – the voice of the people is the voice of God.'

They said afterwards the roar of the people could be heard right across the Charles River, in Cambridge and Charlestown. Adams was shaking from head to toe.

But he also knew, as Hutchinson knew, as he sat in his room in somebody else's house; as John Pownall knew, as he sat alone working by lamplight in his cheap lodgings; as John Wilkes knew, as he plunged into the fleshpots of Medmenham; that the British would try again.

John Pownall warned Hutchinson in his next letter that next time, whatever legislation they passed would be enforced by executive officers sent from the mother country.

Hutchinson feared he was right.

CHAPTER 18

John Pownall burst past the clerks in the outer office of the American Department, as they toiled away, supervised, as ever, by the stately presence of the Chief Clerk, William Pollock. In high good humour, he swung open the door and dashed at full tilt into the cramped office he shared with William Knox.

He was not certain whether he would find Knox there or not. The Irishman had been away from the American Department, suffering the effects of an over-vigorous purging. His absences from the Department were frequent. They were part, Pownall thought, of a scheme of affected indolence.

But the Irishman was at his allotted place, feet up on the desk, reading a book, radiating contented calm into which was launched the storm of John Pownall.

Pownall gripped Knox's shoulders, knocking the book sideways, then kissed him twice, once hard on the cheek, once softly but fleetingly on the lips.

'What are you reading?'

'Hello John! And a good morning to you, too. I am reading, since you so kindly asked, *Revolutions of Sweden* by the excellent Mr Vertot. Our good friend Wilkes has contributed a foreword to the new edition. We learn of Gustavus Vasa fighting for the liberty of his country against oppressive tyranny. I think by oppressive tyranny he means people like us, John. You and me. My ears were burning as Pliny says they do when you are discussed.'

John Pownall laughed delightedly.

William Knox went on: 'So what news from the greatest auditorium in the kingdom? I heard they were going to clear the Colonial Agents and the merchants from the gallery while Townshend spoke.'

'Yes, they did. Good idea. It made more room. Great news, Billy boy. The splendid shuttlecock has spoken.

Charles Townshend was on his feet for upwards of an hour. Ho-ho-ho.' Pownall gave a passable imitation of Townshend's famous braying laugh, shoulders heaving. 'The fool has been appointed Chancellor, for some reason.'

'Fool indeed. And not even a steadfast fool. He has betrayed every leader he has ever served.'

'Yup. You can call him Champagne Charlie now. New nickname. He was slurping down champagne all through his big speech on America. Good stuff, too, by the look of it. The champagne, that is. Not the speech.'

Knox's face took on a deadly serious look. He put his book down on his near-empty desk and held up a peremptory hand.

'Now, hold your horses, my good sir. Hold it right there. You raise a fundamental philosophical question, on this fine summer day. Namely. Stop laughing, boy! Namely, can a man, any man, maintain two nicknames? Townshend has been known as Turnip Townshend ever since he was born in a turnip field in Raynham, which I believe is in Norfolk.'

Pownall was heaving with laughter. 'Stop, stop, stop. You disappear into labyrinths of your own creation, as ever. Now, do you want to hear Champagne Charlie's words of wisdom or do you not? I offer you the very latest from this yellow-haired buffoon, with his unexampled lack of judgement, discretion and sense.'

'Go ahead.'

They were both suddenly serious. Pownall sat at his desk and consulted the notes he had made.

'They are finally sending in Customs Commissioners. And about bloody time. The new Revenue Act creates an American Board of Customs, with headquarters in Boston.'

'Interesting. That makes Boston the de facto capital of the colonies, ahead of New York and Philadelphia.'

'I hadn't thought of that.'

'New York heard of it, wanted it. Offered money for it,

so I heard tell.'

'Really?'

Knox smiled. 'Adams will be pleased as Punch. He'll think Christmas has come early. Or Pope's Day, or whatever he believes in. And Young. And Hancock. They'll all be delighted, secretly of course. Oppression brings the revolution nearer.'

'The word is that one of the new Customs Commissioners, Charles Paxton, helped Townshend draft the bill. Paxton's from Boston himself, of course. And so is John Temple.'

Knox nodded, serious now. 'That's good. Temple's a good choice as Commissioner. He must have been in Boston for at least twenty years now. A seasoned, sober fellow. The Bostonians see him as one of them. And Charles Paxton, too. But the others have got to be honest. And sufficiently paid. If we keep sending them crooks who cheat and take bribes, we are asking for trouble.'

Pownall sighed. 'I know. I know.'

'And has this new Revenue Act really simplified payments? Until they simplify the system, the American merchants, especially Hancock, will just keep on with that hoary old chestnut that they don't pay because they don't know how much to pay.'

Pownall smiled. 'Yes, the new measures are quite straightforward. They should succeed. The new Customs Commissioners, five of them, will need a special building. They can't work from Castle William.' Pownall consulted his notes. 'They have money to set it up.'

Knox smiled. 'Adams and his bully boys will love all that.'

'My esteemed brother is not too keen either. He spoke against the Revenue Act, of course. He is actually becoming a bit better, as a speaker in Parliament, though not much. Mother could never understand a word he said when we were boys. He came up with a couple of good phrases, though. Just a minute ...' Pownall burrowed in his notes, his spidery writing, full of crossings-out, covering a sheaf of papers. 'Yes, here it is: "It is my opinion that this kingdom has no right to lay a tax upon the colonies. The Americans are the sons, not the bastards of England."'

'Yes, that is good. What tax?'

Pownall sighed. 'Oh yes!' He searched through his notes again. 'There is to be a tax on various products, some of them bizarre like painters' colours, but most importantly tea.'

'Tea? Under the Revenue Act?'

'Yup. It has been calculated that if ... IF ... tea duties can get round the bloody American smuggling, they could bring in a small fortune.'

Knox nodded. 'It's inevitable, isn't it?'

'Yes, it is crucial, William. We cannot manage without it. Some of the money will go to pay the Royal Officials – Francis Bernard, Hutchinson, the judges. And the soldiers.'

Knox smiled. 'The Sons of Liberty will howl, of course. Only their Assembly may control payments, remember? Freedom under the Charter. John Locke has moved to America. Our money is our property, our property is inviolable. No thingummybob without thingummy.'

John Pownall clenched his fists, white in the face. 'It's intolerable! Isn't it, William? May we not pay our own officials and soldiery ourselves?'

'Apparently not,' Knox said. And then, quietly. 'John, you know as well I do, they fear their Assembly will be dissolved if it has no purpose.'

'That is our decision, not theirs. No, I've had enough, William. Ridding America of the French has near bankrupted us.'

Knox shook his head in mock sorrow. 'We are in dire need of assistance, if not divine intervention.'

'All we ask the American colonies to pay is about a third of the cost of administering their own land. At the moment, of course. Townshend wants to increase it gradually until

America is finally paying for itself. All taxes collected in America stay in America. For God's sake, what else do they want?'

'Freedom?'

There was a deferential tap on the office door. When Pownall roared 'Come in!' the Chief Clerk, William Pollock, hovered in the doorway, hands submissively over his crotch.

'Excuse the interruption, gentlemen. There is distressing news from the Commons, which I think you should be aware of. Mr Townshend had a fall after his big speech.'

'Epilepsy?' Knox said. 'He gets seizures.'

'I have no idea of the precise diagnosis, sir,' said the Chief Clerk. 'But apparently he is sitting on the floor covered in blood with a patch over one eye.'

'Poor Champagne Charlie,' said Knox. 'I'm sorry we laughed at him now.'

'A little sorry,' John Pownall said. 'Not too sorry.'

Thomas Hutchinson sat alone in his study in his country place at Milton. The shutters were down over the windows. Outside, an autumn wind howled, whipping the waves in Boston harbour to a spiteful frenzy. It was raw-cold; snow was on the ground.

Hutchinson read the letter in his hand, then stared at it blankly. The letter was an official communication of the Crown, signed by the hand of King George III. It informed him of the sad loss of the Crown's loyal servant, Charles Townshend, who had died of a putrid fever at the age of forty-two.

He had, thought Hutchinson, not long outlived the passing of his Revenue Act, already known as the Townshend Act in his honour.

But it was the next paragraph of the letter that devastated Hutchinson beyond what he thought possible. After all, he believed himself half-dead after the destruction of his house and the manuscript of his life's work. Were they now kicking the corpse?

Townshend had been succeeded as Chancellor of the Exchequer, the letter informed him, by the man he knew to be the King's favourite, Frederick Lord North. North's first action in his new role was to give him, Hutchinson, as Chief Justice of the Court and Lieutenant Governor, a monthly payment from the new customs duties to be collected under the Revenue Act – the Townshend Act.

An eldritch noise broke from somewhere inside Hutchinson. It was a noise he had never made before, a deep-voiced agony somewhere between a prolonged groan and a scream. He heaved up and down in his chair. Finally, he did scream, but smothered it as Peggy was around somewhere, as ever not very far away.

Wide-eyed, Hutchinson wondered how *anything*, anything, could make the so-called patriots hate him even more. But by directly associating him, Thomas Hutchinson, with this soon-to-be-hated tax, they had achieved that. They had made him a beneficiary, for God's sweet sake, a clear and public beneficiary, of the abhorred measure.

Hutchinson had never met Lord North, but he had corresponded with him. He held North to be a decent, albeit limited, man with unrivalled sway over the King.

But how could a man entrusted with any dealing at all with colonial matters have such fundamental ignorance as to do this? Hutchinson was the best friend the loyalists had. He was also, he reflected bitterly, the best friend the patriots had, if they only knew it. He was certainly the one man who could form an effective bridge between the Crown in England and the Assembly in Massachusetts.

And now £200 per annum paid directly by the Crown, bypassing the Assembly, would end any role he could have played in healing the chasm between Britain and the American colonies. Nobody in Boston would ever listen to him or trust him again. They would never believe he had not asked for this money, paid in this way.

How could Lord North be such a fool? Hutchinson prayed to God that North would have no further influence on events as far as the colonies were concerned.

Shortly after Thomas Hutchinson sent his prayer up to God, the Customs Commissioners arrived in Boston. As luck would have it, they arrived on November 5, the old Pope's Day, when the North End under William Molineux used to fight the South End, under Ebenezer Mackintosh, before Adams and Young unified and organised the patriots.

The first Wednesday after they landed, one of the Commissioners with a Boston background, John Temple, threw a dance at the Salutation, on the corner of North and Salutation Streets. It was designed to be the first of regular dances every other Wednesday.

This transparent attempt to flatter the Bostonians was lashed by Samuel Adams, writing as Mucius Scaevola in

117

the *Massachusetts Spy*. Adams warned the 'Young Ladies of Boston' not to attend the dance. They would forfeit their reputation and good name by associating with the profoundest enemies of the country.

The Mucius Scaevola article caused Thomas and Mary Young great amusement when Thomas read it aloud to Mary, while she was practising the harpsichord in their parlour, the day before the dance. It did not prevent Thomas and Mary going to the dance, an enjoyable occasion attended by about sixty couples. Thomas kissed Mary passionately in full sight of everyone as they spun to an Allemande.

The week after the dance, the merchant John Rowe threw a dinner party for the two Bostonian Commissioners, John Temple and Charles Paxton, at his gracious house in the South End, just east of Devonshire Street. As all Boston knew, this was the moderate merchants' attempt to come to terms with the Townshend Act and the officials who were to implement it.

Gathered at the Rowe place on a still night, with powdery snow deep enough to cover the oyster shells that paved the streets, was a motley cross-section whose lives would be affected by the Commissioners.

Representing the military was General Thomas Gage, Commander of all British forces in America, visiting from his headquarters in New York. He had brought along his wife, Margaret, a New Yorker sixteen years younger than him. The British Admiral, John Montagu, a frequent guest at Rowe's house, was not in Boston at the moment, so Rowe kept the numbers down by letting Gage speak for the navy, too, which he technically did anyway.

The merchants were represented by John Rowe himself, sometime patriot, sometime loyalist but always a merchant. His wife, Hannah, however, had excused herself from the gathering. She had just had her cataracts couched by Dr Young and was lying on her bed with a cold-water compress over her eyes. This left Margaret Gage as the only woman present.

John Rowe had invited Theophilus Lillie so the small shopkeepers were represented. Lillie, the loyalist dry-goods seller, was just beginning as a tea trader. He was a taciturn man, so Rowe was not expecting him to say all that much, especially in this company.

There was no question of inviting Thomas Hutchinson or his circle, even though they were the most powerful merchants in Boston. Nobody had any contact with Thomas Hutchinson any more. The man was a pariah.

Rowe had invited John Hancock because he thought he had to, but Hancock had brusquely turned down his invitation to parlay with the Commissioners. Hancock had called one of his ships *Liberty*, and no longer even drank the loyal toast.

Rowe was secretly relieved Hancock would not be there. Like most of the merchants, Rowe privately believed Hancock could not go on evading the customs dues he should legally pay. They feared he would provoke a destabilising revolution against the British that none of them wanted – not least because they could never win it.

John Rowe often thought back to Governor Pownall, his dear friend Thomas, now so sadly departed from Boston. Rowe missed him personally and regarded him as representing better times and better ways of doing things than they had now. There was less conflict, less hatred, in Thomas Pownall's time.

In his last letter, Thomas had sounded, not pessimistic exactly, he was never that, but sad. He had warned that John Wilkes's influence over the patriots was strong and direct, through George Hayley and Hancock. He wanted John Wilkes to work through Parliament only, but doubted he would. He had also warned that the French could not be counted on to stay out of American affairs for ever. They were watching and waiting, Thomas thought, biding their time.

Economic circumstances were helping them in their aim. Boston's trade was doing badly. Rowe had been shocked by the recent collapse into bankruptcy of all the ventures of a leading merchant, Nathaniel Wheelwright.

Boston businesses, dependent on trade as industry was forbidden them by the British, were all so interlinked. Wheelwright's collapse into Poor Relief had brought down the businesses of four other leading merchants. John and Hannah Rowe had many tense sleepless nights fearing they could be next. Nobody was safe. Well, maybe Hancock, maybe Hutchinson, but nobody else.

Was this meal now the last chance to set the ship on an even keel, getting the Commissioners and merchants to work amicably together, so avoiding a revolution? It may not have been the very last chance, but in Rowe's opinion there would not be too many more.

Of the Commissioners, the best hope by far lay with John Temple. He was married to the daughter of a leading Bostonian, the wealthy James Bowdoin. Although British-educated, Temple had spent more time in Boston than in London; he gave generously to Poor Relief and had children at the Dame School in Boston. By and large, he was a popular figure.

Popular was not a word that could be applied to Charles Paxton, who was detested in Boston, being regarded as little better than a British spy. Some of the virulent reaction to him shocked John Rowe, who had been civil and emollient to every man and woman who had ever crossed his path. That was the way he had been brought up, back in Chagford, Devon, in the dear old mother country.

Over a meal of what Margaret Gage later generously described as 'the finest haunch of venison I ever saw' washed down by a splendid Burgundy, the company congenially got down to business, some of it veiled as small talk.

'You will need a headquarters,' John Rowe murmured,

wanting to help, starting at a safe, uncontroversial place. His Devon burr was overlaid now by flat Boston vowels.

'We want to build a completely new place, from the ground up, maybe at the old Concert Hall on Hanover Street,' John Temple said, reminding everyone that the Commissioners were not only being paid well themselves, but also plenty of money had been put at their disposal.

'I'll have a word with some people,' said Rowe. 'I shall send three or four builders round to you.'

'Thank you, John,' said John Temple. 'That would be most helpful.'

The Commissioners were also finding it difficult to attract staff. Those prepared to work for them, like Benjamin Hallowell, had a long history of being customs informants for money. They were so detested, nobody on the Boston seafront would even talk to them. Nevertheless, Hallowell had been signed up as their first employee.

'Needs must ...' as John Temple dryly put it.

Charles Paxton knocked back his wine and banged his glass on the table to have it refilled. 'We made our first seizure,' he said. 'We had nowhere to deal with all the documentation. We ended up in Temple's study.'

'I heard about that,' General Gage said.

There had been a near riot. Gage had sent word to the Assembly, asking if they wanted him to call out the guard.

Rowe smiled apologetically. 'Captain John Homer is ... a well-liked personage in the community. And his ship was stopped before it had left Boston harbour. Much of his cargo was perishable.'

Margaret Gage was looking at each speaker keenly as he spoke. She was dressed formally, some Boston ladies would have said overdressed for a private occasion, in a Turkish-style red taffeta ball-gown with lace at the low neck and on the unfashionably wide sleeves.

But then, as Margaret had said herself before they left Castle William, her husband was all dressed up like an Easter lamb before the kill, in his best scarlet dress uniform, complete with epaulettes and sash, so why should she not look equally smart?

Margaret Gage fanned herself with a half-opened fan, smiling. 'That is quick work, isn't it?' she said, referring to the seizure, in her New York drawl, aiming the remark at Temple, who she sensed was the most susceptible to her charms. 'How on earth did you manage that so quickly?'

'We were acting on information, ma'am.'

'Were you, now?' Margaret Gage was all wide eyes, her sharp intelligence well masked behind blinking eyelids and that beating fan in front of her face. 'And how does that work?'

'Benjamin Hallowell is an informer,' Paxton blurted out, gulping wine, then looking hard at her beating fan and heaving bosom. 'He's one of many.' Paxton spoke as if credit for the system of informers were largely due to him.

'And this Hallowell,' Margaret Gage purred, 'does he act for love or money?'

Rowe wondered whether Margaret Gage knew Hallowell had been with the patriots for a while. She seemed to know, by her manner, but heaven knew how.

General Gage had been gazing at his much younger wife with indulgent admiration, rather as if a talking bird he had been training for some time had finally said a few words.

'Margaret,' he said, softly. 'That is indiscreet.'

The Commissioners fell over themselves to assure the lovely young Mrs Gage that her question was not only permissible but of interest to them. They both spoke at once but Charles Paxton spoke loudest.

'People like Hallowell have no principle, Mrs Gage. He does what he does for money.'

'How much?'

That got a laugh. John Temple replied. 'Usually a percentage of anything we sell the seized goods for. Even two per cent can be quite substantial. That is what they usually get.'

'He is hated for it. Hallowell's house was attacked at the same time as Hutchinson's, Margaret,' General Gage said.

'Scum!' Charles Paxton muttered morosely. 'Illiterate rabble.'

Drunken tears came to his eyes. Charles Paxton's own house, back in Newport, had been attacked by a mob of dock workers. Paxton had set his footmen on them and ended up being jailed himself. The bitterness was fresh; this was only a couple of years earlier.

Paxton spoke, looking at Margaret Gage only. 'The mob broke Hallowell's windows, tore down his fence, broke into his house and drank all the wine and brandy in his cellar. You are among barbarians here in Boston, Mrs Gage. It is not like New York at all.'

'They stole his money, too,' said the taciturn tea trader, Theophilus Lillie.

'So that will make him all the keener to inform, to get his money back?' Margaret Gage accompanied this with a furious fanning, most of it aimed at John Temple.

'He was keen enough in the first place, ma'am,' Lillie said, to more laughter.

'We had to make him Comptroller of Customs,' Charles Paxton blurted out. 'Put him on a salary.'

John Temple looked none too pleased. That was supposed to be confidential; even Rowe looked surprised.

'That's enough, Charles,' John Temple said to Paxton.

John Rowe decided to make his move. He had calculated that any enforcement of payments of a customs excise would be tolerated in Boston, albeit with grumbles and mutterings. It was not excise on goods traded that was objected to, but the raising of so-called external revenue in taxes.

Rowe spoke bluntly: 'If you do it in the right way, a move to get Hancock to pay excise might not be condemned too much in Boston, outside the Sons of Liberty, especially if Hallowell were not involved.'

Temple shot Rowe an admiring look. He glanced round the table. If that got back to Hancock ... But in Temple's opinion Rowe's shrewd choice of guests might see him get away with it.

There was silence for a moment. Then John Temple said. 'We would like to do that, John. Though it may take a little time.'

By this time, the footmen and Negro slaves were clearing away the Boston apple pudding flavoured with nutmeg that had been served after the haunch of venison. Finest Madeira was flowing freely. Rowe had timed this well.

'Would you apply to the Assembly to ratify the Customs Commissioners' appointment through the General Court?' Rowe said softy. 'I can guarantee it would be approved.'

Margaret Gage shot him a sharp glance, indicating she had understood. The Charter between King William III and the people of Massachusetts that had brought Massachusetts into being empowered the General Court to appoint all Crown officers.

To the people of Boston, the Commissioners finishing off their Boston apple pudding were not even here legally. Putting their appointment through the Assembly would legitimise it, but more importantly establish Assembly control over Crown appointments to Massachusetts, taking the situation back to what it was in the days of the Charter.

'John, that is ingenious,' John Temple said. 'Even brilliant. But ...'

'But we're not that drunk,' Charles Paxton said, with a sneer.

CHAPTER 20

Thomas Hutchinson also made a last-ditch attempt to keep the issue of the Commissioners in constitutional channels and away from the streets. He put a motion to the Assembly requesting a reduction on the tea tax part of the Townshend Act, attempting to assert Assembly control over a revenue tax imposed by the British Parliament.

Samuel Adams arranged for the Assembly debate on the matter to end in uproar. He was greatly aided in this by Thomas Young. Young controlled the Liberty Boys, Boston schoolboys who included his two sons, Rosmond and John. The Liberty Boys had grown out of the organised trips to the Liberty Tree made by the boys of the South Writing School. Young had them highly organised, in a manner imitative of the Mohucks.

Young called the Liberty Boys to the gallery of the Assembly to barrack Hutchinson and any other loyalist speakers. As Clerk of the Assembly, Adams promptly ended the session before there could be any discussion of the tea tax issue.

The Liberty Boys liked going to the Young house for many reasons. Mary Young made them bowls of porridge and smiled at them, which made them feel warm. Dr Young made them laugh and taught them interesting things they had not known before.

Most of them also liked the house itself; the peace of it, the look of it, the atmosphere of it. The Young place on Wing's Lane stood on a quarter-acre plot near Faneuil Hall. It was narrow but it went back a long way. It had to be sizeable, to accommodate the Youngs' six children, two boys and four girls.

The Liberty Boys met there every Thursday, market day in Boston when the schools were closed. The Thursday after they brought the Assembly to a halt, over thirty of them, in buoyant mood, crowded in to the Youngs' big front common room downstairs, sitting jammed up against each other on the floor. In age, they went all the way from ten or eleven to some who were old enough to be thoroughly distracted by Mary Young's Negro slave sewing girl, Martha, who was a comely wench.

The boys waited expectantly for Dr Young to start his entertaining mix of instruction and briefing to action. All of them liked him, some adored him. His two sons, Rosmond and John, basked in the reflected glory.

Thomas Young beamed. He stood out front, facing the boys, huge, haloed in the light from the window, against a white-plastered wall. Befitting his work as a healer, the wall was adorned with a Hogarth print of *The Consultation* and a portrait of Galen, who Young ranked ahead of Hippocrates, if only because almost everybody else put them the other way round.

He was silent for a moment, then picked up his violin and played a few snatches of Bach's violin concerto in A minor.

'Who wrote that?'

There were a few cries of 'Bach, sir.' Nobody got it wrong.

Thomas Young then played snatches of 'Yankee Doodle', tipping the fiddle around like a peddler playing for pennies at an inn. 'Who wrote that?' And then before anybody could say anything: 'I did.'

That drew laughter. One of the boys said 'No you didn't.'

The boy who had spoken up was a raw-boned youth, all knuckles, knees and Adam's apple, called Christopher Seider. His family were brewers. They were of German stock, like Mary Young, who was playing the harpsichord in the next room, they could hear it. Mary Young's father, Captain Garret Winegar, was from Hanover, same as the British kings.

Like Mary Young, Christopher Seider was blond

126

with a clear complexion. Both of them blushed easily. Cristopher Seider was blushing now. Thomas Young took a step towards him. He towered over the seated youth, even though he was just about the biggest boy in the group. Thomas pointed dramatically at him.

'Christopher Seider is questioning me,' Young thundered. 'He is expressing doubt at what I said about me composing "Yankee Doodle". Is he right to question me?'

'Yes, sir!' the boys bellowed back as one, grinning, laughing, knowing they were on safe ground.

'Good boys! And why was Christopher right to question me?'

'Because we should question everything, Papa,' piped John, Young's second son, still a head shorter than Rosmond but growing like Indian corn.

'Good! Yes, you should even question important people like physicians. You know, in Ancient Greece physicians were highly respected, but in Rome they were not even admitted to citizenship. Which was better, Greece or Rome?'

'Greece!' yelled the boys.

'Yes, Greece. But Rome had its moments. For example, the essence of religion was revealed long before the Gospels by its sages, especially Cicero, who, by the way, regarded Customs Officers as sordid. He ranked them with money-lenders as occupations the public detests.'

That got a cheer and some Indian whoops. Flourishing in the sunshine of their approval, Thomas Young began his party piece, as he called it.

'Christopher?' he began with studied innocence.

'Yes, sir!'

'Christopher Seider, go fetch me my Bible, please. It is next door, with the ladies. I believe Martha may have it.'

The boys hooted with laughter, even Christopher himself, through his blushes. Christopher was nearly sixteen and found it difficult not to dream of Martha. Young strode up and down, giant strides, while Christopher was gone. The boys kept discipline. Christopher was back quickly with the Bible, handing it over reverently with a 'Here you are, sir.'

'Thank you, Christopher,' Young said. 'That was most kind. Now if you would like to continue your service to the group, I would ask you to open the Bible at random and quote me a heading from it.'

Christopher Seider, still standing, took the Bible back, opened it and read out, 'The revelation of St John the Divine, sir.'

Young stopped pacing, thinking hard, or rather acting thinking hard.

'St John the Devine. Good. Well, at least that isn't one of those ridiculous fables, like Moses. St John the Devine. Now, if I remember correctly, there is a passage there which runs: "And to the woman was given two wings of an eagle that she may fly into the wilderness, into her place, where she is nourished for a time and times and half a time." And then you get an angel who swears "There shall be time no longer." Well then, the solar system must have ceased its motions, must it not? For that is how we compute the succession of time.'

There was silence in the room. 'So,' Young continued. 'How do we avoid this vagueness and unintelligibility of the prophecies? Hmmm? I will tell you, boys. We do not proceed from deduction à la Mr Descartes. Oh no! We proceed from empirical observation, like Mr Isaac Newton. Why? So we are not guessing, we are proceeding according to the evidence of our senses, which is verifiable. And after we observe, what do we do?'

'Classify,' said Christopher Seider.

'Correct, Christopher. And how do we classify? We find what Aristotle called the essence in every category. We get the species right, then the genus right. Then we will understand what it is we are dealing with because we have classified it correctly. In classification we follow Linnaeus, or Carl von Linné to give him his correct name.

And having classified correctly, then what do we do?'

'Differentiate,' said Rosmond Young, obligingly.

'Correct, Rosmond. Only yesterday I was able to cure a patient because I differentiated between an exanthematic fever and a critical fever. I did this by empirical observation. Did the patient have a fever with spotty skin eruptions? No. Did she have febrile illness with red sediment in the urine? Yes. A critical fever, therefore.'

There was silence in the room. They were listening.

'Now! From Charles Bonnet's *Contemplation de la Nature* we learn of the interconnectedness of all things. Every human being is an organic part of that whole we call society. What is the study of society called? I will tell you. It is called politics, after Aristotle's *ta politika*, affairs of state. In order to improve the health of a society you first have to understand the system in all its parts, just as you do with a person. Understand?'

There was a roar of 'Yes, sir!'

'And who is our guide to the political system, the body politic, as Linnaeus and Galen are to the physical body?'

They knew that one. There was a chorus of 'John Locke!'

'Yes, boys. John Locke was an Englishman. But we will forgive him that because he had a lifelong interest in medicine. He was physician to Lord Ashley, as well as his secretary. Did you know that?'

The boys did not know that, as Young had not mentioned it before. They were silent, shuffling about a little. There was some coughing.

'Now, Locke teaches us that there are various types of rule of society. There is rule by constitutional right, rule by custom, rule by force and so on, in the body politic. How do you distinguish, say, rule by right from rule by force? What do you look for, as I looked for the symptoms of fever?'

'The consent of the people,' Rosmond Young said.

'Yes, good. You look for the will and consent of the

people. And if it is not there you have rule by force, colonial rule, which is a poison because it is foreign and alien to the body politic, the body politic did not produce it naturally from within itself.'

There were some cries of 'Yes, sir!'

'The British have no right to rule us. They never did. We never consented to it. The Massachusetts Bay Charter was given as a financial arrangement, it was never intended as the constitution for a colony. What was it never intended for?'

They chanted it back, loving it. The trick never failed. 'The constitution for a colony!'

'Excellent! What good boys you are. So, gentlemen, let us get to our feet. The Earth is the Lord's and the fullness thereof. So let us kick every British backside out of Boston.'

The cheers were even louder than usual. They all knew which of three crews they were in. They collected the leather buckets from outside the house. They were borrowed from the Fire Companies and contained Hillsborough Mixture, a mixture of urine and faeces, enthusiastically supplied by the boys.

By now they all knew where the Customs Commissioners and Customs Agents lived, but they obediently awaited orders from the crew leaders or from Young himself.

Nobody broke discipline.

CHAPTER 21

To Samuel Adams's quiet satisfaction, the old days of furtive small-group meetings at the Green Dragon or the Long Room had given way to mass gatherings involving most of Boston. Adams organised the public protest against the Customs Commissioners to start at the Liberty Tree. Despite the rain turning the snow to slush, a crowd of over a thousand gathered there, to be docilely marched to Faneuil Hall, at the other end of Main Street.

No sooner were they settled in Faneuil Hall than Adams decided there was not enough room there. So he got them all up again and marched his obedient army through the drizzle to the Old South Church, which was massive.

It was all Young could do not to burst into applause. The route from the Liberty Tree to Faneuil Hall to the Old South Church took the Bostonians – actually it took them twice – past the Province House, in which cowered the Governor, Francis Bernard, but crucially it also took them past the Town House, where the Assembly sat.

The Assembly was closed when they passed by, thanks to Young and the Liberty Boys disrupting its business at Adams's bidding. So Samuel Adams had just made a vivid propaganda point without a word – using sight and movement only. As the huge crowd surged past the defunct Assembly under Samuel Adams's orders to hear him speak, Samuel Adams ruled Boston.

Thomas Young always thought that meeting at the Old South Church, the first one to be called a Town Meeting, was almost Athenian in its pure democracy, as every segment of Boston society excepting only the destitute-poor and the slaves was represented.

Sam Adams stood at the front, in the pulpit, to address them. He began with a blistering attack on Hutchinson, whose acceptance of a pension direct from England

– 'Judas gold' – he had found out about from John Wilkes, via George Hayley.

Wilkes and Hayley had also told him the pension was a private arrangement with Frederick, Lord North, which it was, as it was coming from the King's Privy Purse. With an irony not lost on Young, this meant North was bypassing the hated British Parliament, just as Adams and Young wished to do.

'Mr Hutchinson …' Adams began, waving a shaking arm at the absent Lieutenant Governor so convincingly that many looked round for him. 'Mr Hutchinson, let me tell you something: he who is void of virtuous attachments in his private life is void of all regard of his country.'

Adams paused to let the cheers subside, then continued: 'Private and public vices are in reality connected. The people cannot be too curious concerning the characters of public men. So let us see who the British Parliament, in their wisdom, have sent to our shores. These Customs Commissioners are prostitutes and whores!'

This was drowned in a clamour of delirious cheering. Many of the crowd jumped to their feet. There was stamping, whooping and whistling. Adams remained impassive, waiting for the noise to subside, his head shaking slightly. As an afterthought he added, 'And they are empowered to appoint as many other prostitutes and whores as they want.'

Young applauded vigorously at that. He had not thought of it himself. There were only five Customs Commissioners at the moment, but they themselves were permitted to create more of their number. They could self-perpetuate without limit. Boston could be swarming with an endless number of officials, checking every shipment, entering every house it pleased them to enter.

And that was the other open sore of a grievance. Adams turned his full force on it: 'Writs of Assistance,' he shouted at the assembled throng of Bostonians, hanging on his every word. 'The Customs Commissioners can issue their own Writs of Assistance on a whim. Do you know what that means? It means our houses, and even our bedchambers, are exposed to be ransacked; our boxes, trunks and chests broken open, ravaged and plundered by wretches who no prudent man would venture to employ even as menial servants.'

As they roared with anger at that, the crowd at the meeting knew Adams's rage was directed not only at the Commissioners but at their local 'lackeys and lickspittles', the likes of Benjamin Hallowell, who would likely do the dirty work of entering offices and homes.

'Laws they are not, which the public approbation hath not made so,' quoted Adams.

Young looked round the glowing faces of the crowd to see their reaction to that. Many of them clearly knew the quotation from John Locke and nodded at it, as if greeting an old friend. Adams then continued to draw on Locke in a passionate defence of the Assembly he had just shut down, and the right of that Assembly to make laws for its people.

'The supreme legislative power is, as Mr Locke says, the first and fundamental law of the commonwealth. The Assembly has full power and authority to make all such laws as it thinks fit. All else is tyranny. Oppression. Slavery.'

He was brought to a halt by applause and cheering from every corner of the Town Meeting. Young thought how much Adams had improved as a public speaker since that first time he had heard him speak at Pope's Day, just after he first arrived from Albany.

Adams gave a curt nod of acknowledgement before continuing: 'Our compliance can be of no benefit to our sovereign, any further than as he interests himself in his subjects.' Adams murmured this as if the thought had just occurred to him, maybe as an afterthought. The near-treasonable utterance, unthinkable before the Stamp Act, received a lusty cheer.

'And what of Parliament? The colonies are prohibited

from importing anything except from Great Britain, saving a few articles. This gives the advantage to Great Britain of raising the price of her commodities, and is equal to a tax *over there*. Is it reasonable, then, that the colonies should be taxed on British commodities *over here*?'

Adams waited for a response, even cupped a hand over one ear. And a response he got, with a rousing roar of 'No!'

'No!' echoed Adams, nodding away. 'We colonists must act according to the voice of reason, against another revenue act. Against this Townshend Act. What a man has honestly acquired is absolutely his own, which he may freely give, but cannot be taken from him. We must defend this right. The fate of unborn millions depends on it.'

There was a roar of approval. There was a stamping of feet on the wooden floor.

'The Crown taking away from our Assembly payment to judges and the Governor completes the tragedy of American freedom,' he said. 'We must have no further truck with these Commissioners. Do not build them a building in which to carry out their nefarious work. Do not join the trade in taxed goods. Do not buy from shops that sell taxed goods. Give these revenue men neither shelter nor succour. If we do not protest we consent.'

As this climactic grew, Adams was looking directly at Young. He was telling him to try non-co-operation against the Commissioners, rather than violence, like the violence of the Liberty Boys, with their buckets of Hillsborough Mixture. Young was not convinced.

Adams was drawing to a close: 'We will not accept subjugation to as arbitrary a tribute as ever the Romans laid upon the Jews, or their other colonies.'

The applause and cheering echoed round anew, bouncing off the near hundred-year-old bricks of the holy building.

CHAPTER 22

Thomas Young, without consulting Adams, organised a protest march to fife and drum through the streets of Boston, from the Exchange Coffee House to the Liberty Tree. It was like the protest marches against British rule he used to organise back in Albany. The 200 or so marchers, all sporting Wilkes cockades, bore effigies of all five Customs Commissioners, each with the slogan 'Liberty, Property and No Commissioners' hung round his neck.

The effigies had been crafted by Mary Young, working through the night. When Thomas pleaded with her to sleep, Mary said, as she always said, 'The revolution comes first. We must not weaken, Thomas.' And she succeeded. The effigies, made to her husband's descriptions – though she had seen Temple and Paxton before – were astonishingly lifelike, but mocking, too.

There were fires burning in the streets, against a winter cold so bitter Sam Adams feared his ink would freeze before he finished his newspaper articles excoriating the Commissioners. The fires added to a feeling of anarchy, wildness on the streets.

Spontaneous acts of violence broke out all over Boston against the Customs Commissioners and their agents. Much of this was against Adams's will. He still believed that uncontrolled mob violence put the patriots in the wrong, and they were not yet ready for what he called real violence, by which he meant armed revolution. Young disagreed, and by and large Young prevailed. Relations between the two men cooled.

Any shop selling taxed goods was surrounded by a crowd, sometimes made up of Liberty Boys, sometimes Mohucks, keeping customers away. Warehouses where taxed goods were stored were also surrounded. Some of the traders, including Hutchinson's sons, Thomas junior and Elisha, tried to move their goods away but the Mohucks caught them and destroyed the goods. Any trader importing taxed goods had his house smeared with Hillsborough Mixture by the Liberty Boys, on Young's orders.

Every night, the disorderly boys, as the Commissioners called them, laid siege to the houses where they were sleeping. They beat drums, they blew horns, they blew conches, they howled like Indians. They had a high old time. The Commissioners got no sleep before dawn, if then.

Commissioner Charles Paxton was caught in the Bunch of Grapes by William Molineux and some of his Mohucks out looking for trouble. He was hauled on a hurdle to the Liberty Tree. A crowd gathered at Liberty Hall, wearing Wilkes blue cockades.

Henry Bass forced a drenching-horn into the screaming Paxton's mouth as he lay on the hurdle. It was a practised gesture, just as Bass used to do in the good old days in London. Molineux produced a teapot full of the hated tea – subject of the monstrous tax, the instrument and symbol of America's slavery at the hands of the hated British. Customs Commissioner Charles Paxton was made to drink the tea, poured down the drenching-horn into his throat until he choked.

Then, directly under the Liberty Tree, Charles Paxton was taken off the hurdle, stripped, beaten, then tarred and feathered. Benjamin Edes put a rope round his neck. To cries of 'Wilkes and Liberty' he was put back on the hurdle, then hauled round the town in a London-style Skimmington Ride.

At the end of it, before he was released on the big area of open grassland known as the Common, Paxton was told that next time he would be made to resign as a Customs Commissioner.

Next day, John Temple's house was smeared with Hillsborough Mixture, his garden was pillaged and his fruit trees cut down by fifty or sixty of Molineux's Mohucks while he was at Castle William for talks with an increasingly helpless Hutchinson. Governor Bernard was too frightened even to come to the talks.

Windows were broken at the house where another Customs Commissioner had found temporary shelter. Two more Commissioners were chased away when they attempted to board a ship at Long Wharf to search it for smuggled goods.

Customs Comptroller Benjamin Hallowell was the easiest target, being well known to the crowd. Hallowell's house was ransacked once again by a drunken mob while he was out. He was forcibly prevented from boarding a ship and pelted with ordure. On his way home he was seized and beaten up by a completely different group of Mohucks.

Next day, somebody posted a paper on the Liberty Tree advocating an armed uprising. Nobody ever found out who it was. Even Young thought the call was premature; Adams was furious.

Within a month, all five Commissioners and what was now four Customs Comptrollers, including Benjamin Hallowell, feared they would be marched to the Liberty Tree by the crowd and made to resign – the threat made to Charles Paxton by Molineux's Mohucks. They also feared their own houses, or the houses where they were staying, would be pulled down. So they fled first to the warship *Romney*, Admiral John Montagu's flagship, then, under cover of darkness, across the Neck to Castle William.

A terrified Governor Francis Bernard kept telling the Commissioners the rioters could not be prosecuted. He appeared too frightened of the patriots to help the Commissioners in any way at all, or to appeal to London for extra troops. So the Commissioners wrote to General Gage themselves. By then Gage was back at his headquarters in New York. They also wrote to Lord North. The letters were drafted by Charles Paxton, but signed by all of them.

'The government in Boston,' Paxton wrote, 'is quite ineffectual and impotent. Governmental rule is in the hands of the people. The garrison moulders, the troops are helpless. There is not one single soldier ready to fight within miles of Boston nor any artillery in any part of the province. At so-called Town Meetings, mechanics discuss upon the most important points of government.'

The Commissioners asked for a large force of battle-ready troops to be sent to Boston.

CHAPTER 23

John Pownall was possessed to the point of mania by the need to send a top regiment to Boston to enforce the work of the Commissioners. He hardly slept for mulling it all over, desperate to promote action against Boston.

He knew British indifference to America all too well; it boiled in his blood. When the American colonies were noticed at all, their needs and interests ranked well behind India, the Caribbean and the other colonies administered by the six Ancient Departments, as they were called, each of which was three times the size of his American Department.

Pownall consulted as widely as he could among any military men who would talk to him, especially those who had served at Castle William. The 6th Regiment, currently at their base in Plymouth, were recommended to him. As Lord Hillsborough was away at his estates in Gloucestershire, Pownall decided to arrange the transfer of the 6th to Boston on his own initiative.

'Don't do it,' was William Knox's smiling but firm advice. 'Sending soldiers in is a bad idea anyway. It won't be made any better by sending good soldiers.'

John Pownall laughed, relaxed for a few moments, but ignored the advice. He set off on the arduous three-day journey to Plymouth. There, he held detailed discussions with the 6th's Commanding Officer, who assumed he had Lord Hillsborough's full authority. They planned every detail up to and including embarkation.

Pownall then returned to London, to find a curt note from Hillsborough demanding to see him. At the meeting in Hillsborough's office at the Board of Trade, his Lordship tore into his subordinate for exceeding his authority.

The 6th, Pownall was informed, were being sent to Nova Scotia. Boston was to get the 14th and the 29th. Pownall was secretly pleased two regiments were being sent, not one as he had expected. But the level of the soldiery confirmed his worst fears. They were among the worst regiments in the British army.

The 14th, in particular, had had hardly any training. They were little more than a motley group of desperate men who had joined up to get a square meal. They had been given a musket and a scarlet uniform and told to make the best of it. They could barely do the basics, like form a square, let alone manage a firing manoeuvre like an enfilade.

'You are to arrange sea transport in private ships ...' a furious Lord Hillsborough ordered Pownall.

'But ...'

'As far as possible. Now get out of my sight before I dismiss you from your post altogether.'

Pownall left without a word, slamming the office door behind him. Hillsborough would not dare dismiss him; they could not manage without him. But his Lordship's revenge was ingenious.

As Hillsborough and Pownall both knew, private shipping for that number of troops would be near-impossible. Merchants were nervous about hiring out their ships. There was growing fear that the landing would be met with armed resistance by the Boston Militia. Among those who had expressed this fear was General Gage, who had been ordered back to Castle William from New York.

In the end, having made him sweat, Hillsborough relented, agreeing that Pownall might arrange the conveying of the 14th and 29th to Boston in navy transports and aboard men-of-war.

John Wilkes reacted to the news with outrage in a letter to Samuel Adams, conveyed by George Hayley aboard one of Hancock's ships.

'I have read with grief and indignation of the proceedings of the ministry with regard to the troops ordered to Boston, as if it were the capital of a province belonging to our enemies,' he wrote. 'Asiatic despotism does not present a picture more odious.'

Chapter 24

Captain John Parker had had the Boston Militia training on the Common for weeks. Just about one in two of Boston's men were militia-trained anyway, but the remainder were clamouring for inclusion. Boston's hardware stores sold out of muskets and ammunition completely, though the training on the Common was carried out without arms.

Most of the women, doing their spinning and weaving out on the Common in the weak autumn sun, watched indulgently as their menfolk strutted about, though some demanded, and received, training with the men.

Mary Young was among them. She and Anne Hayley formed the Daughters of Liberty, as determined to end British enslavement of them as the Sons of Liberty were. The Daughters of Liberty had no official leaders and never held a formal meeting, but they looked to Mary Young and Anne Hayley for a lead, because of their strength and popularity and in Anne's case because of the family connection with John Wilkes, who continued to be their inspiration over the water in England.

Meanwhile, Samuel Adams wanted to organise the cleaning and repair of the muskets gathering dust in the cellar at Faneuil Hall. This idea pre-dated the rumours of the arrival of troops.

Governor Francis Bernard found out about the proposed cleaning of weapons from Thomas Hutchinson, who got it from John Pownall, who in turn had it from one of William Molineux's reports – an accurate one this time. In a gesture of open-eyed contempt and with brazen insouciance, Sam Adams told Governor Bernard the muskets were needed in case there was another war with the French. Governor Bernard believed him, or at least pretended to.

Adams wanted the Liberty Boys rounded up to clean the muskets, pulling them out of school if necessary, not waiting for the next Thursday – market day. He contacted the Liberty Boys' crew leaders with his order.

The crew leaders politely but unequivocally gave him to understand they took orders from Dr Young only. Adams convinced himself this was because one of the crew leaders, Rosmond Young, was Young's son, but actually it was not. It was because they looked to Young as their popular leader, while they were at best indifferent to Adams, many of them actually detesting him.

Young insisted the cleaning and maintenance of the muskets took place on a Thursday only, as the boys – and a few girls too by now, including Young's older daughters – must not miss school. Adams had no option but to agree. The temperature of relations between Young and Adams cooled still further.

Most of the Liberty Boys and Girls had brought clean cloths, oil and tallow from home as instructed. They enthusiastically set about wiping the Brown Bess musket barrels, muzzles and butts, and the ramrods, even polishing the pouch bags for the bullets. The brass barrel bands and triggers were handled delicately, as they were cleaned. There were a few pistols, blunderbusses and cutlasses to be spruced up, too. The Liberty Boys and the Liberty Girls efficiently took care of it all.

Naturally, there was a bit of fooling around, marching up and down with the guns and pretending to shoot them at the hated Lobster Backs, as the British Redcoats were called, but the crew leaders dealt with any tomfoolery sternly.

Young and Adams, looking on benevolently, had neither to intervene nor instruct. Indeed, it occurred to Young while he was watching that even the youngest of the Liberty Boys knew how to use weapons. The only one in the room who did not, Young thought to himself, aware of the irony, was Adams. The Publican was a stranger to all forms of practicality.

'Can we help give out the muskets, sir?' Christopher Seider addressed Young only, as the Liberty Boys tended to, ignoring Adams completely.

Young smiled a little grimly at the misapprehension, which pretty much all of them shared, that the revolution was imminent.

'The time is not yet right,' Adams growled.

The Liberty Boys fell silent at that.

'We are not yet ready,' Young confirmed, gently.

Many of the older boys understood what that meant, though some of the younger ones did not. The phrase 'we are not yet ready' was pretty much a code in Boston. It meant the French were not yet supporting them. But one day …

CHAPTER 25

The first British troop-carrying men-of-war were spotted by the lookouts Molineux and his Mohucks had posted on Beacon Hill. A tar barrel full of turpentine in a skillet was lit atop the Hill. This was the standing signal for the Massachusetts farmers to come into Boston from the countryside as reinforcements.

Molineux then ordered the flag flown from the flagstaff put through the Liberty Tree elm. The flag was a white sheet of cotton with a large blue Wilkes cockade lovingly sewn into it by Mary Young and Anne Hayley. The flag was another pre-agreed call to action, though everybody knew that on this particular day only warning was being signalled, nothing more.

Over at the Province House, Lieutenant Governor Hutchinson was unsuccessfully attempting to calm Governor Bernard. Hutchinson sent for Sheriff Stephen Greenleaf. He told the Sheriff to gather the watch, then have the tar barrel on Beacon Hill seized and the flag on the Liberty Tree taken down.

The Sheriff went straight to Samuel Adams to ask for orders. Adams told him to wait a while, then tell Hutchinson there were too many men round the tar barrel and the Liberty Tree, so he and the watch had been forced to retreat.

Sheriff Greenleaf did as he was told, but by the time he got back to the Province House he was told Hutchinson had been taken ill. So the plump Sheriff gave the imaginary account of his failure to Governor Francis Bernard.

'Matters now,' the Governor pronounced, 'exceed all former exceedings.'

'Indeed they do, sir,' the Sheriff agreed, politely.

The crowds gathering at Long Wharf saw the topsails of the *Romney* first, the huge square-rigger fifty-gun ship of the line. As the near-silent throng of Bostonians watched in unseasonal heat, another eleven ships appeared behind the *Romney* – a massive show of sea-power by the British. The dockworkers and shipbuilders, especially, were familiar with most of these ships, some of the merchants too.

First into view behind the *Romney* was the *Launceston*. Then the three-masted *Glasgow*, a thing of sinewy grace. Many of Boston's Scottish merchants had first come to the city aboard the *Glasgow*. Then there was the *Mermaid*, a sixteen-gun sloop. Then the *Bonelton*, an armed cutter. Behind her an armed schooner, the *St Lawrence*.

And so it went on as ship after ship, sail after sail, gun after gun came into view. This was the mightiest sea-power the world had ever seen, all massing to subdue Boston.

When they had disgorged their soldiers, the mighty galleons were rowed back out into Boston Bay where they manoeuvred into a semi-circle, their cannon pointing at the centre of the city. But by then the citizenry, nearly every man Jack of them down at the harbour, were no longer watching the ships. They were watching the troops, their occupiers, as they disgorged across gangplanks onto Long Wharf.

On the stroke of noon, hundreds of troops marched into town and nobody seemed to have the faintest idea where they were going. Where were they going to sleep? Bostonians feared soldiers would be forcibly quartered on them, perhaps taking the very beds they slept in. What were they going to eat? Were they going to live off Boston's food supplies? There was hardly enough to go round as it was.

Deliberately, the first troops off were the Grenadier regiment of the 29th. Grenadiers were chosen for their height; they were all over six feet tall. They were the first of an apparently endless force, marching their way off the ships.

As its name implies, Long Wharf was a jetty going further out into Boston harbour than any of the other dozen or so jetties jutting out into the water, each leading to its own wharf buildings, owned by a merchant or a group of merchants.

So it seemed to take for ever to the Bostonians lining the route along Long Wharf and on to where Long Wharf runs into King Street for this mass of troops to get any further. At the top of Long Wharf they passed Minot's T, a T-shaped tie-up point for ships. *Stamp stamp stamp* went the boots, coming towards the people of Boston.

Then the soldiers paused before entering King Street. They waited in formation, all menace in red jackets, white trousers, black boots and busbies or caps. On command, they fixed bayonets. On further command, they drew their swords from their waist belts. It was an open gesture of the utmost hostility.

A rumour rapidly spread that each soldier had been issued with sixteen rounds of powder and ball. As the militia-trained citizenry could see, their muskets were ready, dog-heads screwed, flints in. No soldiers in battle, let alone out of it, had ever been more effectively primed to fire.

Among the weapons seen in Boston for the first time on that day were espontoons, half-pikes that did not look that dangerous until they were brandished at the crowd by sweating street urchins in uniform, who clearly enjoyed scaring the locals.

The Grenadier officers all had fusils, carbine-like light muskets, much more modern than the dated Brown Besses the patriots had stashed away back in Faneuil Hall.

On into King Street went the fearsome force. *Stamp stamp stamp.* Each corps was preceded by fife players and grinning Negro drummer-boys banging at drums tied round their necks. They wore white bearskin caps with a badge and motto. The good folk of Boston watched wide-eyed and tried to read the motto.

On they marched, past Richard Clarke's warehouse, on their right at the very top of King Street. Then past the Customs House. *Stamp stamp stamp*. Then past the Royal Exchange Tavern and on into Queen Street. They were going right through the centre of Boston, heading for the open land of the Common to the south-west, streaming sweat in the sticky heat under their thick woollen Bloody-Back blood-red coats.

The open threats of swords, bayonets and charged muskets brought a rare smile from Samuel Adams, who was buried in the bowels of the crowd outside the Royal Exchange, wearing his red cloak even on such a balmy autumn day. He was already composing in his head one of his articles as 'Puritan' for the *Boston Gazette*.

'The troops corrupt our morals and are in every sense an oppression,' Puritan would shortly be writing. 'An affront to our rights *as Englishmen*,' he thought to himself. Yes, that was a good touch.

Thomas Young, at the front of the crowd at the top of King Street, said, 'Why did they do that?' out loud, truly bemused at the foolishness of such open hostility. John Rowe thought of his boyhood in Chagford, when he saw the naked swords. Who could imagine British troops in such warlike mien in the streets back home? He shivered in the sticky heat. He recognised nearly all the British commanders. They had been posted to Boston before, many of the senior commanders had broken bread with him at his home.

The soldiers of the 14th were led by a man Rowe knew well, Lieutenant Colonel Francis Smith, then aged over fifty and seen as an old man by most of his men. Second-in-command, marching at his side, was Major John Pitcairn, who was the same age as Smith. The idea was that the worst regiment in the British army, just about, should at least have seasoned commanders.

Back at the disembarkation point at the sea-end of Long Wharf, the biggest threat was yet to come. Last to disembark, rolling out of the *Mermaid*, was half an artillery regiment, the 59th, with five pieces of field artillery.

They were massive 6-pounders. Nobody in Boston had ever seen one before; they were the most powerful munitions on God's earth. As they clanked on their way through the centre of the town, pulled by teams of straining horses, the crowd fell silent. Two of the huge cannon were drawn up outside the Assembly building, great maws of muzzles threatening the elected representatives. The others were taken to the Common.

This was an army of occupation, an army without end. As Puritan put it in the *Boston Gazette* next morning: 'Using force without authority creates a state of war with the people. How many regiments will be thought necessary to penetrate the heart of a country and subdue a sensible, enlightened and brave people to the ignominious terms of slavery?'

CHAPTER 26

One of the few Bostonians not to witness the arrival of troops in the town was Thomas Hutchinson. On being taken ill at the Province House, he had himself driven in his phaeton back to the Reverend Mather's house in Garden Court Street, where he was still staying. There he experienced another stroke of God's hand; the paralysis in his left arm more pronounced than before, the stiffness on the left side of his face even worse.

Peggy nursed him while he miserably contemplated events. The British had made a huge error, in Hutchinson's view. Even now, few in Boston understood that Governor Bernard had no power to command these newly arrived troops and neither had he. To act legally, British soldiers could be ordered into action only by the Assembly. Parliament had just sent the largest impotent military force ever assembled.

Unfortunately, one of the few people in Boston who understood that only too well was Wilkes-Adams, damn his black soul. And the patriot faction now had a majority in the Assembly, when they deigned to allow it to sit at all.

Most of the time they controlled Boston by calling one of their Town Meetings, herding the rabble into the largest available space, then rigging the result of deliberations by arranging a so-called caucus meeting first to decide into what shapes the malleable clay of the people should be moulded.

Mob rule rests with those who harangue best, those who have the best simple slogans – 'An End to Slavery', 'Hurrah for Freedom' – those who know how to raise the temper and stir the emotions of the people with meetings, marches, singing, anniversaries of events marking martyrdom, celebratory dinners, anything that stops the mob from thinking too deeply.

Was this better than rule by those representatives who

genuinely had the people's interests at heart, be those people artisan or merchant, pauper or prince? Bostonians looked back on the time when he – Thomas Hutchinson – and Thomas Pownall ruled Boston as a Golden Age, and with good reason.

Thomas Hutchinson began to weep. But his bitter thoughts were interrupted by a commotion, which sounded as if it was coming from the Common.

CHAPTER 27

When the troops had finally finished their extended march into Boston, Thomas Young made his way home through the thronged streets. His house was empty. The children were at school; Mary was spinning with her Daughters of Liberty women on the Common.

Young began to gather medicines into a battered leather bag given him by a grateful patient. He determined to set out on his house calls, but there came a thunderous knocking at the door. It was a Negro slave runner, sent, he said breathlessly, by Mrs Young. Mrs Young and her ladies, said the slave, were trapped in the Manufactory House. He himself had escaped through a window but all the ladies were locked inside.

Thomas Young thanked the slave, gave him a penny, then hurried towards the Manufactory House on Tremont Street. He could imagine what had happened. Nobody knew where the British soldiers would end up. When they occupied the Common, which many of them clearly had, the Daughters of Liberty must have gone to the nearby Manufactory House.

What had happened to the spinning wheels? They were valuable, and they were essential to the colonists' war effort, as Thomas Young thought of it. He decided to head for the Common first at a steady run.

The Common was so thick with milling Redcoat soldiers, you could hardly see a blade of grass. But there were no spinning wheels. Had Mary and Anne Hayley and the other women managed to get them into the Manufactory House in time? It looked like it.

Young thought about it, analytically. A linen spinning wheel was heavy; a woollen spinning wheel – where the wheel was bigger – was even heavier. It would take two people per wheel but apparently they had managed it.

But having got the spinning wheels into the Manufactory House, Mary, Anne and the other women would never abandon them to the soldiers, they were too valuable for that.

Clothes for the patriots, their women and their children, depended on the spinning wheels, the more so since the refusal to buy goods imported from Britain. It was the Daughters of Liberty's proud boast that every stitch they wore they had made themselves. It made them independent of the British oppressors.

Thomas Young made his way, at a run, from the Common to Tremont Street, all the while picturing the Manufactory House in his mind. It was a brick-built edifice set up for the people to make their own artefacts and clothes, everything from worsted hose to metal buttons. There was weaving, spinning, pressing and dyeing set up there, using skilled men recently arrived from England as well as the local women.

This artisan co-operative gave the Bostonians a degree of freedom from the British ban on manufacturing anything for themselves. It had been established by William Molineux mainly, now quite the leading merchant. He had chosen his London-born fellow patriot Elisha Brown to run it, day to day.

Molineux was a man Thomas Young had little time for normally, but he admired him for this. He and Henry Bass and a few others, mainly London-born, had even got the project through the Assembly by setting up an excise on carriages and other luxury goods to fund it. Thomas Young liked the idea of that very much. If he had his way, they would sell the Province House and the Governor's and Lieutenant Governor's carriages tomorrow and give all the money to Poor Relief.

When Thomas Young reached Tremont Street, he crossed the grassy knoll in front of the Manufactory House to find a scene of considerable chaos. There were soldiers everywhere, something he was quickly getting used to. Some concerned Bostonians were banging on the doors and windows of the Manufactory House, which was obviously locked.

But Young had the impression there were people inside. He hoped and simultaneously feared Mary was one of them. He was concerned for Anne Hayley, too. Being John Wilkes's sister made her vulnerable to British reprisals.

He strode through the crowd to the front door, only to be stopped by two soldiers and a haughty-looking middle-aged officer. The officer, red-faced and sweating profusely, wore a silver-laced cocked hat and a crescent-shaped silver gorget on his chest – it gleamed in the sunlight. He sported the crimson and buff sash of the 14th.

'Damned peacock,' muttered Thomas Young, attempting to push his way past the officer and the two men. One of the men gave him a push in the chest. Young squared up to him. Another fight?

'And who might you be?' snapped the officer, in a Scottish accent. The tone was intemperate but he was clearly trying to stop a fight breaking out.

Young hesitated. He heard Mary in his head, counselling calm, as she always did, usually in vain.

'I am a doctor, sir,' Young said, drawing himself up to his considerable full height. 'I have been called to treat the sick in the Manufactory House.'

'Name?'

Name? His name demanded in that peremptory fashion in his own city by an invader just off the boat. Young wanted to call him an arrogant knave. He wanted to pick him up and shake him. He wanted to drive him and his kind out of Boston. But he ground his teeth and said 'My name is Dr Thomas Young. What is yours?'

'I am Major John Pitcairn.'

Young grinned mockingly. 'Are you, now?'

Major Pitcairn took a step back, then blinked furiously. 'Wait a minute. Young? Did you say Dr Thomas Young?'

'I did.'

'You are the thorough-paced infidel.'

'I beg your pardon?'

'You are the Deist opposer of our holy religion. Let me ask you plainly, sir. Do you believe the scriptures of the Old and New Testament or any part of them to be truly a revelation from God?'

Young was amazed. He had no idea his heretical views were so well known. In this he was being modest. John Pownall had made sure every officer sailing to Boston knew every detail of the lives of Adams, Hancock and Young. Know your enemy. The senior officers also had dossiers giving carefully selected information on William Molineux and Ebenezer Mackintosh.

Young was recovering from his surprise: 'A revelation from ...? If you wish to put it in those terms, sir: no, I do not.'

The two soldiers accompanying Major Pitcairn moved menacingly nearer, and a crowd was beginning to gather round them, sensing the prospect of a fight. Colonel Francis Smith, attracted by the noise, came hurrying up to them. Major Pitcairn and the soldiers saluted him, Pitcairn crisply, the soldiers sloppily with their palms facing outwards, not inwards.

Young knew who Francis Smith was; John Rowe had mentioned him often, with affection. 'What is going on here?' Smith's clear high voice carried over the grass. 'Ah, Dr Young. What brings you here?'

This was said with a touch of irony. Young smiled. The tension was broken. 'I wish to enter the Manufactory House.'

'So do I.' Francis Smith gave a wry smile. 'But Elisha Brown has put himself at the head of the tenants and is denying us entry. Mr Molineux is assisting us. I believe he understands that little is to be gained from keeping my soldiers out in the open, as they have to sleep somewhere.'

This was the first inkling Thomas Young had that no

preparations at all had been made for the quartering of the troops. That filled him with a strange tingling excitement. If the British planned as badly as that we could beat them. Meanwhile, Young felt that Francis Smith was right. No good would come of denying the soldiers quarters; eventually they would simply seize what they needed.

'I will do anything in my power to help,' Young told Smith. 'But first I must ascertain that my wife is in the Manufactory and that she is unharmed.'

'I can reassure you on both points, Dr Young,' Francis Smith said. 'Mrs Young is inside with the other ladies. So is her slave girl. Martha, isn't it?'

Young could not stop himself looking impressed at Smith's grasp of detail. Smith gave a small smile, creasing his parchment-grey face, then went on. 'Both of them are well. And the spinning wheel is by her side and undamaged.'

'Thank you!'

'Not at all. Look, why don't you go and shout to her through the window. Then you can help Molineux with the intransigent Mr Brown. Time is drawing on, I'm afraid. I don't want to take the Manufactory House by force but I will if I have to.'

'All right.'

Thomas Young strode past Major Pitcairn, just catching the smaller man with his arm. He reached the nearest grimy window of the locked Manufactory, knocked on the glass and bellowed 'Mary! Mary are you in there? Mary, it's me, Thomas!'

'Thomas! We are fine, in here.' Her voice was clear through the dirty glass. 'Remember your Virgil, Thomas. The golden age advances slower or faster according to how the women spin. *Talia saecla, suis dixerunt, currite fusis.*'

Thomas burst out laughing. 'Oh, you wonderful woman. I don't deserve you.'

'True. Hey, this is like Pyramus and Thisbe, isn't it? In *A Midsummer Night's Dream*.'

'All right, Mary. Enough joking now. What is happening there?'

'That fool of a sheriff, Greenleaf, appeared. Francis Bernard sent him. Bernard authorised the troops to use the Manufactory, the scoundrel. But Elisha Brown wouldn't allow it. He was so brave, Thomas. He said we needed to work here. So Greenleaf tried to arrest Elisha Brown and some of the workers seized him. He's tied up somewhere out back, the fat idiot.'

Thomas Young tried not to laugh but failed. Adams must have ordered Greenleaf to do this. Greenleaf didn't move without Adams's say-so.

'What's happening now?' Thomas Young yelled through the window.

'I think Molineux has organised a truce,' Mary shouted back. 'We get to leave. The soldiers can sleep in the churches in town, at least for now. That way we can continue to use the Manufactory. Thomas, you must not let them stop us working here, it's vital.'

'I know. It sounds as if Molineux has done sterling service. I'll find him and come back to you.'

'All right. Good luck!'

For the first time, she sounded a little anxious, her voice fading as she shouted through the window. Thomas turned and caught sight of Molineux and Lieutenant Colonel Smith deep in conversation. Molineux touched the British commander's arm, asking him to wait, then strode over to Thomas Young.

Molineux's handsome face looked serious. "Ello, Thomas. We're gettin' there. It looks like Smith brought tents and field equipment for the 14th, so they're all right. But some aristocratic arse they put in charge of the 29th forgot. Still, it's the 14th Smith wants sent to Castle William, or as many of them as possible. That's the 'old-up.'

'Why?'

"Cos they're fucking useless. He wants them out the way. The 29th are going to Brattle Street Church, the New

157

North, the Friends Meeting and a few smaller churches. Just for a while. Any that can't get in the churches are sleeping on the Common in the 14th's tents.'

'Sounds as if you've got it all sorted out.'

There was a moment of tension between them. William Molineux bit his lip. 'I set up the Manufactory in the first place, chum. I don't want it buggered up now.' Molineux was obviously uneasy. With a muttered 'I gotta go. Make arrangements.' He turned away.

Thomas Young watched him go. Smith came up to him again. 'All right, Dr Young? Your wife in the pink, is she?' There was something forced in his manner.

'Thank you, Colonel Smith. Yes. She's fine.'

'Good-oh. I saw you talking to Molineux. We've sorted it all out. Molineux has rented his warehouse out to us.'

'Fine.'

Why had Molineux not mentioned renting the warehouse? Was it just guilt at dealing with the enemy so soon after the troops' arrival? Or was it more than that?

But at that moment the Manufactory House doors opened. People started coming out, some of the Daughters of Liberty among them. Thomas rushed to meet Mary.

But all the while he was wondering at how smoothly William Molineux had worked with the occupying soldiers. It was as if he was on their side from the beginning. As if he knew them. And they knew him.

CHAPTER 28

On the very night the British troops arrived, the frame of the half-built guardhouse on the Neck was destroyed. This was at the top of the narrow causeway over the water to Castle William, at the entrance to the town. The guardhouse was meant to stop the Boston mob attacking Castle William. Governor Francis Bernard offered a reward for the discovery of the culprits.

The carpenters and coopers, led by John Newell, the Youngs' landlord, publicly refused to rebuild the guardhouse. They put an announcement in the *Boston Gazette* to that effect.

Young applauded this, but of greater interest to him, at least privately, was that nobody had told him about the attack. The attack on the guardhouse was a skilled job. It must have been carried out by Molineux and his Mohucks. And Molineux would not dare mobilise the Mohucks without Adams's say-so.

Mind you, Young reflected, he himself had not told Adams about the march he organised in protest against the Commissioners. He still felt Adams was his blood brother in the battle to rid Boston of the British, but they hardly spoke these days. Adams was a difficult man to like, let alone love.

Hutchinson was still indisposed, too ill to deal with the issue of quartering the troops in his capacity as Chairman of the Assembly. So it fell to Adams, as Clerk to the Assembly, to negotiate with Governor Bernard and General Gage, now permanently based at Castle William, over precisely what to do with all these soldiers.

As negotiations opened, in a meeting room at Castle William, it quickly became evident that Adams had memorised the entire Quartering Act, the relevant statute for the quartering of British troops: 'The Act says "troops are to be quartered in inns and public houses or barns or outhouses must be hired for them ...'"

Governor Bernard and General Gage listened in stunned amazement as Adams droned on, seemingly ready to keep quoting the entire statute until the last British soldier left Boston.

'The Quartering Act specifies,' Adams further quoted, from memory and apparently without needing to breathe, 'that "any officer who takes it upon himself to quarter soldiers in any way other than provided by the Act, or who uses menace or compulsion, would upon conviction before two justices of the peace be ipso facto cashiered and utterly disabled to have or hold any military employment."'

Faced with Adams's blatant use of Britain's own laws, Gage consulted Colonel Smith. It was becoming clear that Gage was reluctant or unable to take any decision whatever himself, so Smith cut the Gordian knot: the 14th would stay at Castle William. Most of the 29th would stay in churches or in tents on the Common for the next couple of weeks. What would happen in the depths of winter nobody knew.

Adams resolutely opposed any attempt to convert the Manufactory House to a barracks. He told Smith, truthfully enough, that there would be a riot if the British even tried that, because it would stop even the limited manufacturing Boston had managed to achieve.

Adams truly did not want a riot because the patriots were not ready to fight yet and they would get a bloody nose when the riot was put down. But he did allow the officers to find rented accommodation in Boston. He allowed that because he realised he could not stop it.

The richer merchants were quietly pleased at the development. Within days, Major Pitcairn was lodging with Hannah and John Rowe, paying a not insignificant sum.

Although some of Dr Young's work among the poor and

sick of Boston involved them coming to his house, mostly he went to them. They paid him what they could, when they could. Sometimes they paid nothing, more often some food, like a plum cake or a stew.

So Young was out and about in the streets of Boston all the time. And the main difference he noticed in the first days of occupation was the ubiquity of British soldiers in the streets. You could not miss them. They were there, walking along in the street in their bright red uniforms. They exercised in Brattle Square. They converted the Old South Church to a riding school for British light horse. They stabled their horses at the ropewalks.

The Redcoats also took part-time jobs to supplement their meagre pay, so they popped up in all sorts of unexpected places. To Young's secret amusement, Adams's first article in the *Boston Gazette*, protesting at the troops, was partly type-set by an Irish soldier from the 29th who had found a part-time job at the *Gazette*'s printing presses.

In that first week of occupation, as he went round Boston visiting patients, Young found soldiers working at a wig-maker, a cordwainer and a baker, all at the poorer South End.

This caused friction. Work at the waterfront or at the ropewalks was on a casual labour basis. The Redcoats were prepared to work for a pittance, even less than the needy locals, who had little enough as it was.

It was often the wives who complained most bitterly to Young about the soldiers taking work from their husbands. The complaint was usually accompanied by an expression of regret that there was nothing to pay the doctor with. In the first week of occupation alone this happened to Young three times.

Trouble quickly escalated after that, from a hundred pinprick sources. The free people of Boston were not used to being challenged by sentries. These were suddenly everywhere. They were outside the quarters of senior officers – so there was one outside John Rowe's house.

There was a sentry guarding the two cannon pointing at the Assembly. There was a sentry outside the Customs House on King Street, which Young passed all the time.

The sentries stopped carriages as well as people on foot. They were there by day and by night, stopping everyone they saw with a 'Who comes there?' Sometimes the challenges were less polite than that. Hurrying home from a call-out to a fever late one night, Young hurried impatiently past a sentry's challenge and was told 'You'll have your brains blown out, mister, unless you stop.'

'I live here,' Young said.

'So do I,' said the young soldier.

'I am from Boston,' Young said.

'No you're not, Dutch,' said the sentry. 'Now state your business.'

Young burst out laughing. Then he made a grab at the sentry, intending to throw him in the air for his cheek.

One of the Scottish merchants found fame right across the city by refusing a sentry's challenge, then bringing charges when he was detained at bayonet point. He was the toast of the town when he won his case, which was heard before the patriots' tame judge, Richard Dana. But that was a rare success.

The British appeared to take delight in goading the Americans. They stopped every Negro slave they saw, encouraging them to demand their freedom. Mary Young had a long talk with their slave, her sewing girl, Martha, about this.

Mary Young said straight out that Martha could have her freedom, but she could not stay as a servant because they had no money to pay her. Martha said one day it would be fine to have her freedom, but right now it would be freedom to starve and be molested by British soldiers, so she would rather stay with the Young family where she was safe, fed and clothed. And anyway she loved the children and they loved her.

The slavery issue was one of the few that Thomas Young and Samuel Adams agreed on, these days. They both wanted an end to the regular slave sales at the Green Dragon and to slavery in Boston in general.

But Adams had matters of greater weight on his mind. He set about drawing up a list of grievances to put through the Assembly and on to General Gage, as official complaints.

There were serious cases of licentious and outrageous behaviour by soldiers, sometimes involving women being beaten with cutlasses, fists or muskets. There were many incidences of soldiers getting drunk on cheap rum, and then being disorderly in the streets.

The religious folk of Boston were offended by the foul oaths of the soldiery. Women of ill repute had gathered in the town, attracted by the troops, to the outrage of the merchant classes.

General Gage, losing patience with the list of complaints, suspended the Assembly. Adams was ready for that. He reminded the occupying power that with the Assembly suspended, there was no way of authorising money to supply the soldiers. So any Boston merchant who supplied the troops with anything at all could not expect guaranteed payment.

Some Boston merchants took the risk, especially loyalists like Thomas Hutchinson's sons, the rest of the Medici, the Scottish merchants and some small shopkeepers like Theophilus Lillie. But from that time onwards, Gage and his soldiers found getting supplies much more difficult.

CHAPTER 29

John Pownall brandished the letter he was reading in William Knox's face, then resumed pacing their tiny office in the American Department, declaiming from it: 'I don't believe there was ever an instance of so large a body of troops, three regiments ...'

'Actually, it's more like two and a half. Half the 59th artillery are still in Ireland.' William Knox shifted his boots more comfortably on his desk, leaned further back in his chair and treated John Pownall to a narrow-lipped seraphic smile.

'Bloody Irish pedant. Be quiet man! "... an instance of so large a body of troops ... quartered in a town so *licentious* as this ..." Mark that, William. "Licentious" is his word, not mine. "... behaving in so *orderly, decent* and *quiet* a fashion as these soldiers have done." There, William! There you have it. And that from Governor Bernard, who is in situ.'

'But hardly a neutral witness, don't you think? Do you intend to send out for lunch, by the way? I could eat an ox.'

'To hell with lunch. Britain is a nation under the law. If the colonists were under French or Spanish rule, Samuel Adams would be twice his current height, stretched on the rack. Or his head would be marched round the town on a pike by now.'

'You appear to relish the thought.'

'I do, as a matter of fact. That man, that ... Adams reptile, is using British law, British respect for the rule of law, and British decency and restraint to make our every task more difficult, not least our task in apprehending him.'

William Knox's seraphic smile grew wider. 'Aah, but you have to admit he's good. I do believe that man could whip up discontent among the angels in heaven. Have you read his latest pronouncements on the troops? Oh, of course you have. You were probably up all night reading them.'

Pownall laughed. 'Just to show you how wrong you habitually are, no I haven't read them. I wasn't up all night reading them because the latest batch only came in this morning.'

'Well, I have read them, you sluggard.' Knox stretched for the pile of newspaper articles which had arrived that morning from Boston. Even that much physical activity made him groan. William Knox did not like movement.

'Apparently,' he said, absently, 'without provocation, British soldiers wantonly attack Boston citizens on the street, they insult, molest and rape their daughters, they turn the town into a veritable bedlam of chaos. That's the gospel according to Sam, anyway.'

'Of course there have been incidents with women,' said Pownall, hotly. 'There have been with every occupying force of troops in history. And as for fights between soldiers and the citizenry, it always seems to be patriots who are involved. I wonder why. The latest was Young.'

The Irishman's eyes opened wide. 'Was it, now? I missed that. What happened?'

'Young was roughed up by a sentry at night, according to a report by Richard Silvester. Young had refused the sentry's challenge. According to Silvester, Young attacked the sentry, not the other way around. But he came off worse.'

'Aah. The gallant and romantic Dr Young! Such a tilter at windmills.'

'Indeed!'

William Knox was still burrowing in the newly arrived newspapers from Boston: 'Ah, here it is! I give you Mr Samuel Adams.' He read Adams's words aloud: '"Here, Americans, you may behold some of the first fruits springing up from that root of bitterness, a standing army."'

William Knox put the newspaper cutting down and applauded. 'Very clever, Mr Adams! Calling the troops a standing army is as much for readers here as in Boston. He

165

knows full well the Boston papers will arrive in London inside a month. We think, how would we like it, now? Knowing perfectly well a standing army is anathema to an Englishman. He'll be using that phrase, "standing army", again and again, you mark my words.'

John Pownall nodded in agreement and picked up Adams's *Boston Gazette* article. '"Troops are quartered upon us in a time of peace ..." Oh, nicely said, Sam. Everything was peaceful and the troops were sent on a wicked British whim, eh? No Customs Commissioners abused? All customs dues paid, were they Sam?'

'What's happened to the Customs Commissioners, in the end?'

'They have left Castle William for their abodes in Boston and resumed work, apparently. But soldiers can't protect them every minute of every day. Young's Liberty Boys are still tormenting them, to great effect.'

There was silence for a moment, then Pownall read on from Adams's article: '" ... in a time of peace ..." Ha-bloody-ha! "... on pretence of preserving order in a town that was as orderly before their arrival as any one large town in the whole of his Majesty's dominions." Stand clear of your desk, William. I wish to void the contents of my stomach on it.'

He resumed reading. 'And a little time will discover whether we are to be governed by the martial or the common law of the land.'

William Knox clapped his large hands together in loud, not entirely ironic applause. 'Oh, very clever! If Boston is under martial law, the patriots can use the militia against the army with impunity, as they would be at war. He is readying the people for just that.'

Pownall nodded. 'You know, William,' he mused, 'what is oft forgotten? Any positive act by a soldier. You remember that fire in the gaol in Queen Street, not long after the soldiers arrived? Some of the 29th rushed there from the Common. They arrived even before the

Fire Engine and the nearest Fire Company. The soldiers rendered great service. Three of them were burned, one nearly died. Adams was furious.'

John Pownall fell silent, reading with trance-like concentration. This was another newspaper article, included by Richard Silvester. Pownall went white in the face.

'What is it?' William Knox said.

'Listen to this: "This day, two of the soldiers concerned in stopping an inhabitant of the town the other evening and beating the said inhabitant were by warrant brought before Mr Justice Dana, who considering the nature of the offence bound them over to answer to the court of general sessions for this county ..."'

Pownall paused, still white in the face. He stared at William Knox, then spoke slowly.

'The Sons of Liberty have somehow managed to ensure that one of their number, Justice Dana, can put our soldiers on trial for going about their duties.'

'I agree with you, John. That is a worrying development.'

John Pownall did not reply but tore open the last packet in this latest batch from Boston. 'Aah! This is from our star turn, William Molineux.'

'What does he have to say for himself?'

Pownall shook his head in wonder. 'Well, for a start, he says Young organised and led the attack on the guardhouse, the evening the troops arrived.'

'Young?' Knox looked dubious. 'That's hardly the good doctor's style, is it? A talented polemicist, yes. Almost as good as Adams himself. And he organises marches. And he encourages tarring and feathering and Skimmington treatment, but he does not get involved in military action, no matter how minor. He has no training for it. It is well outside his compass. How sure is Molineux?'

'Very sure.'

Working through the late morning, into the afternoon and

on into the evening, without food or taking any sort of break, John Pownall wrote up the reports from Boston, copying and unifying them into one long report. He left off the names of the original informants, to maintain secrecy.

He read the start of the report aloud to himself by lamplight in the now empty office: 'Dr Thomas Young was guilty of organising the attack on the guardhouse at the Neck, on the night of the troops' arrival in Boston. Possibly as a result, he was involved in an altercation with a soldier of the 29th. He managed to have the soldier and others concerned arrested and tried by the civil authority, represented by Justice Richard Dana. This has set a dangerous precedent for any British soldiers to be tried by the colonists under a judge appointed by them.'

When John Pownall's report was complete, he called for the Chief Clerk, William Pollock, whom he had instructed to stay in the office for as long as he was required. He ordered his report copied five times. One copy was sent to Lord Hillsborough, one to the Northern Office, another to the Southern Office. The remaining two copies were to be kept in store in the Clerks' Office.

John Pownall then burned the original reports from Boston in the grate of his minuscule office. This was a routine measure to preserve secrecy generally, and especially to keep the names of the spies as secret as possible. Ideally knowledge of them was to be limited to himself, William Knox and the Chief Clerk.

CHAPTER 30

As soon as the Customs Commissioners and the locally recruited Customs Comptrollers left Castle William, they resumed work from their newly rebuilt, heavily guarded office at the Concert Hall. Their first act was to seize John Hancock's sloop, *Liberty*. They did this at the behest of Admiral John Montagu, commander of the massive British naval force aboard his flagship, *Romney*.

Like the army when they first landed, Admiral Montagu had been subject to mass desertions as soon as his fleet of ships docked. Montagu intended to impress some local sailors into the British navy – seize them by force and enlist them. Impounding the *Liberty* and its crew from Boston's leading merchant was a deliberately inflammatory and confrontational way of doing it.

Despite his cordial relations with Boston's leading merchants, especially John Rowe, Admiral John Montagu hated and despised ordinary Bostonians as much as any Briton who ever landed there. He snarled at the very thought of them.

The *Liberty* was taken from Hancock's Wharf on charges of smuggling twenty-five caskets of wine. It was towed to the lee of the *Romney*, where its ties were cut. An incensed crowd gathered, most wearing Wilkes cockades. They began throwing stones and rocks and set up a rhythmic chant of 'Wilkes and Liberty'.

The crew of Hancock's ship had to be released before they could be impressed into the British navy. The first of them were carried on the shoulders of the crowd from dockside to the Province House where they defiantly chanted at the Governor, even though he had prudently fled to Castle William yet again.

When news of the seizure of the *Liberty* reached London, sent by George Hayley on the fastest of Hancock's ships, it fed into the near-permanent Wilkes riots. The seizure of the *Liberty* rapidly became a cause célèbre on both sides of the Atlantic. This was thoroughly resented by both Adams and Young, who felt that fights on behalf of Hancock, with all his riches, were a distraction from the main business of revolution and getting rid of the British. As a result, Adams and Young were barely talking to Hancock.

Relations between Adams and Young themselves remained frosty but they were at least on speaking terms.

To the secret relief of Adams and Young, another seizure was quickly added to that of the *Liberty* to keep outrage raw but with a worthier cause.

The sloop *Bonetta* belonged to the merchant John Rowe. Rowe was a popular figure throughout Boston, seen by most as a cool-headed, reasonable middle way between the loyalists and patriots.

The *Bonetta*, unlike the *Liberty*, was trading when she was seized. She was taken at Braintree, still in Boston harbour but a few miles up the coast. She was making her usual run, carrying corn, candles and oil from the local spermaceti wax works.

On the orders of Customs Commissioner Charles Paxton, a customs cutter boarded the vessel. The Master was told he must produce clearance – letters to show duties had been paid, and an invoice showing the paid duties.

The captain of the *Bonetta* could produce none of this, so the vessel was seized. The captain was forbidden to unload. Later the vessel was boarded again by soldiers from the 29th with swords drawn and pistols loaded. Their lieutenant had obeyed an order from the Commissioners, setting a precedent for the Commissioners to use British troops without permission from the Assembly.

Sam Adams saw the significance of that immediately. He made sure Boston erupted in rage. This was deep, long-lasting fury, a blaze from the spark lit by the seizure of the *Liberty*. John Rowe publicly demanded the return of his ship.

Sam Adams called a caucus meeting in the Long Room, fuelled by free 'flip', a mixture of rum and beer, to drink and free tobacco and clay pipes. The most effective retaliation, Adams, Young and Molineux agreed, was non-importation of British goods.

As Adams put it to the caucus, speaking quietly as he always did when deadly serious: 'We can easily avoid paying the tribute by abstaining from the use of those articles by which it is extorted from us.' The caucus murmured its wholehearted assent, puffing at their free clay pipes, sipping at their free flip.

The citizens of Boston would refuse to assist the import or sale or consumption of any British goods whatsoever, but especially of goods taxed under the hated Townshend Acts; and of those, especially tea, which is where the British were getting most of their extortionate tax revenue.

As Adams put it, 'The Tea Duty is the sliver which keeps the wound of British power open.' That got a round of applause and foot stamping and a rousing cheer from the caucus.

The caucus was followed, as ever, by a Town Meeting. Attendance was enormous, even the Old South Church, the biggest meeting place in Boston, was overflowing. Relayers had to be appointed to keep those standing outside informed of what was being said. What especially pleased Adams was the attendance of nearly all the significant Boston merchants, including John Rowe.

Thomas Young stood before the crowd, exalted, impassioned, enjoying himself. 'This is the critical moment to play off the whole force of America in every shape it can safely be exerted, to show a despicable ministry how little they have to expect from a continuation of their absurd and villainous measures.'

The applause thundered round the massive Old South. Thousands of feet stamped on the wooden floor.

Samuel Adams spoke second, in support. Adams had realised early that the provisioning of the British army and navy was an alluring bait for the richer merchants. This was a bigger threat to the patriots than the small shopkeepers and inns profiting from the day-to-day sale of rum and suchlike to the soldiers. The merchants had come to the meeting, so far so good, but persuading them to support his cause was a much bigger step.

So when he spoke, Adams charged at the issue directly, explicitly linking the non-importation issue with the withdrawal of troops, thus inviting the merchants to put patriotism before profit: 'We are more than ever determined to relinquish every article, however dear, that comes from Britain, till the Acts are repealed and the troops removed.'

Adams did not need to manipulate the result, at that heady Town Meeting: a Non-Importation Agreement was drafted and signed straight off by over a hundred traders, big and small. For one year, all signatories would not import any European commodities. American colonial manufactures were to be encouraged. Preference in trading would be given to traders who had signed the Non-Importation Agreement. A Committee was formed to oversee Non-Importation.

The Committee was pre-packed with Adams's caucus men. However, to Adams's fury, there were still some merchants and even more small shopkeepers who refused to sign the Non-Importation Agreement. Battle lines, thought Adams, were drawn as never before between the patriots and loyalists. There was nowhere to hide in the middle.

In a way, that suited Adams. He detested those trimmers who would not choose a side as much as he detested his enemies, except for the Medici. They had their own degree of hatred beyond all mercy and redemption.

Chapter 31

Thomas Young started a drive to stop consumption of all imported tea. On his regular doctor's rounds, he preached the virtues of tea made from the leaves of the shrub *Ceanothus americanus*, growing wild in many places along the Massachusetts coast. He instructed his patients on the gathering of the small leaves required and its subsequent cleansing and brewing. He carried out demonstrations, then proudly presented the patriotic tea.

Unfortunately, the resultant Hyperion Tea, sometimes known as Labrador Tea, was a deep brown colour, which invited bawdy comparisons. Young's claim that it tasted of wild rosemary was not always confirmed by the people who drank it. Most of them thought it tasted vile.

But Thomas Young persevered. He told the good folks on his rounds that the tea was good for many pains, including rheumatism and disorders of the spleen. This claim, which Young had invented, was widely repeated when the tea was produced commercially and advertised.

In the final analysis, though, Bostonians drank Young's tea because they liked Young and because he praised them as patriots for avoiding the hated Hyson and Bohea teas, which the detested British were using to wring out every last drop of Boston's blood in the form of extortionate taxes. This appeal to their sense of being Americans, rather than colonists, went deep to the heart of Bostonians and once there it tended to stay there, despite the taste of the tea.

However, Young reached the limits of Boston patriotism with his recipe for burnt barley or small field peas, to be toasted gently with butter and then ground. Young's claim that the result could be called coffee, and indeed was equal to the best West India coffee, defined the limit of patriotic revolt.

One thing that did strike Young, though, on his rounds

as the days of Non-Importation became weeks, was the increase in the necessary use of barter for payment. Barter had always been part of the lower levels of Boston trade, as the shortage of ready money had lasted as long as anyone could remember. But now the situation grew markedly worse.

Like many households, the Youngs measured their prosperity, or rather the lack of it, by however many days ahead they could afford to feed the children, themselves and the sewing girl, Martha. They used to reckon on maybe two weeks' food ahead. But right now, Young calculated they had enough to eat for only three days ahead, if that. After three days at most something had to turn up, even if it was only a plum cake from a grateful patient.

The call to patriotic duty to replace luxury items – all imported from Britain – with homespun, homemade, simple artefacts, was seen as a necessity, not a choice. Almost as inevitable, in a Boston under British occupation, was an inability to pay taxes.

The main beneficiary of this state of affairs was Samuel Adams. His large backlog of uncollected taxes was now rivalled by the other three tax-gatherers. Tax payment and gathering was near collapse in the spreading poverty. Adams was secretly relieved of his tax collecting duties by the Assembly, despite the fact that it was not even officially in session. The matter of his uncollected dues was quietly dropped.

Adams had got away with letting Ebenezer Mackintosh, William Molineux and a goodly part of the old Pope's Day fighters off their taxes to keep them under his control.

Young's work with the Liberty Boys on Thursdays continued. But there was a problem, now: before, the boys had been gleefully attacking the houses and disturbing the sleep of Customs Commissioners only, or Customs Comptrollers, traitors like Benjamin Hallowell. Now,

Young wanted the same tactics applied to the merchants who were importing British goods in defiance of the Non-Importation Agreement, and the small shopkeepers who were selling goods from Britain, likewise in defiance of the Agreement.

Many of these shopkeepers were facing hardship, even hunger. And they were local people, Bostonians in good standing. The Liberty Boys were becoming unhappy about the idea of tormenting them, even if they were selling imported British luxury goods, because they had to sell those goods to keep going. Not to mention that some of the Liberty Boys and Girls were the sons and daughters of those very same small shopkeepers.

The first to ask to see Thomas Young about this was the big crew leader, Christopher Seider, at the head of a small deputation of Liberty Boys. There were about half a dozen of them, but not John or Rosmond Young. There had been some talk of picketing Christopher's own family brewery for importing hops, but nothing had so far come of it. Seider and most of his crew of Liberty Boys would likely refuse to do it.

Thomas Young soothed Cristopher Seider. The next Thursday he called a meeting of the Liberty Boys in the Young front parlour. Thomas and Mary stood out front. They asked Christopher Seider to speak first.

'What's wrong, Christopher?' Mary Young said, gently. 'Tell us how you feel.'

'We are fighting our own people,' a tearfully defiant Christopher Seider said. 'And it's not fair. The little guys are getting hurt the most.'

This was undeniably true. Non-Importation was much easier for the larger merchants. They could store imported luxury goods in warehouses they often owned and sit tight, waiting for the hoped-for repeal of the Townshend Acts, which was rumoured almost as soon as they were passed. The small shopkeepers, on the other hand, soon had nothing to sell. They faced destitution.

Thomas and Mary looked at each other. Thomas spoke first: 'Christopher, we have to do this because as long as Massachusetts remains within the British Empire we can never compete with their textiles and hardware coming in by sea. And certainly not while they force us to sell what little we *are* allowed to produce to them or through them. So we have to throw off the yoke once and for all and leave the Empire.'

'We are fighting for a better future, Christopher,' Mary said. 'There will be casualties. Some people are going to get hurt. But it will be worth it in the end.'

Mary Young and Anne Hayley expanded the Daughters of Liberty, keeping them independent of the men. They held a meeting at the Young place, followed by an announcement in the *Boston News-Letter* that they would not buy ribbons and other luxury items and would shun shops selling taxed goods. Anne Hayley copied out the announcement and sent it to her brother. John Wilkes wrote back saying he was proud of her.

John Hancock argued furiously with Young and Adams over the amount of pressure being put on the shopkeepers and merchants. He saw no justice in the patriot case, in such instances. Young – especially – saw his point but said there was no other way.

However, he continued to give medical treatment to the families of importers, often without charge, as they had nothing to pay with. This was in defiance of the demand from Adams and the Committee to cease all contact with them. So yet another rift developed between Adams and Young over Non-Importation, an addition to their myriad other disputes and niggles with each other.

Meanwhile, force against the larger merchants was meeting with some success, even against the Medici. After his house was smeared with excrement, Thomas Hutchinson's oldest son, Thomas junior, was among the merchants agreeing not to sell items prohibited by the Non-Importation Agreement. Thomas junior agreed to hand over chests of tea and other British goods to the supervision of Adams and his Committee.

As to the Lieutenant Governor himself, Thomas Hutchinson was to some degree restored to health at this point, but had handed over all business affairs to Thomas junior and his second son, Elisha. He was, as he put it, past caring about anything they did.

Chapter 32

The commander of British land forces in the American colonies, General Thomas Gage, started writing reports to John Pownall at the American Department as soon as he moved to Boston from New York. He did this because he believed John Pownall, and only John Pownall, knew Boston's affairs well enough to advise him from Britain. (Gage had heard of William Knox but did not trust him, in part because he was Irish.)

Gage's reports were much valued by John Pownall. They were concise, well written and arrived at frequent regular intervals. In this they were very different from the few reports written by Governor Francis Bernard, which were rambling, fearful and unclear. Governor Bernard, apparently, feared Armageddon daily.

General Gage, by contrast, thought the patriots only a faction. The royal officials, he felt, were too timid. This was what John Pownall wanted to hear. Gage named the five Customs Commissioners as among the timid, not Governor Bernard. But Pownall knew perfectly well he meant Bernard too.

Reports from Lieutenant Governor Thomas Hutchinson, which also arrived frequently, were clear and clever, but John Pownall never acted on them. There was always plenty of material about the black arts of Samuel Adams, which Pownall did not disagree with, but there were never any practical plans for action to oppose these black arts.

John Pownall's underlying attitude to Hutchinson was and remained one of mistrust. He always felt the Lieutenant Governor was acting to promote the family business interests, via sons Thomas junior and Elisha. This feeling grew even stronger when Thomas junior arrived in London to develop the family's tea imports.

Thomas junior met all the leading London tea traders.

With one of them, he arranged for pre-paid consignments of sixty chests of tea at a time, to be landed at Braintree, up the coast from Boston, which made avoidance of duty easier.

Go ahead, serve your own interests, John Pownall thought to himself. But how did that square with the Hutchinsons signing the Non-Importation Agreement at Samuel Adams's behest? It was duplicitous hypocrisy on the Hutchinsons' part, thought Pownall, and the man of straight lines did not like it, even if the Hutchinsons were outwitting Samuel Adams and doing him down, at least for now.

There was no question of John Pownall copying Hutchinson's reports to his older brother, because the fewer people caught in Hutchinson's webs of lies and half-truths, as John Pownall saw it, the better. But General Gage's reports were occasionally, by no means always, copied out by the clerks for his brother.

Both the Pownall brothers were, after all, on the loyalist side, in John's opinion, because they both wanted Adams and his so-called patriots stopped. In any case, to John Pownall's own great surprise, he felt a need to see his older brother occasionally, to chew things over, private matters and public matters. He was still leading the life of a hard-working hermit but occasionally needed a break from it. His meetings with Thomas were a welcome chance to relax, as far as he was ever capable of that.

They met at the Cock, just behind the Royal Exchange, where they had eaten turtle soup together at their first meeting in London, just after Thomas returned from Boston.

John handed over General Gage's reports and any other papers he felt it was in the American Department's interest for Thomas to see, anything that would help them both bring down Wilkes and Adams. Thomas, for his part, would update John on his latest efforts to help Boston and

179

its people. And those efforts were considerable.

Thomas had been working like a plump but scurrying beaver. He had even lost weight, to some extent. This period of his life, as he belatedly reached a growing maturity, was the hardest-working. It outstripped even his time as a student at Cambridge, the only time up to then he had worked with systematic discipline: rising before sunrise, breakfast at a local coffee-house, in class at seven o'clock, lectures until twelve noon, then a dinner hour, then study and disputation until chapel at five.

Thomas still kept up the landscape painting he had taken up in Boston, in desultory fashion, but only briefly between bursts of work and with much less aspiration. Indeed, when he looked at his early Boston landscapes he grimaced, mocking his earlier view of himself as an aspiring artist.

The conduit for Thomas's new-found systematic industry on Boston's behalf was the Massachusetts Trade Agent in London, Dennys de Berdt. All the American colonies had trade agents in London; de Berdt was one of the most effective. Thomas and de Berdt quickly decided on the best way they could help Boston: boost shipbuilding. Some of the best shipbuilding timber in the world grew close to Boston's shores. Britain had tried to send it back to the London shipyards, but the wood was too heavy and the process too costly. So they allowed the Bostonians to build the ships, but ruled that any ships built in the Boston shipyards counted as British under the Navigation Acts.

Through de Berdt, Thomas arranged for a consortium of Glasgow traders to build four 230-ton vessels in Boston. That would keep the seafront in work for years. Thomas was ecstatic at his success.

Then de Berdt died. Concealing his bubbling excitement under pretended grief, Thomas tried to have himself appointed Massachusetts Agent in de Berdt's place. His brother John had no objections, though he did not help Thomas as much as he claimed he had. Thomas spoke to

Lord North, pleading his cause, desperate to be back in an official capacity, helping Massachusetts.

As far as Thomas knew, Lord North supported him to Governor Bernard, but Thomas was stymied by his old nemesis, Lieutenant Governor Hutchinson. Hutchinson refused to back him to the Massachusetts General Court, the body responsible for making the appointment. Someone else was appointed, a nonentity who did almost nothing for Boston.

Thomas's stubborn streak had been poked. Dominated, as ever, by heart not head, his blazing desire to return to Massachusetts was rekindled and inflamed by his failure to obtain a post which, while serving Massachusetts, was firmly based in London. From the day of his rejection as Trade Agent, for the rest of his life Thomas Pownall dreamed every day of returning to live in Boston again.

But until the longed-for day of his return, with that characteristic mix of tactical shrewdness, strategic ineptitude and personal and political naiveté, Thomas Pownall spent every waking moment battling for Boston. And he came up with a plan, or at least a well-developed idea.

Boston possessed great natural advantages – it had raw materials in abundance: wood, wool, flax. The number of skilled artisans was increasing. But Britain's ban on any manufacturing was the key problem, as Thomas had understood ever since he was Governor. He set about an ingenious solution, encouraging skilled artisans to start a new life in Massachusetts, causing pressure to start manufacturing by their very presence.

These were the people – the cordwainers, coopers, skilled shipyard workers, carpenters – who were the backbone of Boston life. Most British newspapers were in full cry against America, but Thomas paid for advertisements in the few London journals which supported the Americans – mainly the *Monthly Review* – advertising work in Boston. He started an assisted passage scheme, until his defects as an administrator caused it to collapse in debt. Nevertheless, the plan to steadily promote and develop Boston's manufacturing was beginning to work.

Thomas's cause was helped by the unpopularity of Non-Importation among the London merchants. Trade was down. The London merchants did not like that at all. They wanted Boston's squabbles and grievances, whatever they may be, ended. They disliked trouble because trouble affects trade.

So when Thomas tried to pull out the Non-Importation thorn in Parliament, the effort had the London merchants' blessing. Thomas stood in a half-empty chamber. He pleaded for the use of a Royal Prerogative Order to settle the intractable problem of troop billeting and the collection of the Townshend Taxes. This would have put Massachusetts directly under the control of the Crown, bypassing Parliament, returning to the days of direct royal rule under the Massachusetts Charter, as many patriots in Boston wanted.

Thomas understood the urgency of having soldiers camped out on the Common with nowhere permanent for them to go more clearly than Governor Bernard did, or even than General Gage did. And he was at least proposing a solution to collecting Townshend Taxes, which was proceeding as badly as it had been before the troops arrived.

Watched from the gallery by his brother and William Knox, Thomas predicted an armed uprising in the American colonies if nothing was done. He pleaded with an indifferent House of Commons to make an agreement with these Englishmen who lived outside the realm, as he put it. Americans were friendly and loyal subjects of the Crown, Thomas pleadingly told the Commons.

William Knox, and even Thomas's younger brother, were moved by his words. And Thomas's pleas for use of a Royal Prerogative Order were at least listened to in the Commons – if only for the ingenuity of the idea. Thomas would never make an orator, but he had improved somewhat since his first disastrous speeches. His argument was at least clear.

But, as William Knox understood all too well, and whispered as much to John, his basic argument fell into the same error the Bostonians made and did not stop making.

Thomas Pownall and the Bostonians never understood King George III. He was not like his distant predecessors, the Stuart monarchs who ruled directly over the people with devices like the Massachusetts Charter. George III regarded himself as a modern Hanoverian monarch, proud to be a spiritual child of the Glorious Revolution, proud to rule through Parliament, and only through Parliament – a Parliament he and North controlled. Direct rule was an abomination to him.

Not to see this showed a special kind of naiveté on Thomas's part – the naiveté of a sophisticated man.

Several of Thomas's correspondents in Boston, including John Rowe, had told him Governor Francis Bernard could not go on operating at this level of incompetence. Crucially, General Gage had turned against Bernard.

Thomas Pownall began a frenzied flurry of activity to seek backers to return for a second period as Governor. Yet again, he elicited support from North and his brother, John. Disingenuously, he even wrote to Francis Bernard himself, trading on the Lincolnshire heritage they shared, offering to replace him as Governor.

It was all for nothing, leaving Thomas shrivelling up inside with burnt-out hopes. Francis Bernard was indeed recalled, but he would be succeeded as Governor by the Lieutenant Governor, Thomas Hutchinson.

A despairing Thomas then felt he had nothing more to lose by acting on a long-standing grievance: he went to see Lord North and complained that his letters to America were being opened. He had already complained in the

Commons about this infamous breach of trust. Could North either have the practice stopped or perhaps, Thomas said with heavy jocularity, ensure that His Majesty read Thomas's opened letters, thus increasing his influence?

North smiled. His eyes twinkled. He muttered some pabulum without pointing out that it was Thomas's own brother who was having his letters opened – something that had not occurred to Thomas.

CHAPTER 33

After years of badgering requests from John Pownall to find concrete proof of wrongdoing against John Wilkes, Nathan Carrington, the head of the King's Messengers – the Secret Service – had finally come up with something. He was presenting his findings to John Pownall and William Knox at the American Department.

The Secret Service chief was known for the contrast between his foppish dress and his plebeian speech and manners. Today, touches of gold lace on his hat and waistcoat and a gilded sword and dagger confirmed the first part of the reputation. His opening speech confirmed the second.

'That traitorous bugger Wilkes has been a governor of the Foundling Hospital for ages,' Carrington began sonorously. 'As you may know, gents, the Hospital takes in foundling babies off the streets and provides for them until the boys can join the navy and the girls go into service. Waste of bleedin' time if you ask me. But anyway, when the Hospital opened a branch in Aylesbury, on Wilkes's patch, so to speak, Wilkes was made Treasurer of it.'

Nathan Carrington paused for dramatic effect. Pownall had his eyes closed, believing heaven to be within reach. William Knox put his feet up on the desk.

Carrington continued. 'Wilkes had incurred debts from another of his positions, as Colonel of the Buckinghamshire militia.'

'He has had that position removed from him,' Pownall said.

'Indeed, sir. That is what caught our Jonny on the 'op, so to speak. Left with debts of £800.'

Knox whistled. His bright blue eyes were shining.

'He is also behind with bills, our Jonny is. That is in addition to the debt. His supporters keep giving him money, but he spends it faster than they can give it. So he used his position as Treasurer to help himself to Foundling Hospital money.'

'Can you prove that?' Pownall was shouting.

'Yes, Mr Pownall, I believe I can. Here is a statement signed by a Mr Dancer and a Mr Hamar who are governors of the Foundling Hospital at Aylesbury.' Carrington passed the statement to Pownall. 'It confirms that the Governors authorised the payment of £224 3s 3d to John Wilkes as Treasurer for payments to tradesmen at Aylesbury for sundry articles.'

Knox put his arm round Pownall as they both silently read the document. The tension in the room thickened.

Carrington went on. 'Now 'ere in this second document is a bunch of signed statements from all the tradesmen, saying they never got no money. There's ten of the bleeders, which is why it took us so long. I 'ad two men up in Aylesbury for a week.'

Carrington handed over the ten signed statements, held together in a clip. Pownall started to read them aloud. '"Thomas Roger is owed £4 13s 8d, James Lee is owed £36 11s 1d, James Austin is owed £2 16s 2d ..." Carrington, you have won the lottery for us.'

'It is all there, guvnor. It all adds up. Balances, like.'

There was silence for a moment. Pownall turned to Knox. 'We have got him, William. Embezzlement, clear as day. And against a public charity.'

Knox nodded, trying to contain his excitement, but failing. 'Agreed. Carrington has brought us the Holy Grail, all right. Well done, Mr Carrington.'

'Yes, well done!' Pownall shouted.

The Head of the King's Messengers gave a modest smirk.

'Do we prosecute?' Knox said, half to himself.

'No,' Pownall said, firmly. 'It will take too long. His supporters would rally to him. There will be even more instability In London. And Lord North wants him gone. Off the scene. No, I shall confront him with this evidence and demand he leaves the country, under threat of prosecution. As soon as he is clear of our shores, we claim he fled justice, then have him declared an outlaw, so he may not return.'

'Where do we challenge him?' Knox asked, deferring to Pownall, as he usually did on practical matters. 'Do we summon him here?'

'No. Too public. He will agree to flee more readily if he thinks it will be hushed up. I shall visit him at his home, confront him with the evidence. I shall tell him he must leave England immediately.'

Carrington beamed. 'I'll come with you, sir. With a couple of my best men.'

'No!' Pownall shouted. And then more softly: 'No, thank you, Mr Carrington. As I say, this must be kept discreet.' Pownall turned to Knox. 'We've got him, William. We've got him.'

John Pownall sat opposite John Wilkes in Wilkes's luxurious house in Great George Street. He stared at Wilkes's face. It was practically deformed. He squinted badly, screwing up his face. His smile of welcome had revealed gaps in stumpy yellowing teeth. The tongue which could weave those verbal spells of magic was too big for his mouth, resulting in a lisp over smilingly insincere words of welcome and offers of refreshment.

Pownall thought of Wilkes's well-known boast that he could make any woman forget his ugliness after twenty minutes in his company. Having forgotten his ugliness, the boast continued, the woman, any woman apparently, would be willing, even eager, to disrobe.

Pownall himself had never seen a woman naked. Indeed, he did not expect to until his wedding night, an event awaited as part of the usual order of things rather than anticipated with any pleasure.

He handed over the papers Nathan Carrington had produced at his office, laboriously copied out by two of his clerks.

'These documents are clear evidence that you have embezzled money from the Aylesbury Foundling Hospital.'

Wilkes took the papers with a crooked smile.

'To avoid proceedings as a common felon on these charges, Mr Wilkes, you are required to leave the country. Leave immediately, stay away for two years or until we tell you to come back.'

Wilkes studied the papers without a word.

'You can go to Paris,' Pownall continued, conversationally, while Wilkes was reading. 'I believe you have a daughter there.'

Wilkes snorted, giving Pownall a crooked smile and a beady-eyed gaze, mainly through a right eye which was considerably higher than the left. 'Well nooow, Mr Pownall. Let me see nooow. Let me seeee.' Wilkes was giving a satirical imitation of Pownall's Lincolnshire burr. It was faint, unless John was talking to Thomas or his mother, but noticeable nonetheless.

Wilkes abandoned the imitation, his manner hardening. 'Now you listen to me, boy.' Pownall recoiled. He and Wilkes were approximately the same age. 'Before you come blundering in here, making allegations, you need to check your facts. I knew there were people sniffing around in Aylesbury. And I have sent word to Mr Hamar and Mr Dancer.' Wilkes slapped the papers in front of him. 'They accept that the tradesmen concerned did not appear when requested to collect their money. They are prepared to swear an oath to that effect.'

'What, all of them? All ten tradesmen did not appear? That is absurd!'

'I think you will find all the tradesmen will support my story, Mr Pownall. I am well known in their community. One word from me and ...' Wilkes mimed throat-cutting. 'Do I really have to spell it out for you? The tradesmen have withdrawn the statements they made.'

John Wilkes handed over a bundle of papers, ready

on a small table next to him. A brief withdrawal of the earlier statement was written in one hand and signed with a scrawl in various different hands. John Pownall counted the identical withdrawal statements; there were ten of them.

Pownall was silent.

Wilkes continued. 'Mr Pownall, would you say you were a popular figure at your place of work?'

The question hung in the air.

'Popular? Popular? I do not seek ... What has that got to do with ...?'

Wilkes smiled. 'Your clerks don't seem to like you very much. Information about you was quite easy to come by. They didn't even want paying. Happy to give it for nothing, if it would harm you.'

'What information?'

Wilkes got up – he was well made – and strode athletically to a small, beautifully inlaid Sheraton desk. He took some papers from it, then sat down again. He gave a mock theatrical sigh. 'It seems, Pownall my boy, that you are doing rather well in the King's Service.'

'What does that mean?'

'It means, you country bumpkin, that your salary for your old position at the Board of Trade is still being paid on top of the £500 for your post in the American Department. Does poor old Mr Knox know you are getting two salaries?' There was silence in the room. 'Well, does he? Does? He?'

'No.'

Wilkes resumed the mocking country accent. 'No. He don't knoooow. Do he? He don't knooow because you are the only person in colonial service drawing two salaries.' The accent stopped, so did the mock smile. Wilkes's hideous face contorted further with hatred. 'What did you do to earn that, eh, little boy? Let Hillsborough give it to you up the arse?'

Pownall had always assumed the double payment was

Hillsborough's way of surreptitiously rewarding him for his invaluable work. It was easier than finding him another sinecure payment.

'You move against me, little boy Pownall, and you are finished. *I* will be prosecuting *you* for embezzlement. You hear me?'

'Yes.'

Eventually, as Pownall always believed he would, Wilkes overreached himself. His journal, the *North Briton*, printed a scurrilous accusation that the King's mother and Lord Bute were lovers. Lord North loved George III dearly and was as wounded by the charge as the King was. That the allegation was almost certainly true made North's outraged detestation even stronger.

Lord North denounced Wilkes in the Commons for obscene libel, forcing him to flee to France, enabling North to have him declared an outlaw, as Pownall had originally intended with the Foundling Hospital charge.

But even absent, John Wilkes haunted Pownall's days and nights as much as Samuel Adams did. Pownall took to visiting Mrs Salmon's waxwork of Wilkes in Fleet Street. He stood there staring blankly at the devil Wilkes. It was the only time he stopped work.

CHAPTER 34

John Wilkes's sojourn in exile in France was by and large pleasant. He adored his daughter Polly, who had adopted Paris as her home. For her part, Polly admired her papa, the fiery champion of the people's freedom. She was proud of him. She was only too happy to have him living with her, rent free, in her tasteful apartment overlooking the Bois de Boulogne.

Neither the proximity of Polly nor the advancing years, however, curbed John Wilkes's need for the pleasures of the flesh. He was a frequent visitor to the brothels and bagnios of Les Halles, where he lost himself in debauchery as extreme as the practices of his youth in Leiden with Charles Townshend or at Medmenham in his middle years. He also took two mistresses on the Faubourg Saint Antoine.

When not at play, he settled to work, weaving his new contacts into a network. The Court and the government in Paris showed little interest in an outlawed representative of the English Parliament. But his notoriety made him a magnet for the *demi-monde* on the outer fringes of public life.

He made early contact with the Chevalier d'Éon, who had fought as a soldier against the British, was a spy for Louis XV in London, and who was as passionately dedicated to the American cause as Wilkes was. Although at their first meeting, Charles d'Éon dressed as a man, thereafter he wore women's clothes and he and Wilkes quickly became lovers.

Through d'Éon, Wilkes met the extensive pro-American patriot faction in Paris. He reported all these contacts to Samuel Adams by sending trusted messengers, French female friends of Polly's, to London to meet George Hayley, whenever one of John Hancock's ships docked. There, Wilkes's messages would be repeated, with nothing written down.

Wilkes reported that the French pro-patriot faction were ready and willing to help, whenever they were called on. They had the means and the capacity to deliver weapons for use against the British, even if no formal war was declared. Adams had no need to wait until the French court or the French government backed him.

Wilkes kept himself closely informed of events in America and in Britain via George Hayley, who still maintained his London house in Great Alie Street, Goodman's Fields as well as a house in Boston. Wilkes had become even closer to his brother-in-law in exile, and Hayley naturally knew better than anyone the aspects of life in England Wilkes most wanted to hear about.

He most wanted to hear about trouble, preferably trouble that would lead to revolution, and there was plenty of it. An especially severe winter had forced the Common Council of the City of London to open subscriptions for the destitute. Wilkes had given the tightest of smiles at the news – the destitute would swell the ranks of protesters at the next rampage of the mob, whatever the cause.

And indeed Wilkes did not have long to wait for the next riot. The Spitalfields weavers took to the streets once again when the master weavers lowered the price of their work. Hayley reported that the weavers had joined forces with the coal heavers of Shadwell and the merchant sailors. He excitedly added that all three groups were supporting Wilkes by demanding the rescinding of his outlawry. His mistreatment, as they saw it, was linked to their demands for better conditions.

Wilkes had long been waiting for this. When the three groups stopped all outward-bound traffic in the Port of London he could barely contain his excitement.

And there was more. There was a disturbance at the pleasure gardens at Ranelagh by coach footmen and other attendants who had been forbidden to take vials or tips from their masters. They hissed at them and pulled up palings and piles in protest. Surely, Wilkes reasoned, if the lackeys of the rich were in revolt, revolt could turn to real revolution in Britain very soon.

George Hayley reported rumours that the state was running out of money. Building work had stopped on the new Adelphi. London was swept by rumours that George III had withdrawn his money from his bank in the Strand and put it under his bed. Prices were up for meat and, crucially, bread. The price of coal was prohibitive. When a mob at the docks found out it was being exported to Bordeaux for less than it cost in London, there was a tumultuous and bloody riot. Wilkes was in a near-permanent state of tumescent excitement.

Encouraged by Wilkes, George Hayley had called the first of a series of Public Meetings in London. These were based on the Boston Town Meetings. There were industrial marches on Parliament. The Commons was stormed and very nearly taken by the mob.

It was a commonplace, Hayley reported to Wilkes, that the Wilkesites held the streets, even without a visible Wilkes to lead them. In Wilkes's constituency, Aylesbury Town Hall lowered the Royal Standard and flew a flag inscribed 'Wilkes and Liberty' in gold – just like the one on the Liberty Tree in Boston.

The established system of government was under threat. Revolution was in the air, revolution was on the way. That is why John Wilkes left Polly and the American patriot faction, left Paris and returned to London. By then d'Éon was already back in England and Wilkes knew he would see his ally, lover and friend again there.

Wilkes left with a smile on his face. He said he would raise a dust or starve in gaol. At first, the latter looked more likely. The outlaw was arrested as soon as he set foot in Britain. The King's Bench prison was in Blackman Street, overlooking St George's Fields. Although it had thirty-foot-high prison walls, inside it resembled a village, having both a public garden and a recreation ground. Wilkes was allotted two comfortable rooms overlooking the fields. The turnkeys arranged a celebration for him on his forty-third birthday, which occurred while he was a guest at the prison.

The Chevalier d'Éon sent him a dozen smoked Russian tongues as a birthday gift. His accompanying note regretted that the tongues did not have the eloquence of Cicero so he and Wilkes could rejoice properly. Wilkes, recalling only too well what Charles-Geneviève-Louis-Auguste-André-Timothée d'Éon de Beaumont meant by rejoicing, bellowed with laughter.

John Hancock and George Hayley visited Wilkes in prison.

'Last night we were at a meeting of the London Friends of Liberty at the New England Coffee House, in Fleet Street,' Hayley reported to Wilkes. 'All the leading London patriots were there. Our former Governor, Thomas Pownall, sent greetings to you.'

John Hancock had more news: 'The *London Journal* has published the names of two hundred Members of Parliament ready to defy North and his King's Men and join the Friends of Liberty.'

Borne aloft on this swell of support, Wilkes told them to start the revolution outside his window, in St George's Fields.

On a fine spring day, the day of the opening of Parliament, a mob of well above a thousand gathered at St George's Fields, all sporting Wilkes cockades and chanting 'Wilkes and Liberty'. The authorities were expecting this and quickly diverted one hundred troops of the 3rd Regiment of Foot Guards, predominantly Scotsmen, who had been guarding Parliament.

The mob, many fuelled by a couple of hours' drinking at the Dog and Duck, on the edge of St George's Fields, cheered and whooped at the appearance of the soldiers, many of whom had just been ordered to take off their own Wilkes cockades.

A rumour quickly spread that the prison was to be stormed and all the prisoners released. The Foot Guards drew up inside the prison. The mob's chants were more hostile than usual. In addition to 'Wilkes and Liberty' there was 'Damn the King, damn the Government, damn the Justices'. Some of the mob threw dead dogs and cats at the soldiers. John Wilkes, watching from his window, waving to the mob, felt a thrill of the deepest contentment.

A Justice was called who read the Riot Act, requiring the mob to disperse. Inflamed, the mob started throwing stones, one of which hit the Justice in the face. The bloodied Justice panicked and shouted 'Open fire!'

The soldiers fired. Men fell wounded and dying. A group of soldiers chased the journeyman who had sparked the riot by throwing a stone at the Justice. The journeyman, who was wearing a red waistcoat, ran away over a rail, round a windmill, and through a cowshed with the soldiers running after him but hampered by their muskets. The soldiers lost sight of him, caught sight of a red waistcoat again near the Horseshoe Inn and one of them opened fire.

Their quarry fell. As he fell, another soldier ran up to him and bayonetted him as he lay on the ground. There was a scream of anguish: 'My son! My son!' as the publican of the Horseshoe Inn ran towards the body.

'What have you done?' screamed the publican. 'He was not at the Fields. My boy was here. He was working in my barn. What have you done?'

The soldiers looked at each other, one of them glanced at his bayonet, still dripping blood.

'Leg it!' one of them said.

They all ran away.

The boy who lay dead on the ground behind them was the publican's son, William Allen, aged fifteen. His now bloodied red waistcoat had cost him his life.

Allen's body was taken on a slab to Parliament, where there were further fury-filled riots. While soldiers battled the mob at the gates of the Commons, the streets burned in Limehouse, the Spitalfields weavers rioted and the coal heavers turned on the merchants, attacking and burning their houses, beating them when they caught them. The King was besieged in Buckingham House.

London was in a state of civil war.

The day after what was already known as the St George's Fields Massacre, King George III told his wife Charlotte that he no longer commanded his own capital. He had no choice but to abdicate. Charlotte immediately sent for Frederick, Lord North, who eventually talked him out of it. But it was a close-run thing.

John Wilkes had to be released from prison, to prevent London from going up in flames. He sent a message to Samuel Adams, via Hancock and Hayley. He told Adams to learn from the St George's Fields Massacre and its martyrs, especially William Allen.

CHAPTER 35

The Boston newspapers carried the story of the St George's Fields Massacre as front-page news. Writing as Mucius Scaevola in the *Massachusetts Spy*, Adams fulminated against British callousness.

Adams noted with interest that Wilkes had succeeded in getting what was originally known as the St George's Fields riot called a massacre by absolutely everybody, even loyalists. The story rumbled on for days, weeks, and not just in the patriot press.

There was a spectacular funeral for the slain boy, the martyr of the massacre, William Allen. This took place at St Mary's in Newington churchyard, Southwark. It was packed with the London patriot faction, including Thomas Pownall.

Two years went by after the St George's Fields Massacre and no opportunity presented itself to Adams to find martyrs for the cause. But Adams was patient. His enemies did not call him a basking lizard for nothing. Adams waited on his rock, seeking out the sun of discontent.

Meanwhile, events appeared to be turning against the revolution. The Non-Importation Agreement was dead. Adams had always had secret doubts about the enterprise. Non-Importation was turbulence, not proper revolutionary activity. They were shaking the branches of the tree of oppression, creating breeze, when they should be cutting the trunk down.

And he knew Non-Importation was flawed, the very idea was flawed. It was impossible, in practice. How do you police every ship unloading in Boston (or more likely Braintree) with imported goods, whether or not that particular merchant had signed up to Non-Importation?

And Hancock! That Judas. He had put profit first as he always did, continuing to import from Britain by the ton, knowing the patriots could not say a word because of his closeness, through the Hayleys, to Wilkes, and because he financed the patriots, almost single-handedly.

Another factor in the death of Non-Importation, Adams thought bitterly, was the defection of New York, especially, but also Philadelphia, pulling out of their respective Non-Importation Agreements.

Adams maintained relations with patriots in other colonies, mainly New York and Philadelphia, but also to some extent Georgia. Nobody else wanted to do this liaison work. It was tedious and brought little gain. But with a movement like Non-Importation, unity was all, as the merchants could always switch their banned British goods to another port in another colony. No unity, no Non-Importation.

Adams had let Thomas Young lead some stupid victory parade celebrating their defeat, the end of Non-Importation, pretending it was somehow, mysteriously, a victory. Young was good at parades; he played three or four musical instruments, including the fife. Parades let him show that off. And he normally wrote a terrible ditty of praise or blame to suit the occasion.

So off they all paraded, flags flying, drums beating, Trumpets blowing. Young was pleased with himself after the parade, as they attracted such good numbers – above 3,000.

Adams, who had stayed away, could not even bring himself to look pleased. He increasingly regarded Thomas Young as someone playing at being a patriot, attracted to the gaudy trappings of turbulence but never getting to the substance, the real business of revolution.

The patriots even lost control of a Town Meeting for the first time ever. A report to implement agricultural reforms and support vital home manufacturers was turned down by a sparsely attended meeting, even though he himself, Samuel Adams, was one of the authors. Was the revolution dying?

It got worse. With Non-Importation at an end, and troops available to guard them as they went about their business, the Customs Commissioners were newly emboldened, newly active, newly effective. Thomas Young still put his Liberty Boys onto them, which was fine, and there were still occasional attacks by the Mohucks, but by and large the patriots were losing.

Until they finally had a bit of luck and got just the martyr John Wilkes told them they needed – their own William Allen.

Feelings had been running especially high against Theophilus Lillie, the dry-goods seller and tea trader. He had been at the centre of the loyalist faction. Now his name had been published in the *Boston Gazette* as a violator of Non-Importation, even though he was not breaching the Agreement – he had refused to sign it.

Rather than just waiting for the anger to turn elsewhere, Lillie had hit back in the pages of the *Boston News-Letter*, almost as if a dam was breaking on his years of taciturn near-silence. He wrote that he would rather trust the Crown than the mob: 'I own I had rather be a slave under one master; for if I know who he is, I may perhaps be able to please him. If I am a slave to a hundred or more who I do not know, then I also don't know where to find them or what they will expect of me.'

This enraged the patriots. Their rage was compounded by Lillie's closeness to a leading customs informer and Comptroller of Customs, Benjamin Hallowell. After several attacks on him, Hallowell openly boasted of keeping a musket at home: 'Let 'em come for me, I've got guns loaded.'

Theophilus Lillie was close to Benjamin Hallowell personally and geographically; they were next-door neighbours in Middle Street. To the Liberty Boys this was especially convenient as both could be tormented at once by making a noise at night. The same batch of Hillsborough

Mixture could also be used to smear both sets of windows.

This particular frolic, as the boys called the attacks, started with Christopher Seider and his crew putting an effigy of Lillie outside the three-storey gabled building that doubled as Lillie's house and shop. The effigy had the word IMPORTER in huge black letters on a sign round its neck.

They also put up a board with a paper pinned to it depicting Lillie and three other violators of Non-Importation. The boys – eight of them – stood around the effigy and the board, effectively deterring, if not actually blocking, anybody from going into Lillie's shop and buying anything.

The truculent Lillie, driven beyond his natural character, lost his head and began screaming at the boys. Benjamin Hallowell heard him and emerged from his house to offer support. Hallowell's wife came out as well and a general exchange of screaming abuse took place.

'It'll be too hot for you before nightfall,' Benjamin Hallowell yelled at his tormenters.

The eight boys retreated, then advanced again, more or less in formation, as they had seen the militia do, throwing anything that came to hand – lemon peel, eggs, horse manure, dead dogs.

Hallowell and Lillie retreated indoors, from where Lillie threw a brick at the Liberty Boys crew. Christopher Seider threw it back and it broke one of Lillie's windows. Hallowell also had his windows broken and feared for the safety of his wife and two daughters. Lillie and Hallowell both fetched blunderbusses and fired swan-shot into the group of boys.

Some of the shot, lead about the size of a pea, hit Christopher Seider's chest, going into his lung. Seider went down in a heap.

The boys sent a runner for Dr Thomas Young, who ran pell-mell through the powder snow from his home, medicine bag clutched to his side. There was nothing he could do. Christopher Seider died in his arms, just as his own boys, Rosmond and John, came running to help but were in time only to add their tears to his.

Young was instrumental in stopping the mob that gathered from hanging Lillie and Hallowell on the spot. He disarmed Hallowell, who was waving a cutlass about. Then he held Hallowell and Lillie safely, his imposing bulk shielding them, until Sheriff Greenleaf arrived to arrest them.

Christopher Seider was widely held to have given his young life for the patriot cause. Samuel Adams fanned the righteous outrage, writing large the parallels with William Allen, who had also had his life taken before he reached manhood while fighting for freedom and a patriot victory, in England: 'The blood of young Allen may be covered in Britain,' Adams thundered in the *Boston Gazette*. 'But a thorough inquisition will be made in America for young Seider, which cries for vengeance like the blood of the righteous Abel.'

Christopher Seider's funeral procession began at the Liberty Tree. The venerable elm was bedecked with a sign that said: 'Take no satisfaction from the life of a murderer. He shall surely be put to death.'

Hutchinson, who was present though not prominent, later told Peggy he thought it was the largest funeral ever held in America. Five hundred schoolboys walked ahead, leading a crowd of at least two thousand, headed by Christopher's German immigrant parents, following the coffin, borne aloft. The slowly marching procession was half a mile long. It was followed by no fewer than thirty carriages and chaises.

Interment was at the Granary Burial Ground. Dr Thomas Young gave the address, choosing as his theme the 6th Chapter of Romans, 16th verse: 'Know ye not, that to whom ye yield yourselves servants to obey, his servants ye are to whom ye obey; whether of sin unto death, or of obedience unto righteousness.'

Samuel Adams also spoke. Staring straight at Thomas Hutchinson, he read from the Epistle to the Hebrews, 9th Chapter, 27th verse: 'And it is appointed unto men to die, but after this, *the judgement.*'

All Boston's church bells rang out. The ships in the harbour flew flags at half-mast. The city mourned.

CHAPTER 36

The death and martyrdom of Christopher Seider was never going to be enough on its own, Samuel Adams knew that. It was the spark, the flash in the pan, but not yet the opening shot, let alone the opening volley.

So he walked the streets alone at night – Sam the publican trudging through the snow in his red cloak and his dirty grey wig, worn boots thumping on the oyster shells on the frozen cobbles. He was, in the most literal sense, looking for trouble.

And with impressment of Boston men onto British navy ships getting more and more frequent, amid bitter resentment, and deserters from the army roaming the streets, trouble was not hard to find. The first British soldier to be killed in Boston – a lieutenant, at that – died days after Christopher Seider's funeral, as Boston sailors on a brig belonging to John Rowe resisted impressment.

On this particular evening, Samuel Adams was heading for the ropewalk, a frequent flashpoint. It was a massive building just off Milk Street on the South Side. It was a flashpoint because so much casual labour was needed to lay rope. That attracted soldiers, sailors, deserters, the indigent poor, all looking for jobs.

They were all supposed to work harmoniously together in bands of twelve or so to weave yarns of hemp together into heavy ropes, which could be hundreds of yards in length. They were called spinners and were paid a miserly rate. Fights broke out near nightly, with one of the tools of the trade, a willow wand for straightening rope threads, making a useful weapon.

The night of Samuel Adams's visit, the fight was pretty typical.

A Redcoat private from the 29th had come to the ropewalk looking for work to supplement his meagre soldier's pay.

A rope-maker said 'Looking for work, eh?'

'Yes,' said the private.

'Then go and clean my shithouse,' the rope-maker riposted.

There was a fight. The soldier got the worst of it, but came back later with six more Redcoats from the 29th, looking for revenge. There was a pitched battle. British sailors working at the ropewalk while their ship was in port sided with the rope-makers because they despised the garrison rats, as they called the soldiers.

Again outnumbered, the soldiers eventually retreated, but not before they arranged a rematch, or maybe a continuation of the original fight, in the open square of King Street next evening.

Samuel Adams arrived at the ropewalk just as they were making that arrangement. Four British sailors were sitting in a circle, drinking a celebration beer after the fight. Sam Adams approached them.

'You boys from the *Heron*?'

The *Heron* was one of John Hancock's ships. Adams knew perfectly well they were from the *Heron*, because he had seen them before. The *Heron* was due to sail for London two days later, early in the morning, which was perfect.

'Yes, mister. We're from the *Heron*,' said one of them. 'Mr Hancock's finest. Jack Tars. All the way from the capital of Empire, at your service.'

They all laughed. Samuel Adams laughed with them. Then he came straight to the point. 'I have a job for you fine buckos. It pays ten guineas each and I'll square it with Mr Hancock.'

There was an amazed silence. The amount was considerable. It was also exactly the amount paid for reporting anybody seducing a soldier from his duty, no questions asked.

'You want us to report a Redcoat?' asked one of the

four sailors.

Adams ignored the question, responding with another one, a technique which had served him well over the years. 'Can you all fire a musket?'

'Of course we can, mister!'

The silence deepened. When Adams broke it, he spoke softly. 'You will meet me tomorrow evening at dusk at the Customs House in King Street. There I shall provide you with a musket each. You will fire it where I tell you to. Then I shall give you ten guineas each. After that you return to the *Heron* immediately. I shall speak to Mr Hancock about the matter. You will be expected aboard. You stay on the *Heron* until she sails, early next morning.'

'You are well informed, sir,' said the first Englishman. 'May we confer?'

'Naturally.'

The discussion was brief. 'We're all up for it, mister. Thank you very much, mister.'

'Good. I now need to know all your names, so I can inform Mr Hancock.'

The Englishman doing all the talking told Adams his own name, and that of the other three. Samuel Adams shook them all solemnly by the hand.

'These muskets, mister? That we are to fire?'

'They will be provided. Never fear. Never fear.'

'You're shaking, mister.'

They all laughed. Adams laughed with them. 'I am shaking with excited anticipation. I am about to fulfil a long-held ambition.'

'And what might that be, sir?'

'Never you mind, young man. Never you mind.'

CHAPTER 37

As a Fire Warden, Samuel Adams had the power to order
the church bells rung. He put the word through that bells
were to ring out at dusk. Adams then put out the word that
the troops were contemplating a general massacre in King
Street just as the first fingers of dusk touched the town.

A soldiery now numbering 600 men – half the 29th
had been sent home as there were no quarters for them –
could not resist a population of 16,000, Adams's message
continued. Tar barrels were to be lit on Beacon Hill to
bring in the Massachusetts farmers from the surrounding
areas. All patriots were to mobilise at King Street, outside
the Royal Exchange Tavern and the Customs House.

From five o'clock, as Adams had instructed, the church
bells starting ringing. As Adams often reminded people,
you could tell the Boston-born by two things: first, if you
cut them they bled salt water. But second, they could tell
every single one of Boston's thirty-two churches from the
sound of its bell alone.

Not one of the ministers in any of Boston's churches
refused to ring the bells. Adams expected no less.

As early dusk approached, Samuel Adams set off from his
home in Purchase Street to walk to King Street. He was
swathed in his red cloak, with his grey wig keeping off
the light flurries of snow. He swung his sword-cane in his
right hand almost jauntily.

He had spoken to John Hancock, who had willingly
provided the money he needed to pay the four British
sailors from the *Heron*. As he walked, he noted with
satisfaction that the streets were thronged, packed with
people, hurrying and scurrying in the general direction of
King Street.

Thomas Hutchinson heard the din of the gathering street

riot from the Reverend Mather's house on Garden Court Street. He fetched his wig, sword and cloak. Peggy pleaded with him not to go. As she knew but did not say, the simmering near-universal dislike of Hutchinson could boil over at any time. The crowd might attack him on sight.

But Thomas Hutchinson did not care. He did not wish to die, that would have been a blasphemy against God and Christ. But he was not overly worried whether he lived or whether he did not. Peggy was his only reason to stay alive; she tipped the balance. He gave her a fond kiss goodbye and walked out into the street.

As he walked through the snow, and the sky grew heavy and dark, Thomas Hutchinson reflected that his expected appointment as Governor of Massachusetts, succeeding that nincompoop Francis Bernard, still had not matcrialised.

He shrugged indifferently as he walked along. He was still *Acting* Governor Hutchinson, then. So be it. What would once have been the pinnacle of his ambition no longer mattered to him. He thought of his house, now gone, of his *History of Massachusetts*, now gone, then he stopped thinking altogether.

People were running past him, ignoring the stooped figure of the Acting Governor. Thomas Hutchinson felt for these people, out there in the street, in the snow. He wanted to help them, reach out to them. But he could not do that. They did not want him, the people of Boston, not in their heads or in their hearts. Sam Adams had seen to that.

Bitterness was spreading in Hutchinson, spreading inexorably like the grey in his hair. He realised it himself, but as self-pity rose up in him, he was distracted by the start of a fracas. There was trouble. Hardly surprising. With the febrile atmosphere in Boston since Christopher Seider's funeral, less than a week ago, there was bound to be trouble.

The Mohucks had instructions from Adams to create a

fracas in King Street. Led by Ebenezer Mackintosh, they took up a shout of 'Fire! Fire!' The fire-fighting machine, the Newsham Engine, manned by Mackintosh's fire company and pulled by four heavy dray horses, arrived in King Street, churning up the mud and snow.

Ebenezer Mackintosh was accompanied by his brother-in-law, young Samuel Maverick. Maverick had been dragged along against his will. His job as an apprentice to a wood turner and part-time dentist was going well. As someone of part Negro blood, Samuel Maverick felt himself fortunate to be doing so well. He had no time for frivolous diversions, as he saw it, like mobs and riots.

He had been eating a peaceful early supper when Ebenezer Mackintosh had banged dramatically on his door. He insisted Samuel Maverick accompany him to the riot at King Street, aboard the Newsham Engine. His wife, Mackintosh's sister, had said, 'Oh, go along, Samuel,' more or less to keep the peace.

Having arrived in King Street, Ebenezer Mackintosh prompted Samuel to shout 'Fire!' by whispering in his ear. 'Go on, cry it out loud. Go on!' Mackintosh was drunk and looked ridiculous in that uniform he always wore, but Samuel Maverick always wished to oblige. He half-heartedly shouted 'Fire!' as required.

The chant was rapidly taken up by the crowd. As the fire bells began to ring, Mackintosh took up the ancient cry of 'Town born, turn out.'

They wanted to create confusion and they did. The start of the riot also left the Customs House without a sentry, as the private guarding it had left his post to try and help put out the fire, wherever it was.

Unnoticed in the growing clamour, Samuel Adams led the four British sailors into the unguarded Customs House and up to the second floor. William Molineux was waiting for them up there with four muskets taken from the store at Faneuil Hall, together with lead ball and powder.

'You can start priming the muskets,' Molineux told

the sailors. Adams looked at him questioningly; he knew nothing about guns. But Molineux nodded, confidently. 'I'll give you the word,' he said to the sailors.

The four British sailors started priming the muskets, biting the ends off the cartridges and pouring powder into the pan.

'That'll shut you up!' Molineux said, watching with satisfaction as the sailors held the cartridge ends in their mouths.

Down below in King Street there was the most utter confusion. Everybody thought there was a fire but nobody knew where. People were running, meeting other people running towards them, then running back. People who were indoors came out when they heard the bells, a summons no Bostonian could ignore. Many brought leather buckets to carry water against the fire. These people, too, started running.

As the din grew, the guard was called out at nearby Murray's Barracks. The six soldiers, led by a captain who answered the call to turn out the guard, were Grenadiers – tall but not especially able. They reached King Street to find the private guarding the Customs House, who had returned to his post, under threat from a crowd advancing on him.

The guard of Grenadiers fanned out in a semi-circle round the private with their backs to the Customs House, guarding it. They pointed muskets charged with ball at the crowd. One of them had been at the fight at the ropewalk the previous night. He had been beaten up and felt humiliated.

The crowd grew at the excitement; surrounding the soldiers on three sides, jeering, shouting, throwing snowballs and mud. The shouts grew louder: 'You Bloody-Backs! You Damned Lobster-Back! Fire if you dare!'

The soldiers began to load to half-cock without waiting for an order to do so. In the din, they would hardly have heard their officer if he had given the order. The youngest of the Grenadiers was at the outer edge of the semi-circle. As he was struggling to load his musket he was hit by a chunk of ice thrown by a rope-maker who had also been at the fight at the ropewalk.

The young soldier's musket went off half-cock. The captain commanding the soldiers was hit hard on his arm with a club, but still desperately shouted 'Don't Fire!' In the hubbub and confusion two of the Grenadiers heard that as 'Fire'. As the crowd surged towards the soldiers, they all fired, some into the air, some at the crowd.

It was the moment Samuel Adams had been waiting for. He nodded to Molineux. Molineux said 'Forward!' to the four British sailors. The Customs House had Yorkshire sash windows – small windows which slid open sideways. The sailors had room to fire but could not be seen from ground level. Molineux eased open four of the six windows.

As a chill breeze with snow flurries swept into the room, the sailors advanced, loaded, aimed and fired down into the crowd from a position immediately above the semi-circle of soldiers. They each fired once.

The sailors stepped back, out of sight. Molineux gathered their weapons and powder into a canvas bag. He was unhurried and calm.

'What shall I tell John Pownall?' Molineux said to Adams.

'Nothing,' Adams said. 'Don't write a report at all. Let him sweat.'

'What about Dr Young?' Molineux waited for his command, obedient as any soldier.

'That Goody Two-shoes? He doesn't need to know anything. Say nothing.'

Molineux gave his wolfish grin. 'Understood.'

Two of the British sailors were looking shaken. Sam Adams gave them a little pouch each, containing ten guineas per man, courtesy of John Hancock.

'Come on,' Molineux said. 'I'll take you out the back

way, then back to your ship.'

As soon as the shots cracked out from the Customs House window, men fell to the ground in the snow, sometimes hitting others in the tightly packed crowd as they went down. One of them was Samuel Maverick. Mackintosh cradled him in his arms, trying to lift him out of the snow and slush, howling softly.

Maverick bled profusely onto the cordwainer's bizarre uniform and even more profusely onto the snowy ground. Thomas Young had been found and was there in minutes, with his doctor's bag. He did what he could for Samuel Maverick, staunching the worst of the bleeding, tying a tourniquet, giving the boy laudanum for the pain. But the British sailor's bullet had gone straight into his belly. Samuel Maverick died as Young and Mackintosh held him.

Young yelled at the mob: 'The soldiers are withdrawing. Go on home, folks. Go on home!'

Adams watched him coolly from the three steps in front of the Customs House. Samuel Maverick was not the only one lying dead or dying in the snow; there were at least five more, he thought, all martyrs to the cause.

CHAPTER 38

Adams swiftly ensured that what was briefly known as the 'King Street riot' rapidly became the 'Boston Massacre'. There were 10,000 mourners at the funeral of the Boston Massacre victims at the Granary Burial Ground. The British were responsible for the slaughter of innocent Boston citizens, massacring them on the streets.

The Customs Commissioners had to flee to Castle William, yet again. Income to the Crown from customs dues in Boston plunged to zero. The Customs Commissioners were dissolved; their new headquarters stood empty, a monument to the patriot victory.

General Gage was paralysed with fear in case the tar barrels still burning on Beacon Hill brought in 10,000 armed and army-trained farmers from the Massachusetts countryside who would overwhelm his soldiers. And even if the farmers did not come in, he feared an armed insurrection from inside Boston to avenge the fallen martyrs of the Boston Massacre.

To keep the peace, the general was happy enough to accede to Samuel Adams's demand that all troops be withdrawn from Boston and confined to Castle William, out of the way over the Neck in Boston harbour.

To Adams's soaring joy, the soldiers were marched out of Boston with an escort of armed Boston militia. The stolen British muskets were virtually brandished in Gage's face before being returned to their store at Faneuil Hall, with Gage not daring to do a thing about it. Adams graciously gave an assurance that the British troops would not be harassed as they marched back to barracks.

But as there were still too many soldiers in Boston to fit into Castle William, Adams then demanded even more of them be sent home, as billeting them in town risked provoking further blood and carnage. This was at a meeting with Gage and Hutchinson at which, as he delightedly reported to the Sons of Liberty later, Hutchinson's knees were trembling.

Gage said nothing publicly, not even to Colonel Francis Smith and the other Staff Officers, but he quietly did as he was told. With no more Redcoats to be seen, the streets were patrolled by the Boston militia, led by Captain Parker, under the ultimate command of Samuel Adams.

In what Thomas Hutchinson viewed as a bitter irony, his appointment as Governor of Massachusetts came through at this time. His sons begged him to take Peggy and move to Castle William, as he was not safe even out at Milton, but Hutchinson refused.

He accepted Boston's fate stoically. 'Government is at an end in Boston, and in the hands of the people,' he wrote to John Pownall. Pownall agreed. He replied that Samuel Adams's rule of Boston exceeded even John Wilkes's grip on London.

On release from prison, Wilkes had stood for public office. He became part of the governance of the realm as an elected Alderman of London. So despite the Wilkesite mobs ruling London's streets, Wilkes was no more than what Adams called an agitator, a wave-maker, a creator of turbulence. He never became a revolutionary, a man who took over.

In that sense, as Adams understood completely, the sometime pupil had overtaken the master. Samuel Adams was well on the way to becoming a revolutionary, and a successful one at that. He knew that full well and quietly rejoiced at it.

CHAPTER 39

Lord North rose to his feet in a noisy House of Commons. North had only recently become First Minister, in addition to his previous role as Chancellor of the Exchequer. He had no desire at all for the post of First Minister. He felt he was not fit to hold the office. He had accepted it because the King wished it and because the new combined salary went some way to easing his chronic financial problems.

He glanced up at the Public Gallery. John Pownall was up there, and William Knox. But the man he was looking for, smiling down at him, was William Legge, 2nd Earl of Dartmouth, his step-brother and his lifelong bosom friend.

North feared that without Dartmouth's financial help he would be declared bankrupt. He might be declared bankrupt anyway, if the Mohuck mob succeeded in demolishing his London house. Twice, the Mohucks had been beaten off by the guards Dartmouth had twice paid for, but it had hung in the balance both times.

North was arranging for Dartmouth to take over from Lord Hillsborough as Head of the American Department as soon as possible. He could really have done with his help now, in the Commons. He was about to introduce the repeal of the Townshend Acts, except on tea.

The tax on tea could not be repealed, North was firm on that, even though there was nobody in Boston capable of collecting it. Leaving the tax on tea asserted Parliament's right to tax the colonies. North said as much to a largely indifferent Commons.

Another reason for not repealing the tea tax, North said, was the behaviour of the colonists. The colonists were becoming more intransigent than ever in their insistence on not importing English goods. While this was the case, he declined to give way.

'The petulance of a weak man,' John Pownall muttered to William Knox, up in the Gallery.

Knox threw an alarmed glance at their soon-to-be Head of Department. The pious, rather solemn and straight-laced Dartmouth was sitting next to him. He grimaced and wished his fellow Under-Secretary would be more discreet.

William Knox harboured the hope that John Pownall's marriage to Mary Lillingston, their lovely house out in the country at Vanbrugh Fields, and now their two sons, might have a mellowing effect on his fellow Under-Secretary. But no. The centre-point of his existence was still the defeat and destruction of Samuel Adams.

Pownall had lost weight, making his face even leaner. He had taken to loping around like a wolf on the hunt, sitting down only when he had to. He was pacing the tiny office at the American Department now – furious, trapped paces.

'How can a jumped-up jackanapes, the penniless son of a failed brewer, order British troops back to barracks? How can he be the instrument, the direct instrument, of considerable numbers of British troops being withdrawn from a colony altogether and sent home?'

John Pownall stopped pacing. He wiped his hand across his lower jaw, a new gesture of his middle age, much used lately, as if wiping some imaginary slate clean.

To William Knox's real alarm, Pownall then strode next door to where the seven clerks were at work, standing at their desks.

'Stop work!' the Under-Secretary commanded.

The Chief Clerk, William Pollock, looked furious. Knox quietly followed his fellow Under-Secretary into the outer office. The clerks looked apprehensive. They feared John Pownall's lashing tongue and sudden rages.

'I want you all to stop what you are doing and find me chapter and verse, legal justification, to have Adams brought back to London for trial. And Young. And Hancock. Something strong enough to go to Lord North

215

with.'

The Chief Clerk spoke: 'Mr Pownall, sir ...'

'No, Mr Pollock. I don't care how busy they are. I want this done now.'

The Chief Clerk shot William Knox a look of near-desperation. 'Mr Pownall, sir. I have some information, germane ...'

'What?'

William Pollock picked a report from a bundle of papers. 'It is from Richard Silvester, our informant, the landlord of the Green Dragon ...'

'Yes? Well? Go on! It's like drawing bloody teeth getting anything out of you.'

'Richard Silvester has formally charged the patriot leaders with treason, Mr Pownall. We have reports that he has had to flee Boston. We ...'

'And when were you going to tell me all this, Pollock? Next week, next month, next year?'

The Chief Clerk shot a glance at his subordinates, some of whom were smirking at this public dressing-down. 'This has only just arrived, sir. I was ordering ...'

'Yes, yes, yes! Well, anyway, it's excellent! We will make use of Mr Silvester's charge. Perfect timing. Now, I repeat, find me a precedent for the arrest and deportation of the patriots under that charge of treason, as Silvester alleges.'

John Pownall stormed out of the outer office, taking the bundle of papers with him, ignoring the white faces of the clerks.

William Knox followed him back to the office they shared. So did the Chief Clerk, who shut the door behind him. 'Mr Pownall, a word, please.'

'Yes, Mr Pollock. A word. Perhaps even two. But more than that would be tedious. Now what is it?'

William Pollock looked strained, but dignified. 'Sir, the Clerks' Office can only function if instructions and delegation of work are put to me first. I shall endeavour to meet your wishes at all times, sir. But for the smooth running of the office ...'

Pownall flushed pink, then red. 'You are forgetting your station, Pollock,' he bellowed. 'Your rank and your station. Don't you dare tell me what to do in my own office. Now get out.'

The Chief Clerk left with unhurried dignity, without another word.

William Knox sighed one of his deep sighs. 'Do you think that was wise, John?' And then, when Pownall said nothing, 'John, I am growing concerned for you.'

John Pownall studied the newly arrived papers. Richard Silvester had evidently gone to Thomas Hutchinson with the accusation of treason against the patriots. Hutchinson naturally supported it, especially the charge against the Machiavelli of chaos, another of Hutchinson's names for Samuel Adams.

Hutchinson had enclosed affidavits supporting Silvester's charge. They were by respected Boston loyalists, accusing Adams, Hancock and Young of treason. Hutchinson had provided no covering letter with the affidavits. That was typical, John Pownall thought, of his arrogant disdain.

However, the Governor had clearly co-ordinated the statements, all of which accused the patriot leaders of urging armed attacks against the Customs Commissioners. And he had obviously consulted the statute books before carefully coaching the main accusers, to make sure the words they reported the patriots for uttering were treasonable.

A slightly calmer John Pownall delightedly read out Richard Silvester's affidavit: 'William, listen to this. "The informant heard the said Samuel Adams say to the said party 'if you are men, behave like men'."'

Knox grimaced. 'That doesn't sound like Sam Adams at all. Sounds more like Molineux.'

217

'William, we are attempting to frame a legal case here, not mount a drama for Drury Lane. "Let us take up arms immediately," Adams said, "and be free, and seize all the King's officers. We shall have thirty thousand men to join us from the country." There! What do you think of that?'

'Very good of Adams to damn himself so clearly. Most co-operative.'

John Pownall's old good humour, now in evidence only in glimpses, returned for a moment.

'You are a cynic, William Knox! All right, try this one. Affidavit about Dr Thomas Young: "Young, trembling and in great agitation cried 'Let us take up arms immediately and be free, and seize all the king's officers. His Majesty has no right to send troops here to invade the country, and I look upon them as foreign enemies'."'

'What wickedness, John. What wickedness!' William Knox's amused twinkle was firmly in place.

'I'll give you one for Hancock.'

'I thought you might, John. I thought you might.'

'Here's John Hancock from Dr Samuel Whitworth's affidavit: "The times were never better in Rome than when they had no king and were a free state. And as America is a great empire we shall soon have it in our power to make our own laws."'

Knox snorted. 'That sounds more like Young than Hancock. If it sounds like a human being at all. Young knows his classics. Hancock would only read a book if you paid him to.'

Pownall smiled his increasingly rare smile. 'You are a hard man to please, William.'

Within days, the industrious clerks of the American Department had unearthed a statute dating from the time of Henry VIII, enabling those committing treason abroad to be brought back to England for trial.

'We've got them, William. Adams, Hancock and Young. We've got them. I'll have warrants drawn up.'

William Knox looked thoughtful. 'This could just possibly work, John. Just possibly. You know, Captain Kidd was arrested in Boston. And his sloop seized. He was brought back to England, tried and hanged. Hanged at the second attempt, I believe. All you need to do now is stiffen Gage sufficiently to execute the warrants.'

But before that could be done, the warrants had to receive parliamentary approval. John Pownall took them, plus copies of the Henry VIII statute, to Lord North. North gave his immediate and unequivocal backing. Pownall was confident North and his King's Men would see the measure through Parliament.

His confidence was justified, but there was spirited resistance from Thomas Pownall, watched from the gallery of the Commons by his younger brother and William Knox.

Thomas Pownall got slowly to his feet in the House of Commons, a poised and confident man now, and plumply prosperous. He was resplendent in lime-green silk, with silver-buckled shoes and a gold sword. His material fortunes had changed greatly for the better. Indeed, they had been transformed. The former Governor of Massachusetts was now a very wealthy man.

The Pownalls' mother and grandmother had died within three months of each other. The mother was near-penniless but the ninety-one-year-old grandmother had left Thomas, as the older brother, a small house and extensive estates in Saltfleetby and Dally, in Lincolnshire. John, as the younger brother, had been left nothing. John affected not to mind, nor to hold his good fortune against Thomas.

Thomas's increased wealth transformed his social standing. Always a gregarious man, he now began to mix in circles that brought him into contact with London's mercantile classes. In due course he married one of them, Harriet Fawkener, widow of the late Sir Everard Fawkener, who had been among the wealthiest men in England, earning his money in the silk trade.

Thomas now had access to a small fortune from his wife's money. He lived in Albemarle Street, the better end, not the end Lord North lived in. His weekend guests there, who became known as the Albemarle Set, included Benjamin Franklin, Samuel Johnson, John Almon and Horace Walpole. He was now able to join London's more exclusive clubs, like White's and Boodle's. All this increased both his already considerable knowledge of American affairs and his political influence.

Thomas spoke for two hours, a speech unkindly compared by John to the droning of hoverflies in summer. The proposed extradition, he said, was alien to the political philosophy of both England and America.

'He has a point,' William Knox whispered in John Pownall's ear, up in the Gallery. 'England and America have the same political philosophy. It can be summed up in two words. John Locke.'

Below them, Thomas Pownall's defence of the patriots ground relentlessly and defiantly on: 'This extradition is punishment of the severest and most cruel nature,' Thomas averred, 'because it would send Americans thousands of miles over perilous waters on the unproven authority of a single man.'

Thomas did not say the single man was his younger brother, but John gave him a big smile and a wink anyway.

Thomas saw the smile and the wink but ignored them. 'I dread the consequences, if Americans should realise the full significance of this measure, which deprives them of the common liberty they enjoy, at a whim from London.'

'You worry too much, old boy,' John said, quite loudly. 'You always did.'

Thomas ended with a warning: 'The thread holding the two countries together is pulling apart,' he said. 'War is the inevitable consequence.'

But by then John Pownall and William Knox had had enough. They had left.

CHAPTER 40

Margaret Gage's meetings with Thomas Young at the Crown Coffee House, at the top of Long Wharf, were among the worst kept secrets in Boston. They had started just after the Boston Massacre.

Margaret Gage cordially detested her husband. But one of the few pleasures of her marriage was her frequent visits to London. The Gages had a house in Crag's Court, just off Charing Cross. Margaret loved it there. She had no wish to see her adopted country, Britain, fight the country of her birth, America.

On the contrary, she wished to work for peace and for prosperity in Boston. The parlous state of Bostonians truly alarmed her, with nobody, apparently, having any money, businesses going bankrupt, and the poor facing real hunger as Poor Relief was not what it was in Governor Pownall's time. Margaret gave all the help she could, including making generous donations to the poor.

She also worked through the Assembly to help the smallpox hospital, on an islet near Castle William, to combat the frequent smallpox epidemics. That is how she first met Dr Thomas Young, who she always viewed as a doctor first and a patriot second. She and Dr Young spent a lot of their time at the Crown Coffee House talking about Thomas's work at the hospital and how Margaret Gage could contribute.

But although Margaret was a free spirit who always went her own way, even she took pause at what would happen if it got out that the wife of the commander of British forces in the American colonies was meeting a leading revolutionary. The meetings would be stopped. So Margaret dressed in men's clothes to meet Thomas Young to make herself less conspicuous.

The problem with that was that Margaret Gage had not been inconspicuous since her girlhood as Margaret Kemble in New York, and she never would be. All the male garb did was encourage the widespread rumour that she was a spy – a rumour that amused Thomas Young no end.

For a start, as Thomas laughingly told Mary when he gave the full accounts of their meetings demanded by his wife, Margaret Gage was not a spy because she knew nothing of any use to the patriots.

As Thomas also told Mary, Margaret's younger brother, Major John Kemble, was an aide to General Gage. He was as smitten by Margaret as just about everybody else was, and he would have told her anything she wanted to know. But the patriots were not an army, at least not yet. Military details were of little use to them, except perhaps where ordnance was stored and they already knew that.

In time, over convivial tankards of beer, Margaret opened up completely about her husband. As a young officer, Thomas Gage had helped destroy the rebel Jacobite army at Culloden, one of the bloodiest battles in history.

'He wakes up screaming in the night,' Margaret said of her husband. 'He sleeps in the next room to me, so I can hear him. In the early days, he told me of his dreams of that time. He dreams the Highland soldiers are about to stab his eyes out with their dirks.'

'I have no sympathy,' Thomas Young said. 'He deserves his haunted dreams.'

Margaret smiled. 'Maybe. His past is consuming him. You know he failed to attack as he was ordered under Wolfe, back in 1759? He has never gotten over that, either.'

'Why did he not attack?' Thomas asked, curious, fascinated, suddenly the doctor and philosopher again.

Margaret smiled, ruefully. 'For fear of making a mistake; for fear of not being able to choose the best course. He was always just a plodder. John, my brother, thinks he has only moderate abilities as a soldier and is deficient in military knowledge. He certainly can't control the troops.'

'John tells you that?'

She shrugged. 'My brother has no fear of him. More like contempt.'

'Why did you marry him, Margaret?'

She sighed, silent for so long Young thought she was not going to reply. But she did, finally, speaking slowly: 'I was inexperienced. A lot of women make mistakes, you know. Dazzled by false appearances. But also he has changed, and very much for the worse.'

'In what way?'

'For one thing, he hates it here in Boston. He gets out and goes on vacation to Danvers whenever he can.'

'And where is Danvers?'

'Near Salem. Being in Boston has made him more brutal. Mind you, all the officers regard Boston as a posting that will end their careers. Apparently, there should never even be a garrison here. It's too far from the principal lines of communication, that's what John says. It has no military value at all, apparently.'

'Good. Maybe the British soldiers will give up and go home.'

Young was half-joking but Margaret took him seriously. 'I think one day they will,' she said. 'My husband cannot wait. He hates you all, right enough. He sees you all as cheap, homespun lawyers, especially Adams. He once said to me, "Every man in Boston studies the law and interprets it to suit his purpose."'

'I take his insult and wear it as a badge of honour.'

'You do that! He also says America is a mere bully and Bostonians are by far the greatest bullies.'

'That's rich, coming from him.'

Margaret drained her tankard of beer. 'I think just being here, in this difficult position, has made my husband even more reluctant to take any decisions at all. He is paralysed in spirit, now. All his aides see him that way: Smith, Pitcairn and John, too. They are always trying to get him to act. He always finds a reason not to.'

'Is that why he has not served the arrest warrants for

223

Adams, Hancock and myself?'

'Pretty much. He says he doesn't dare serve the warrants for fear of civil war.'

'He may well be right.'

'Actually, his aides back him on not serving the arrest warrants. Except Pitcairn. He thinks you and Adams and Hancock should be clapped in irons tomorrow. You first, Thomas, as you are a heretic as well as a rebel.'

Thomas Young raised his tankard in a toast. 'May Major Pitcairn never prevail. Good. I will tell Mary as soon as I return home, that her husband is safe for a while.'

'Tell her I embrace her, Thomas. Tell her I embrace you all.'

Thomas and John Pownall did not mix in quite the same circles, socially, though their circles occasionally overlapped. Both were a part of London society; John at the outer fringes, at the upper-middling rank, Thomas quite close to the centre, glimpsing aristocracy. Both had an entrée to the finest houses, which Thomas relished but was of little interest to John.

Some of John's money came from skilful winning of sinecures from his superiors, first Lord Hillsborough, then Lord Dartmouth. The Governorship of Barbados proved especially lucrative. But his wife's fortune from the wool trade made by far the biggest contribution to his material worth.

Thomas's fortune through the Fawkener connection was much more substantial. It saw him living in a fashionable Flemish-bond brickwork house in Piccadilly with an outer staircase to the first floor, like the Devonshires.

Crucially for the brothers' own friendship, their wives, Harriet and Mary, got on well. Indeed, they became fast friends. It was that, as much as anything, which brought Thomas and John together socially, and when they did meet they were at least as cordial with each other as they had been as young men, possibly more so.

They never discussed politics, that would have been bad form.

John was achieving some esteem as an antiquarian. His article *An Account of Some Sepulchral Antiquities Discovered at Lincoln* had attracted much attention, even being publicly praised by no less an authority than Edward Gibbon. He was on the committee of the Antiquarian Society. To the older brother's delight, he proposed Thomas as a member. Thomas, ever the dilettante, would not have had a solid enough body of work to be elected without John's support, but with it his membership went through on the nod.

'Mr Thomas Pownall,' the Chief Clerk, William Pollock, sonorously announced.

Thomas entered the American Department in a cloud of yellow silk and Cologne, the effect slightly spoiled by dollops of mud thrown at him by a crowd of bread-price rioters outside the Admiralty building. They were still faintly audible in the office.

The Chief Clerk withdrew.

John, at his desk, looked up from his reading. He was alone, as William Knox was away in Ireland.

'Thomas! To what do we owe the honour?'

Thomas perched precariously on the only spare chair. He crossed one plump calf high over the other thigh – the undignified pose which had so irritated Thomas Hutchinson back in the time of the Pownall Governorship of Massachusetts.

'What do you know about John Company?' Thomas brought out finally.

John's eyebrows went up. 'You mean the East India Company? It does not really impinge on my interest.'

'It does now.'

'Do tell.'

Thomas wiped some sweat from his forehead. 'The East India Company is in deep financial trouble, the details of which do not concern us. But they deeply concern the government. So at the East India Company's behest, the Commons has passed a Tea Act for the American colonies, to rescue them.'

Thomas had never seen John so disconcerted. 'Whaat? When?'

'Just now. I have come hotfoot from the Commons.'

'So I have missed the debate?'

'There was hardly a debate to miss. It was over before you could blink. Under an hour. No division.'

John looked stunned. 'Parliament has hardly bothered

with American affairs for years. And now you are telling me a Tea Act has been passed without anybody informing the American Department?'

'Correct.'

'Purely to benefit the East India Company?'

'Correct again.'

'God's bodkin! Was Dartmouth there?'

'No, he's in Staffordshire, at his estates.'

John was chalk-white in the face; Thomas thought him more Cassius-like than ever.

'No vote? No division at all, you are saying? It just went through on the nod?'

'Precisely. Most of the Members were "staying a-fox-hunting", as they say. Only the halt and the lame were there. The place was like the Pool of Bethesda, only white-haired old gentlemen and irritated invalids with gout. More pox than the Lock Hospital.'

'And you, naturally.' John said. 'Mother Pownall's top boy.'

'Yes, and me, John. But not you. Left out again.'

'Oh, shut up! Tell me precisely what happened in the Commons, Thomas.'

Thomas shrugged. 'North had an overwhelming majority among those present. He arose and said "It is to no purpose making objections, the King will have it so. The King means to try the question with the Americans." There are rumours that George is arranging some Hessian soldiers as a show of force.'

'Was there any opposition at all?'

Thomas gave a small sigh. 'Some. I spoke against the measure. I argued that the grand marine dominion should ensure the flow of free trade. It should not be threatened by lesser sovereignties like the East India Company.'

John shook his head in disbelief. 'I'm with you on that.'

'I knew you would be, that's why I came.'

'All right, then, Thomas, cough it up. What was in this Tea Act?'

227

Thomas shifted on his uncomfortable chair. 'The East India Company has a massive tea surplus,' he began. 'That is the problem. To help them out, the government will let them dump their tea directly in Boston, as cheaply as possible, without paying duties in London. As a happy bonus for the government, that will undercut the smugglers. Indeed, they hope to eliminate smuggling by John Hancock and his ilk.'

John Pownall snorted. 'Some hope. So tea will actually be cheaper than before, in the American colonies? The price will go down, with no duties?'

Thomas nodded. 'Yes, John, tea will be cheaper. North expects the colonists to welcome that. But they won't: the tax on tea for the colonies will be 3d in the pound. North again insisted Parliament keep control of tea taxes to maintain its right to tax the colonies.'

'Quite right, too! But Adams will portray it as a new revenue tax.'

Thomas nodded hard. 'Precisely. I tried to tell them that in Parliament. Tea to the Bostonians has become a symbol, I said. Again and again, Samuel Adams calls tea the symbol of American slavery. But that is not understood here at all.'

John looked furious. 'Damn Adams to hell. You wouldn't think they were colonists, would you? Was that it? Or are there any other provisions of this Tea Act?'

'East India Company tea can be sold only to designated consignees, in Boston. Merchants who are on our side. Loyalists.'

John sneered. 'I imagine friend Hutchinson will be in there, extending his business empire.'

'I have no doubt of it, John. Old man Hutchinson himself will not be involved. He is getting too frail for all that. But the sons, Thomas junior and Elisha, will apply to become consignees. So will the Clarkes, the Olivers, the Copleys and all the rest of them.'

'What happens to merchants who are not consignees?'

'Good point. If they do not apply or are not accepted as consignees they may not trade in tea. That system favours the larger traders; the small ones will be locked out.'

John shook his head, impatiently. 'And the moderate merchants who do not become consignees will be driven into the arms of Adams and his ruffians as their livelihoods, or a good part of their livelihoods, will have been removed.'

'Quite so.' There was silence for a moment. Then Thomas spoke again. 'We have to stop this, John. For once, we are on the same side here. The colonists will never stand for it. It could lead to war.'

John nodded. 'I agree. And if there is war, with the French navy massing at their ports to supply them, I fear we may not win.'

Chapter 42

For the first time, in Boston, there was open talk of civil war. At the next Town Meeting, a motion for the citizens to arm themselves was passed. Every hardware store in the city sold out of guns and ammunition.

A watch was kept at Fort Hill, overlooking Boston harbour, by leading merchants and patriots, led by John Hancock. Hancock, the bringer of tidings, was enjoying a surge in popularity, mainly at Hutchinson's expense. He was even being spoken of as a possible replacement for the increasingly frail Governor.

Hancock and George Hayley had just arrived back from London on Hancock's sloop, *Anne*, the fastest ship in the known world. As ever, he brought the latest news from the capital of Empire: that news being that the tea ships were on their way, carrying the first cargo on Tea Act terms, with a revenue tax.

Hancock and his watchers were the first to see the leading tea ship, as it came into view on the horizon. As it grew nearer, clearly heading for the abutment of Griffin's Wharf, they saw it was a ship seen in Boston many times before – the *Dartmouth*.

The *Dartmouth* was an Indiaman with a high poop and ornamented stern. It was a beautiful ship. But it was a slave ship, as the patriots saw it, with the Americans as the slaves.

There had been a formal naming and appointment of consignees, the sole permitted purchasers of tea from the East India Company. Thomas Hutchinson's sons were among those appointed, along with Hutchinson's nephew, Richard Clarke, and Clarke's son, Jonathan. There was also Peter Oliver, of the Oliver family, stalwarts of the Hutchinson clan. And John Copley, who was married to Sukey Clarke of the Clarke family. With only two exceptions, every consignee was dynastically connected to Governor Hutchinson.

The Governor himself argued against the family firm becoming consignees. But he had long ago given up the day-to-day running of the Hutchinson trading empire, so Thomas junior and Elisha easily overruled him. They overruled him quite brusquely. Thomas junior had made his own trading contacts in London. They no longer needed the old man – their attitude to him made that clear.

On the foothills of old age, Governor Thomas Hutchinson was learning the lesson of King Lear: that if you give something away, not only can you not take it back, you can lose more than you gave away in the first place.

The tea ship *Dartmouth* landed at Griffin's Wharf full to the gunwales with tea: it carried eighty chests of strong, black Bohea and sixty-two of the more exotic and refined Singlo, Hyson, Souchong and Congou.

Right up until that point, Governor Hutchinson did not foresee any trouble. After all, the 3d in the pound tea tax had been carried over from the rump of the Townshend Taxes, so it was nothing new.

Samuel Adams saw matters very differently. He saw this as a defining moment for the patriot cause. After the failure of Non-Importation, if the British successfully imposed their slave tax through their tame consignees – all leading Boston men, not outsiders like the Customs Commissioners – then the Sons of Liberty were finished. They would just wither away.

What to do? Adams was only too well aware of the arrest warrant against him, even if at the moment they did not dare serve it. Any further defiance from him and they just might do that. He was in his fifties by now, but looked and felt a decade older. His health, never good, was getting even worse. He had rheumatism as well as ever more frequent attacks of palsy. Did he really want to spend his declining years as a fugitive?

On the other hand, the fight against the Medici was his life's work. If Hutchinson – it was always Hutchinson personally to Adams – managed to land the tea then he knew full well Bostonians would buy it. Who could blame them? It was cheaper! Parliament's machinations, waiving duty at the London end, were a fiendishly clever plot to do him, Adams, down and it could well succeed.

So a fight there must be. Samuel Adams decided to fight the good fight and damn the consequences.

Step one was stopping any of the consignees taking as much as a leaf of tea, then getting them all to resign this ridiculous post. Step two was obtaining clearance at the Customs House for the tea to be sent back to London, in defiance of the British Parliament.

With his tactics decided, Samuel Adams got drunk for the first time in a decade. He got drunk by himself.

The patriot caucus met in the Long Room, above the printing presses of the *Boston Gazette*. Adams felt the Green Dragon was tainted by former landlord Richard Silvester's betrayal of them, even though Silvester had long ago fled Boston.

At this first meeting, letters were drafted to all the consignees requiring them to resign their posts. These letters were pushed under their front doors at the dead of night.

At the next meeting, Thomas Young offered to lead an attack by his Liberty Boys on Richard Clarke's house to put more pressure on the consignees. After that, they would be declared Enemies of the People if they did not come to the Liberty Tree to resign.

'The people would be justified by every consideration if they tore such wretches to pieces,' Thomas Young said.

Young detested the Clarkes as they treated him with lordly disdain and never paid him for his medical treatments. Richard Clarke's daughter, Young reminded them, was married to Thomas Hutchinson junior. 'So we can kill two birds with one stone,' as Young put it.

William Molineux, who as Mohuck leader would normally have led the attack on Richard Clarke's house, made no objection to Young using his Liberty Boys for the purpose.

The Clarkes lived on School Street, in an affluent area, just a few doors down from King's Chapel. The attack followed the usual pattern: windows were smashed, stones thrown, walls smeared with Hillsborough Mixture; chanting, songs and fife-playing kept the Clarke family awake; trees and fences were destroyed in the garden. In a stroke of luck for the patriots, Thomas Hutchinson junior was also in the Clarke house when the attack was mounted.

Although a pistol was fired from inside the Clarke house, accompanied by a terrified if defiant shout of 'You rascals. Be gone or I'll blow your brains out!', Richard Clarke finally cracked and surrendered.

One by one, the other consignees cracked, too. They came to the Liberty Tree and formally resigned as consignees. The Hutchinson sons, Thomas junior and Elisha, were the last to give way, but eventually they did. All the former consignees fled to Castle William.

So far so good. But getting the tea sent back to London, as Adams realised, would be a much harder proposition. They had to get customs clearance for tea they did not actually own.

The Master of the *Dartmouth*, Captain James Hall, was a Boston man. James Hall had settled in Boston after serving in the Royal Navy in the war against the French. The *Dartmouth* was even owned by a Boston family, local whalers who also owned one of the town's leading taverns, the Bunch of Grapes on State Street.

Captain Hall was called to a Town Meeting at the Old South Church. Some of the handbills round the town announcing the meeting had been signed OC – Oliver

233

Cromwell. Five thousand Bostonians braved the pouring rain to come along, with more outside.

Samuel Adams, as Moderator of the meeting, told James Hall in front of everybody that if Boston suffered the tea to be landed from the ship it would be at his own peril. He meant Hall would be tarred and feathered by the Mohucks, and that is what Captain Hall understood him to mean.

At that point, Sheriff Stephen Greenleaf arrived with a message from Governor Hutchinson. In the name of the Governor and the Commander of British forces in Massachusetts, General Gage, the meeting was required to disperse. Sheriff Greenleaf handed the message to Adams. 'Any reply?' he enquired, with a straight face.

Thomas Young read the message over Adams's shoulder from out front.

'Gentlemen, all! We have here a note from Governor Thomas Hutchinson,' Young yelled at the gathered throng. The very name brought cat-calls and war-whoops of derision. Young shouted: 'This is a message from the man who the King privately pays a small fortune for being Governor of Massachusetts. Anything else we need to know?'

There was uproar. Most of the citizenry knew Sheriff Greenleaf was on their side, but he fled anyway, having had the Governor's message returned to him.

As calm was restored by Adams flapping his hands, Captain Hall was requested to hand over the keys to the *Dartmouth* to William Molineux, then and there. This he did, willingly enough. And to roars of approval from the Town Meeting he announced that he had keys to the two smaller tea ships tied up on the wharf as well, and he handed them over.

Adams and Molineux quickly chose a patriot boarding-party from among those present to occupy the tea ships. They chose twenty-five men, mainly Mohuck craftsmen and journeymen, but Adams was also keen to include some of the merchants to add to the operation's respectability.

To Adams's delight, John Rowe, that bell-wether of opinion, agreed to go on board the *Dartmouth*, when Adams requested it, even though he was part-owner of the cargo of one of the two smaller tea ships, the *Eleanor*.

The Mohucks of the boarding-party were divided into three crews, each with a crew leader. They set off for Griffin's Wharf. Rowe and the other merchants went with them. While they were away taking over the ships, Adams read out a Resolve: 'Now that we have humbled the consignees, we will effect a return of the tea to the place whence it came.'

Thomas Young, his blood roaring wildly with the adulation of the crowd, yelled out: 'Hey! Who knows how tea would mingle with salt water?'

The crowd cheered, yelled and stamped. Adams looked thunderstruck.

'Why send it back?' Young added, speaking to Adams only. 'Why don't we just throw it into the sea?'

Young and Adams looked long and hard at each other. Why had they not thought of this in the first place?

By now the crowd were baying 'Throw it in the sea!'

'Keep everybody here a while,' Adams whispered to Young. 'I have arrangements to make.'

Thomas Young nodded and began his task of keeping 5,000 Bostonians occupied, so the tea could be thrown into the harbour with no distractions. He greeted the gathering with a smile, not having the faintest idea what he was going to say.

CHAPTER 43

The *Dartmouth* had been brought to the lee of the British flagship, the massive fifty-gun *Romney*, for safety. The feared commander of the British fleet, Admiral John Montagu, was aboard the *Romney*. His personal pennant flew from its topmast.

Adams glanced wryly up at it as he boarded the tea ship. Then he began an earnest pow-wow with William Molineux about the mammoth task ahead. Molineux reckoned they had almost enough skilled artisans to unload and jettison the tea, but they needed a few more shipyard workers, ropewalk workers or blacksmiths who were familiar with ropes and blocks and tackle. They also had to get the pulley-blocks and the tackle from the warehouses on Griffin's Wharf, so they could haul the tea chests out of the hold.

Molineux named the blockmakers, housewrights and blacksmiths he thought they needed. Some of them had been among the few missing from the multitude at the Town Meeting.

'Go and get them,' Adams commanded, crisply. 'Bring them here.'

Molineux took five Mohucks with him from the ship. The six men split into pairs to summon the extra men. When each Mohuck pair reached the sought artisan's home, the man was summoned by the Mohawk Indian war whoops that the North End, in particular, had used ever since the days of the old Pope Day fights.

While the reinforcements were being fetched, the crew leaders ordered their men to bring blocks and tackle from the wharves. The warehouses along Griffin's Wharf were owned by consortia of merchants, as were the shops, usually owned by the same merchants. John Rowe immediately provided the keys to his own wharf, which stored one heavy block and tackle.

236

Although there was no sign of John Hancock or George Hayley, Anne Hayley appeared out of nowhere in a chaise, with the keys to Hancock's Wharf. She had been at the meeting and realised they would need the equipment. Anne was popular anyway, because she was John Wilkes's sister, but on this occasion her arrival was greeted by a delirium of Mohawk war whoops and cheers. Adams had to stop the more enthusiastic Mohucks from hoisting her aloft and carrying her round the deck.

It was dusk by now, and the light was fading. They needed lanterns brought from the stores on the wharf. It had stopped raining but the air had all the rawness of a Boston winter. The decks were still slippery from the earlier rain.

The holds were opened with the keys Captain Hall had provided, then the blocks and tackles were positioned on deck, at the neck of the open holds, each illuminated by a lantern. When the blockmakers, housewrights and blacksmiths arrived, they supervised the attaching by rope of the first of the chests in the hold to a block and tackle up on deck.

At a holler of 'Heave', men on deck hoisted the massive tea chests up, one by one. Another crew then broke the chests open on deck with hatchets and hand-axes and shovelled the tea over the side of the ship.

The artisans developed a spontaneous song to keep in rhythm as they worked.

> *Rally Mohucks, bring out your axes,*
> *And tell King George we'll pay no taxes,*
> *On his foreign tea.*

As the loose tea hit the water, there were cheers and cries of 'Let's make tea!' and 'Wilkes and Liberty!' Then there were cries of 'Boston harbour's a tea-pot tonight', and 'Hurrah for Griffin's Wharf'.

Attracted by the noise, Admiral John Montagu came onto the deck of the *Romney*. He had been entertaining guests, so was wearing his full dress uniform, minus the tricorn hat. He looked down on the action aboard the *Dartmouth* with interest, then clicked his fingers, summoning a midshipman.

Montagu had a good think to himself, while the midshipman waited for instructions. Although he had armed marines and grappling hooks on the *Romney*, the admiral was in no way inclined to send his sailors over to attack a group of Bostonians, many of whom he knew socially.

He was also aware, as was every British soldier and sailor in Boston, that the town was a powder keg and the last thing they wanted was to ignite it with a pitched battle. The rough-and-ready Montagu sent his midshipman runner to Gage to keep him informed, but bluntly forbade any action by soldiers.

As the runner left, the Admiral caught sight of John Rowe, a distant figure below him on the deck of the *Dartmouth*. Montagu knew the merchant well; he had been a frequent guest at his table. He gave Rowe a cordial wave, which the merchant returned, then he went back below deck to continue his meal.

It never occurred to Montagu that Gage would countermand him and send troops to Griffin's Wharf. But in Gage's quarters at Castle William, Major John Pitcairn wanted to do just that, and argued the point heatedly.

'They never were so brazen before,' Pitcairn said in his strong Scottish accent of Adams and Young. 'We should seize the heretic and his fellows. Make an example of them.'

Major Pitcairn made a point of being foolhardily brave. He walked alone and fully uniformed from Castle William into Boston every day to buy a leg of ham. But on this occasion, his bravery did not prevail. Colonel Smith and Gage's brother-in-law, Major Kemble, were with Gage on the side of caution, and that swung it. No troops were sent. But it was a close-run thing.

Anne Hayley had stayed aboard the *Dartmouth*, watching proceedings with interest. Eventually, John Hancock and George Hayley turned up, too, in John Hancock's luxurious sprung phaeton drawn by six horses. They were rapturously received.

As luck would have it, it was low tide; the water was only two or three feet deep. Thick layers of tea floated from the harbour towards Dorchester Neck and Point Shirley, where it lodged on the shores, sending out its message. It was the cheaper Bohea tea that floated. The aristocratic exotic teas sank. The patriots identified themselves with the cheaper tea and cheered that, too.

Many of the Mohucks on the *Dartmouth* had taken part in the attack on Hutchinson's house, and to them throwing tea into the sea was another blow against the hated aristocracy. It was all the same to them whether the aristocracy was in Boston like Hutchinson or in London like George III.

As night began to fall, some of the artisans went over to the two smaller tea ships, the *Beaver* and the *Eleanor*, which had arrived with the *Dartmouth*. Rowe was pretending sorrow at the loss of his tea, aboard the *Eleanor*, though in secret his heart soared at what he believed was coming freedom.

The two smaller ships had a hundred chests of tea each. They went the same way as the tea aboard the *Dartmouth*. The artisans were still singing as they worked. The merchants watched, leaving the task to those who could do it best.

Finally, the last of the tea from all three ships was thrown overboard into the harbour. Adams was proud that no vessels or other property had been damaged. He was ecstatic at the patriot success; his first real joy in life since

239

before his father went bankrupt, in his boyhood.

Thomas Young arrived by fiacre, having finally let the meeting at the Old South Church break up. He was hoarse from his shouted spontaneous diatribe about the evils of tea, which had kept 5,000 Bostonians amused. Young gripped both Adams's shoulders hard in his huge hands. There was fire in his eyes. Adams felt fragile in his tight grip, like a wood-and-straw effigy of a man.

They were brothers again now, Adams and Young. Both of them looked over the taffrail of the ship, spirits soaring at the sight of the floating Bohea. They were silent for a moment, then Young spoke. He was still in didactic mode, after his public lecture about the health dangers of tea.

'At the very beginning of the Roman Republic, grain from the private land of the Tarquins was thrown in the river. Because the tide was low it piled up on the riverbed, forming a new shape to the city just as the monarchy was overthrown. This is a sign, Sam.'

Adams nodded. 'I hope you're right.'

'Of course I am. Rome fell under the pressure of its own weight. Now we're seeing it again. We have created the perfect crisis in the British Empire.'

There was a long silence. Finally Adams spoke, so softly Young had to strain to catch his words.

'Thomas, I have some news. The French have made contact, just this week. Someone called the Chevalier d'Éon. John Wilkes has played honest broker and put us in touch.'

Young shut his eyes, in a state of near-bliss. 'But Sam, that is … That is truly wonderful.'

Adams allowed himself a smile. 'Yes. Wonderful.'

'Will they land men here?'

'No, no. They are not able to do that. They fear British sea power too much. And anyway we have men enough. But they will send us weapons: modern muskets with

French bullets. And cannon. We do not have nearly enough cannon at the moment. They will send them through the British blockade.'

'When, Sam? When?'

'Soon, I hope. Soon we shall declare the revolution and fight.'

CHAPTER 44

News of the attack on the tea ships in Boston harbour sent London aquiver with discussion and debate. John Pownall devoured the newspapers the moment they appeared, sending the clerks running out to buy them, his face set grim.

The Wilkesite journals stridently supported America. To Pownall's disgust, Samuel Adams was much discussed in every article, spreading his fame throughout London.

False rumours swept the capital from every newspaper, rumours Pownall disdained but knew he would have to counter to Dartmouth, perhaps even to North: Gage was dead, said the *London Evening Post*. Two regiments in Boston had revolted. Six British regiments had been sent to Boston. The army in Boston had been attacked. Many Boston townspeople had been killed by Redcoats. Boston harbour was ablaze. And the one which would have pleased Samuel Adams the most – Massachusetts had 80,000 militiamen ready for war.

Pownall thought this was something like four times too many, but still, he wryly acknowledged to himself, it was easily enough to overwhelm what was left of the British garrison at Castle William.

All the London newspapers were predicting a war with Massachusetts. A minority, mainly Wilkesite, predicted an American victory, as the colonists deserved. But most took the line that the colony was hardly worth the trouble and should be given up without a fight.

The *Morning Post* sniffed that tobacco and rice from the south mattered more to Britain than anything Massachusetts had to offer. Pownall glanced across at the still-empty desk of his fellow Under-Secretary, William Knox, a Georgia landowner. He allowed himself a smile. How Knox would have loved that.

The thought made him miss the absent Irishman even

more. Where was he and when was he coming back? John Pownall had not felt so alone since the long-gone days when Thomas had left their Lincolnshire home for his studies at Cambridge.

He needed someone to discuss these momentous events with. Without moving from his desk, he shouted for William Pollock, bidding him come into his office. The Chief Clerk stood mutely before Pownall's desk, willing to comply.

'Listen to this, Mr Pollock, from the *Morning Post*. "America will triumph and see her own independence, the consequence of Lord North's policy." Spicy stuff, eh? Then we get "Never was Great Britain in a situation so contemptible." What do you think of that, Mr Pollock?'

'A sad day, sir,' the Chief Clerk said, nervously.

'A sad day and the first of many sad days, I fear.'

Pownall glanced at the Chief Clerk. He knew something. Pownall could tell. It was always worth listening to William Pollock. His father had been in the Secret Service and he maintained good contact with its present leadership.

'Come on, William,' John Pownall said, softly but with just a hint of menace. 'You've heard something, haven't you? Let's have it, man. Let's have it.'

'It's Wilkes, sir,' the Chief Clerk said, mouthing the name as if it tasted of henbane and gall. 'He has issued a Remonstrance calling for the removal of Lord North and his cabinet for their iniquitous measures with respect to their fellow subjects in America.'

As part of a spate of lightning-fast armed robberies plaguing the capital, Lord North's coach had been held up by two highwaymen at Gunnersbury. They had snatched North's wallet from about his person and shot his postilion in the thigh, to prevent pursuit.

North's rare moments of sleep were now plagued with lurid dreams in which highwaymen cut off his leg. He would awake screaming, aware, as he reluctantly returned

243

to wakefulness, that the limb being sawn off was America. The debate in the House of Commons on the destruction of the tea was watched by a tense and anxious John Pownall, up in the gallery. William Knox had sent word by messenger that he did not wish to attend.

George III opened proceedings by declaring a most daring spirit of resistance to the law, on the Americans' part. Pownall's superior, Lord Dartmouth, had asked the legal officers for advice on whether the attack on the tea ships was treasonous. He announced to the Commons the advice that it was.

Of more interest to Pownall was Lord Sandwich's request that the fleet be kept at home to protect England from the French fleet. Pownall regarded French involvement on the American side as by far the greatest threat to the realm. He regarded it as his first responsibility to prevent it.

He was therefore pleased to hear the use of force advocated by Sandwich. Immediate, overwhelming force against America might pre-empt French involvement, or so John Pownall hoped. So he was encouraged when North, who naturally spoke first in the America debate, obviously thought so too.

He became less happy when Lord North appeared to be taking leave of his senses, before Pownall's very eyes, on the floor of the Commons. The normally mild-mannered First Minister appeared to be possessed by the demon of somebody else entirely as he launched into a tirade which stunned the Commons, waving his arms about as he spoke: 'The Americans have tarred and feathered the King's subjects, plundered the King's merchants, burnt the King's ships, denied all obedience to the King's laws and authority; yet so clement and so long forbearing has our conduct been that it is incumbent on us now to take a different course.'

The different course proposed was war.

To Pownall's pleased surprise, among those supporting North in advocating force was his lordship's step-brother, the head of the American Department, Lord Dartmouth: 'For the King's dignity and the honour and safety of the Empire, force should be repelled by force,' Dartmouth said.

Dartmouth then demanded that Boston pay for the destroyed tea.

As John Pownall was resignedly expecting, his older brother rose to oppose any idea that Boston should pay for the tea they had destroyed. The noise increased as Thomas rose, John himself giving a loud groan followed by a weary sigh he hoped was audible down in the chamber.

For reasons opaque to John, Thomas attempted to describe the peaceful nature of the Bostonians, based on his time living among them, which added laughter to the raucous cacophony going on around him. He then said, with a catch in his throat, that these peaceable Bostonians were ourselves, if not our brothers, and so war would be civil war of the worst sort, brother against brother.

The fault and blame for this incipient war, Thomas was shouting to a derisive House of Commons, lay squarely with the British: 'The colonists have neither rebelled against nor invaded England, nor stolen from her. There would be no discontent had we not provoked the contest by pushing the principle of authority so far by the duties on tea, and had we not stationed troops in Boston to enforce obedience to unpopular Acts. The chances are that without these two actions there would be no talk of conflict.'

'You are making it worse, my idiot brother,' John Pownall said aloud to himself in the gallery.

But at that point Thomas Pownall was howled down, sitting plumply hard back on Lord North's benches, from which he still spoke. However, he was ready for this rebuff: he had had pamphlets printed of his speech, which he now distributed to any Member who was willing to take one. He even looked up at the Gallery, miming asking John if he wanted one.

John mimed back that he did not.

CHAPTER 45

As soon as the debate was over, John Pownall took action over an aspect of the American defiance overlooked, as he saw it, by everyone but him – the position of Governor Thomas Hutchinson. Pownall had wanted Hutchinson replaced for some time, but now he feared the Governor would be an effective brake on the implementation of firm measures against Massachusetts. He would wait no longer.

Having decided on his aim, John Pownall's tactics were typically labyrinthine: first, he went to his superior, Lord Dartmouth, so he could not later be accused of having gone over his lordship's head. 'I am more and more convinced that it would be both a credit and advantage to Governor Hutchinson if he were ordered home. And that it would be of great utility in any further steps that may be taken regarding that province.'

The pious, unworldly Dartmouth could see the sense of that. But anyway, he left everything to Pownall because the Under-Secretary knew so much more of these colonial affairs and was so much better at implementing policy.

Having reached that objective, John Pownall then gently asked, 'I beg your lordship's direction whether I should put it upon the list of cabinet business next Saturday.'

A relieved Dartmouth, having ascertained that Pownall, not he himself, would address the subject in cabinet, gave his enthusiastic approval.

Pownall then arranged an appointment to see Lord North privately. Given the weight of the Agenda this coming Saturday, Pownall wondered if North would agree in advance to Hutchinson being relieved of the Governorship in such a way that he should appear to be coming to England at his own request, and settling here.

As to how this might be achieved, Pownall suggested the withdrawing of his salary from state funds and its replacement by a pension payable in England only. The Assembly in Boston were hardly likely to start paying the detested Hutchinson's salary now, if the British stopped doing so.

On the contrary, the Assembly would likely be in full support of ending Hutchinson's Governorship. At this point Pownall ingeniously quoted one of Samuel Adams's attacks on Hutchinson in the Assembly.

As North would no doubt recall, Pownall said, the Massachusetts Assembly had formally complained to the King about Hutchinson and about the new Lieutenant Governor, Andrew Oliver, Hutchinson's brother-in-law. The Assembly accused them of a plot to destroy the Massachusetts Charter, on which the King's relationship with the colony rested, by ruling in a sovereign and independent manner, arrogating justice in criminal cases, such as treason, to themselves. They petitioned for Hutchinson and Oliver to be removed from their posts.

Indeed, Hutchinson's stock had sunk so low in Boston that Adams was openly suggesting in the *Boston Gazette* that the Governor should pay for the destroyed tea from his own funds. Hutchinson, Adams said, had both encouraged and provoked the people to destroy the tea by refusing them customs clearance to send it back.

North managed a wan smile at that. He readily agreed, as he already wished to replace Hutchinson with General Gage as Governor of Massachusetts. The myopic North saw General Gage as a mighty soldier, a pillar of strength in a crisis. So he saw Gage's promotion to Governor, while keeping his command of the army, as both firming and simplifying London's dealings with the rebel state.

Seizing quick advantage, John Pownall outlined the powers he wished the new Governor to have. These were powers Hutchinson had never had: Gage was to be the first Massachusetts Governor who could call in military assistance without the advice and consent of the Assembly.

Then a second injustice, as John Pownall had long

247

seen it, was removed: British soldiers were to be given immunity from prosecution in Massachusetts courts, so they could not be arrested and tried as the Redcoats held responsible for the Boston Massacre had been. The fact that they were, by and large, found innocent was of little consolation to John Pownall.

Combining the role of military and civilian governor had not been seen in the colonies since the time of Governor Andros, ninety years before. It was time to return to older and firmer ways, John Pownall shrewdly suggested to the ultimately traditionalist and conservative Lord North, a dreamer who believed in, and sometimes lived in, a golden age from the past.

The matter of Thomas Hutchinson's future was quietly taken off the cabinet agenda. Gage was appointed Governor of Massachusetts then and there. Arrangements were made for Hutchinson to come to London and stay there.

John Pownall was most satisfied, although the irony of having just completed Samuel Adams's life's work and fulfilled his deepest desire by ejecting Hutchinson from Boston was not lost on him.

CHAPTER 46

The cabinet meeting the following Saturday was held in the spacious drawing room of Lord Dartmouth's London house in St James's Square. As the meeting began, two warships were under orders for Boston, with four infantry regiments being mustered, a fraction of the forces the newly appointed Governor Gage had been pleading for.

John Pownall attended the cabinet meeting. This was not unusual for an Under-Secretary. Someone of Pownall's rank would sit against the wall, not round the table, ready to leap forward whenever his Minister, in this case Lord Dartmouth, required information.

William Knox would normally have attended the cabinet meeting with Pownall, but he had once again excused himself by messenger, behaviour that was beginning to both worry and irritate Pownall.

All the men round the cabinet table, ten of them, knew that whatever they decided would easily clear the Commons and come into effect, as North's inbuilt majority of King's Men was larger than ever. There would be some prominent opposition but opposition would, in the end, count for nothing.

Lord North naturally spoke first. He said they were meeting to devise measures to enable His Majesty to put an end to the present disturbances in America. And to secure the just dependence of the colonies on the Crown of Great Britain: 'It is impossible for our commerce to be safe while it continues in the harbour of Boston,' he went on. 'It is highly necessary that some other port be found for the landing of our merchandise where our laws would give full protection.'

There was a buzz of agreement round the table. Tilting his head back against Lord Dartmouth's yellow wallpaper, John Pownall thought the meeting was going rather well. On Lord North went: 'On frequent occasions, the officers

249

of the Customs have been prevented from doing their duty in Boston. The inhabitants of the town of Boston deserve punishment.'

'The whole town should be destroyed,' Lord Sandwich muttered, 'like Carthage.'

John Pownall nodded vigorously at that.

Lord Dartmouth, as the Minister responsible for America, was next to speak. He uneasily cleared his throat, nervous even in his own front room. John Pownall remembered one of William Knox's typically subversive comments: if Dartmouth's chin receded any further, the Irishman had said, he would be in danger of swallowing his nose. Pownall suppressed a smile. He still keenly missed his permanently absent colleague and friend.

Dartmouth said he believed the challenge to the Crown's authority was the work of a handful of self-interested fanatics, which John Pownall knew with great certainty vastly understated the case. This gentle, pious, evangelical Wesleyan believed the unrest in Boston was caused by defects of the spirit, a phrase which had made John Pownall snort with contempt when he first heard it.

But he took a hard line because that was what North wanted. William Legge, 2nd Earl of Dartmouth, loved Frederick North dearly. They had gone on the Grand Tour together as young men, such experiences often forming a lifelong brotherhood even beyond that of blood.

Dartmouth's frequent absences from London and his work were occasionally to his Staffordshire estates but more often to Somerset, saving the North family's estates from bankruptcy. This made him feel protective of his step-brother. So, out of love for him, he followed North's line – the port of Boston should be closed and customs collection moved elsewhere.

This was John Pownall's chance. He knew the cabinet would be discussing other specific measures against the colonies. He did not want the measures against Boston to be swallowed up into a footnote of a sub-clause in the coming flurry of legislation. He stood and whispered in Dartmouth's ear as he sat down.

'May I have the floor, sir?'

Dartmouth looked relieved. 'Certainly, John. Members of cabinet, my Under-Secretary, Mr Pownall, craves your indulgence.'

There was a general nodding and muttering of approbation. John Pownall was the expert on Boston, par excellence. The cabinet, to a man, wished to hear what he had to say.

As ever, John Pownall spoke without notes. In a show of loyalty he stood immediately behind the Secretary of State, Dartmouth, who had to twist in his chair and look upwards to follow him.

'Gentlemen of the cabinet. The latest intelligence from Boston is that an army of no fewer than sixteen thousand from Massachusetts are being trained for readiness.' This received the murmurings of outrage and horror Pownall had hoped for.

'Also other colonies have taken to making treasonable statements. The rebels, Adams in particular, have long been in touch with other colonies, sowing discontent and at times downright treason.' That got a bellow of disapprobation. 'So, gentlemen, I think it may be time to revisit measures first discussed some years ago, under my noble Lord's predecessor, Lord Hillsborough.'

That was audacious. It was an oblique reference to Dartmouth's reputation for prayerful dithering. Dartmouth gave a small smile. Pownall knew he had got away with it.

'Those measures then discussed were as follows: the closure of the port of Boston, the prohibition of Town Meetings, the regulation of colonial juries and alterations to the right of representation in the Assembly. Would the honourable gentlemen wish me to ...'

Pownall left his sentence hanging in the air; he did not need to finish it. He was tasked with drafting a measure to be called the Boston Port Act, unfettered by any need to consult Dartmouth, North or anybody else.

CHAPTER 47

So, where was William Knox? Working on the Boston Port Act at his desk in the tiny office they shared, or had once shared, John Pownall glared at the desk of the absent Irishman. While never exactly cluttered, it was now ostentatiously empty. John Pownall had not seen him for weeks. The Chief Clerk, William Pollock, had heard nothing from him in even longer.

John Pownall swore softly and went back to work. He was working fifteen, sixteen hours a day – sometimes even more – six days a week.

The other Acts against the American colonies, already collectively known as the Coercive Acts, were being given a final draft at the Northern Office, under Lord Sandwich. One of them would make the capture of the ringleaders easier. This was all very promising!

John Pownall lowered his eyes again. The port of Boston would be closed from June 1st, except for coastal ships carrying fuel and necessary supplies. Customs services would be removed to Marblehead. The Assembly would be moved to Salem, which would replace Boston as province capital.

Boston's punishment would continue until indemnities had been paid to the East India Company for the destruction of the tea, until injured royal officers had been compensated, and until the King judged that peace was so restored that trade could continue. But even then only a few wharves would be allowed to reopen.

John Pownall viewed progress so far with growing satisfaction: the chances of George III ever rescinding Boston's punishment were, in Pownall's estimation, nil. The Massachusetts port was to be closed off for ever. Boston was effectively declared dead.

Adams and his mobs would no doubt prepare for war, but the British were already doing so. It was more essential than ever to keep the French out of it.

At that moment, the sound of activity, a flurry of liveliness in the outer office, some talk and even laughter, announced the now unaccustomed arrival of William Knox.

John Pownall was delighted to see him but tried to hide it. 'Ah, our absentee Under-Secretary for the American Department. This is a surprise.'

William Knox looked grim, not a look Pownall had ever seen on him before. He tried the light-hearted tone again. It backfired.

'What's the matter, William? Too much work for you? Too much of that boring day-to-day detail we all know is beneath you?'

'Will you be quiet? John. Please.'

'What?'

'I have had enough. I have transferred to the Civil Service in Dublin. I am here for some books. After that you are on your own.'

'I see. And what, pray, brought all this on?'

William Knox had gone to the shelves behind his desk and was collecting books into a leather bag, but now he stopped.

'You have to ask that, John? You really have to ask that?'

'I just did, William.'

William Knox slammed the leather bag down on what had been his desk. 'What you are doing here is against the Law of God, John. And by rights it should be against the Law of Man. You cannot murder a city. You cannot choke a town by its throat.'

'Have you been watching a melodrama at Drury Lane? What is this popular claptrap?'

'Oh, claptrap is it, now? Is that so? And what are these people supposed to eat, John? Tell me that. It is a port, is it not? And you wish to stop ships landing there with food for every man, woman and child.'

254

'I'm sure they …'

William Knox held up his hand. 'No, John. Don't, please. Please do not insult my intelligence. Yes, food will be brought in from the interior. The hinterland. But you know as well as I, better, that that can never be even nearly adequate. Whatever Adams and his scum of the earth have done, nobody, nobody John, deserves this.'

Tears came to John Pownall's eyes. There was silence for a moment. Then: 'I am sorry you feel this way, William. And I am even sorrier to lose you, as my colleague and, as I thought, my friend. I wish you well in Dublin.'

William Knox left without another word.

The Boston Port Bill sailed through both Houses of Parliament exactly as John Pownall had drafted it. It then received the Royal Assent from an enthusiastic King George, similarly unaltered and un-amended. The King commended Lord North on his excellent work and declared himself truly satisfied.

John Pownall became the only Under-Secretary in British history to construct a complete, unchanged piece of legislation unaided and alone.

CHAPTER 48

The news of the Boston Port Bill reached Boston before Lord North intended it should. The *Harmony*, one of John Hancock's ships, made the crossing in a speedy forty-one days. One item of news not aboard, however, was Hutchinson's replacement by Gage as Governor.

So the visceral rage at Britain's actions against Boston found its target in the nearest royal representative, which as far as the Bostonians knew was Thomas Hutchinson.

The entire front page of the *Boston Gazette* was given over to excoriating Hutchinson. He was called the most malignant and insatiable enemy of his country. He had committed greater public crimes than his life can repair or his death satisfy, was the *Gazette*'s conclusion.

A satirical play, *The Adulateur*, ridiculing Hutchinson, not only played to sold-out audiences in Boston, it was published as a pamphlet by the publisher of the most committed of the patriot newspapers, the *Massachusetts Spy*. In the play, a thinly disguised Hutchinson was lampooned as Rapatio, the rapacious Bashaw – a high official of the Turkish Empire but a term used in Boston for any official considered over-grand or self-important:

> *Though from my youth ambition's path I trod,*
> *Sucked the contagion from my mother's breast;*
> *The early taint has rankled in my veins,*
> *And lust for power is still my darling lust.*

Samuel Adams made sure any opprobrium hurled at Hutchinson himself spread to the other Medici families. Under Adams's influence, the Assembly passed a resolve against the conduct of Peter Oliver, as Chief Justice. He was no longer allowed to try cases.

Andrew Oliver was sickened at his hounding as Lieutenant Governor, both by attacks in the newspapers and by the continuous mobbing of his home by Mohucks. He died within weeks, but there was no peace for him even in death: the *Boston Gazette's* obituary painted him as a member of the cabal which was ruining Boston for personal gain. His disdain for the mob was portrayed as snobbery.

In a final act of revenge, the mob took over his funeral, hooting with delight over his coffin, giving three cheers as it was lowered into its grave before the grieving family, which naturally included Thomas Hutchinson, supported by his daughter, Peggy.

Richard Clarke, whose house had been attacked before the tea was thrown into the sea, had by now left Boston for good. The other sometime tea consignees had also left, except Thomas Hutchinson junior and Elisha Hutchinson, Hutchinson's sons.

This reduction in the numbers of the Medici concentrated the attacks on the ones who were left. Samuel Adams publicly called for Thomas Hutchinson and Peter Oliver to be put to death.

News of his replacement as Governor by General Gage and the payment of his pension in London, where he was required to live, reached Thomas Hutchinson in the first days of spring. He acquiesced immediately.

By now, the battered and beleaguered former Governor looked and acted twenty years older than his sixty-three years. He was so broken in spirit, he would have presented himself at the Liberty Tree for tarring and feathering had that, too, been requested of him. But it was not, though if Samuel Adams had had his way, it would have been.

It was agreed that Elisha and Thomas junior would stay in Boston to take care of the considerably reduced Hutchinson business interests. Hutchinson pleaded with Peggy to stay in Boston with them, not to give up any more of her life for him.

Peggy smilingly but firmly refused. She began an

occasionally brittle but determinedly cheerful extolling of the joys of London life, and how superior it would be to their narrow, provincial existence in Boston. She waxed lyrical over the shopping they would do in the Strand; the cathedrals and palaces they would see; the theatres they would visit, including the famous Drury Lane.

The incoming sloop *Minerva* docked, carrying several London newspapers and magazines including *Town and Country* and the *Public Advertiser.* Peggy read them avidly. They told of even more joys in their coming days in London. Several of the big Whig mansions had public days, Peggy informed her father; they could go, they could visit. Peggy's eyes were wide at their coming joy. And what about the Vauxhall Pleasure Gardens? You could hear concerts by the famous Mr Handel there, how wonderful. And there were salons and coffee houses. The litany of possible pleasures went on and on. Eventually even the battered Thomas Hutchinson managed a wan smile.

The sons, Elisha and Thomas junior, dealt with any business their father's leaving occasioned. Peggy handled practicalities, which included booking their passage on the *Minerva*'s return voyage to London. The *Minerva* was the last ship to arrive before the Boston Port Act took effect – except for warships. She would be the last ship ever permitted to leave.

'Poor unhappy Boston,' Thomas Hutchinson's now gravelly voice croaked out to his daughter when he heard the news. 'God only knows your wretched fate. I see nothing but misery ahead for your inhabitants.'

In the days before he left, the Assembly sold Hutchinson's home at Milton for a song, to get a quick sale. The proceeds went to Poor Relief. Hutchinson and Peggy were allowed to live there until he left Boston.

'I will not see the lights in these posts they are putting along the walkways,' Hutchinson said to Peggy. 'The streets are to be lit at night! An exciting prospect, I suppose.

I hope the Assembly handles it well. If we will still have an Assembly, that is.'

On a mild day in early summer, thirty-seven years to the day since his start in Boston politics, Thomas Hutchinson and his daughter left Milton for Long Wharf, where the *Minerva* was tied up.

As his carriages had been sold at public auction, they travelled on the Burling coach, a new carriage-for-hire service. It was rather a good service, Hutchinson thought. He told the owner as much, as he drove them personally to the point of embarkation.

There, on the quayside, stood the two Hutchinson sons and the captain of the *Minerva*, who saluted Hutchinson smartly.

Peggy supervised the loading of her and her father's luggage. Finally, the *Minerva* put to sea with Hutchinson and Peggy on deck, seeing their last view of Boston. They eased past the tied-up merchantmen and the many men-of-war. Admiral Montagu's new flagship, the *Captain*, was off Hancock's Wharf. Then the *Minerva* passed the *St John* and the *Canceau* which stood ready, awaiting orders to block the harbour and the Charlestown ferry-way.

As the *Minerva* became a speck on the horizon, a hunched figure watched it unblinkingly from the end of Long Wharf. It was a hot day for a red cloak, but Samuel Adams never wore anything else outside the house. He basked in the sunshine without sweating.

Silently, wrapped in his cloak and in his thoughts, the latter-day Savonarola watched the last of the hated Medici sail away, knowing the Bonfire of the Vanities blazed behind him. Hutchinson's houses were gone, his carriages were gone, his wealth was all but gone. All the trappings of power were gone, along with the power itself.

Like the Florentine monk Savonarola, Samuel Adams was in secret contact with the French. The contact was regular, with Beaumarchais as well as the Chevalier d'Éon.

And naturally George Hayley still brought him messages from Wilkes. It would not be long now ... The new order. The new Jerusalem.

Samuel Adams turned hard eyes to the *Minerva*, diminishing and dwindling in size like its hated human cargo, soon vanishing. He felt no sense of triumph. He felt no sense of revenge. He felt no sense of good triumphing over evil, or of the people triumphing over their masters.

He felt nothing. But then he always felt nothing.

CHAPTER 49

The voyage to London was, Hutchinson thought, astonishingly fast – just thirty-four days. He was badly seasick, but he was glad Peggy fared much better. She was eating well, bright as a bird, chatting to the officers and the other passengers, starting a journal.

The *Minerva* finally tied up at Saviour's Dock, between two timber yards on the Thames. As soon as they had moored, the captain knocked deferentially on Hutchinson's cabin door and handed him a note.

Hutchinson groaned; more demands were no doubt being made on his elderly being. Then he noticed with some alarm that the note bore the royal crest. King George III wished to see him immediately; a royal phaeton was waiting at dockside to convey him to St James's Palace to attend His Majesty at a levee.

As Hutchinson was assisted into the six-horse royal phaeton, Peggy's delirious happiness was marred only by the lack of any time to change into a more stylish dress. She feared the yellow and white silk sack-back she had left out for travelling would be considered old-fashioned in London.

Hutchinson, too, regretted not meeting his monarch in his best suit of clothes. Though never as vain as his enemies painted him, Hutchinson had always felt it his duty to present himself well, not stained and creased from a journey. But needs must!

'St James's Palace, papa!' Peggy's eyes were gleaming with excitement. 'Some acknowledgement for your dedicated service, at last.'

'Darling, I do not wish to sound ungrateful,' Hutchinson said with a groan as he settled his aching back against the phaeton's leather bench seat, 'but I would prefer a sleep lasting quite some time.'

The phaeton dashed through London without sparing

the horses, the pitching and swaying of its well-sprung chassis making Hutchinson feel seasick again – or 'land-sick': he corrected his thoughts with a historian's precision. The Royal Steward, now sitting up with the postilion, had already warned they would be hard put to arrive even for the end of the levee.

Hutchinson, like many royalists, regarded a levee as the epitome of democracy – the King appearing *en déshabille* before his subjects, completing his toilette and dressing before them while hearing the petitions of high and low alike. And all the while, the most famous entertainers of the day strutted their stuff, singing, or perhaps playing the harpsichord.

Peggy was already hoping that someone called Manzuoli would return to England from Italy to sing at the levee they were rushing towards.

'Or Tenducci might be singing "Waters Parted from the Sea".' Peggy was squeaking with excitement. 'Or Lovattini! Papa! Lovattini!'

'Indeed. Lovattini. Yes, dear,' Hutchinson said, as he finally managed to drop off to sleep.

As they trotted down Horsleydown Lane, Hutchinson was jerked awake again by the swaying of the phaeton. The old man was struck by the glass-fronted shops.

'Look at that, Peggy!'

Peggy gave her beloved father an indulgent smile, as if she had seen all that before, which she had not.

The Strand was full of huge swinging shop signs with brilliant pictures on them, picturing the shop's wares. Hutchinson feared the postilion would be decapitated as all the shop signs swung past his head in the wind.

How did the Londoners manage in this traffic? Indeed, just as he thought that, they were brought to a halt in a queue of coaches. How many carriages were there in London? Thousands apparently.

They heard the postilion shout out 'Make way for the royal coach!'

The Royal Steward's alarmed voice came in through the windows telling the postilion to be quiet, as they were already being surrounded by a hostile crowd. Some small stones and lumps of mud hit the windows, but then the coach moved on.

'When we are settled in London, Papa, can we go to St Ann, Blackfriars to hear Mr Romaine preach? Oh, please, Papa?'

Hutchinson nodded, hearing only '... settled in London'. He had avoided even thinking about where they would lodge this coming week, let alone where they would live out their days. He had considerably less in funds than hc had anticipated when this plan was first broached to him.

This dark thought prompted another: this city, this London, it belonged to John Wilkes. Wilkes had been elected Lord Mayor, preaching Justice for America. Justice for America, indeed! He, Thomas Hutchinson, had fought all his life for Justice for America and now this exciter of mobs, this twisted devil, steals his clothes and gets the mob behind him.

'Papa! Papa!'

'What is it, darling?'

'You were muttering to yourself again.'

'Was I? Don't worry, my dear. I am sure I was saying something quite profound. If only I could remember what it was.'

Her tinkling laughter exalted his spirit and made his heart light again.

They edged forwards slowly as far as Pall Mall.

'Papa! Papa! Look! Look! A Macaroni. A real London Macaroni.'

'A what?'

Hutchinson peered through the glass window at a ridiculous-looking fop with narrow breeches, a short, tight waistcoat and a wig piled a foot high on his head.

'Don't know how he breathes with his breeches like

that.'

Further along, as their coach was overtaken by another, amid imprecations from the postilion, Hutchinson caught sight of a society woman in a carriage more elegant than the King's. The carriage roof had been made higher to accommodate a three-foot hair tower with miniature ornaments on it.

'That's chiné silk,' Peggy said reverently of her dress. 'It must have cost a king's ransom. Let us hope for her sake nobody throws acid at it.'

'Throws …? Why should anybody …?'

Hutchinson shook his head, sorrowfully. He said nothing, but thought, they are decadent, these people. They are like the last days of Sodom.

'There are posts along the walkways, Peggy,' Hutchinson said. 'They will be lit at night with lamps, hardly any need for link boys any more. We are just about to get them in Boston, too, we saw them as we left.'

They were both silent at that, because Hutchinson had spoken as if they were going back to Boston, at some time. And both of them knew they would never go back.

CHAPTER 50

When they reached St James's Palace, an exhausted Hutchinson was told the levee had just finished. The old man blinked back tears because his daughter was so disappointed.

The disappointments continued: Peggy never met, nor even saw the King. She was shown into an ante-room where one of the Ladies of the Bedchamber sat with her. The Lady of the Bedchamber asked polite questions about Boston, but appeared to think they were in daily danger of being scalped by Indians.

Meanwhile, Thomas Hutchinson was ushered into a small and rather shabby closet with faded green wallpaper. In a corner, a half-finished backgammon game stood on a Chippendale table with a scratched top whose drawer-handles and castors needed polishing. Hutchinson would never have given it house-room in his Garden Court glory days.

George III stood to greet him. He was completely alone. He had changed into everyday clothes after the levee. He was wearing an indoor red tasselled cap, a short blue jacket, a Holland shirt and brown worsted stockings. Hutchinson had the possibly treasonous thought that he could have been anybody, including the gardener.

Then he looked at the King's face. It was a shock. The King bore little resemblance to the many portraits of him which Hutchinson knew so well. But he bore a strong resemblance to the portraits of Lord North.

Hutchinson's eyes grew wide. So the rumours were true! The King and Lord North were half-brothers! They had the same father, Frederick Prince of Wales. He knew they had been brought up together, tutored by the Earl of Bute, but half-brothers! That explained everything, most especially how a mediocrity like North came to be First Minister.

Hutchinson was swept by a wild desire to laugh. His past life passed before him. All that study of history. All that perusal of documents. All that reading of political theory. And none of it matters a fig. Accidents of birth, quirks of the inner nature, webs of connections, that is all that matters. That is the real stuff of history.

To Hutchinson's alarm, the desire to give way to roaring laughter was not diminishing. Was he to be convulsed with uncontrollable laughter at his first meeting with his monarch? Was his career to end in the Tower?

He dimly realised, as if through sleep, that the King was speaking.

'Mr Hutchinson! How good to see you, eh. What?' The King was hopping about from foot to foot like a hare on hot coals. Was he always so lively? 'So sorry, Lord North cannot be with us today. He is off at the Oaks in Surrey for a masque. And there is, oh how jolly, there is a banquet and a ball. Do you know Lord Stanley?'

'I am afraid not, your Majesty. No.'

'No, course you don't. Course you don't. Anyway, he's marrying Lady Betty Hamilton. Scottish. Rich as the bloody Exchequer itself. Pardon my French!'

The King roared with laughter. Hutchinson thought it politic to join in, if only to release the laughter bubbling up in him in any case.

'Now. Cut to the chase. Mr Hutchinson. Your view of the situation in Boston. If you please. Eh What?'

Hutchinson was ready for this. His view was that the American colonies could not possibly stay part of Great Britain. They would secede, probably very soon. But he could hardly say that to the King.

'I believe the situation is grave, your Majesty. I would support Governor Gage in his request for more troops, including, if possible, cavalry.'

'Quite! Quite!' The King looked thoughtful for a moment. 'But what if we were able to arrest the ringleaders? Bring them back to Britain? I mean who … Adams? Or

Young? Or Hancock? The merchants would be delighted if we arrested Hancock. More trade for them, eh? What?'

Hutchinson was impressed by the King's knowledge of the personalities of Boston politics. Did he have this from John Pownall? Probably, yes. Via North.

'Your Majesty is well informed,' Hutchinson said.

The King nodded, his smile fading. Hutchinson's compliment, he realised, had been a faux pas. One did not compliment monarchs. He was nothing but a provincial clodhopper after all. Ah well, in for a penny in for a pound. Hutchinson knew he had been given a chance. He seized it.

'My advice, Your Majesty,' he said slowly, 'would be to arrest Adams, most certainly, as a major priority. Young and Hancock would be a bonus, but they are secondary. Arrest Adams and you cut the head off the dragon of revolution.'

The King nodded, oddly over-vigorous. He looked thoughtful: 'What accounts for Adams's importance? How is such a thing possible? Here, he is rather considered the antithesis of order. A purveyor of upheaval.'

Hutchinson smothered a sigh. 'He is certainly that, Your Majesty' He paused. 'Adams has a great pretended zeal for liberty,' he said, finally. 'He uses liberty as a lever to achieve disorder. In doing this, he deceives the simple people. In Boston, as elsewhere, they do not always judge their own best interests well, nor act in accordance.'

'I see. And how has the recent legislation regarding the New England colonies been received?'

Hutchinson hesitated. 'The people of Boston are much dispirited.'

'Good. It was the only effectual method that could bring them to a speedy submission. It will be a means of establishing some government in that province which has been a crucible of lawlessness and chaos.'

'Yes, Your Majesty.'

'I am convinced they will soon submit.'

'Yes.'

George extended his hand for Hutchinson to kiss.

'Thank you for coming, Mr Hutchinson. At least you escaped before they tarred and feathered you.'

Chapter 51

Thomas and Peggy Hutchinson did indeed visit the London theatres, as Peggy had dreamed. And the pleasure gardens at Vauxhall. And they heard the famous Mr Romaine preach at St Ann, Blackfriars. But it quickly became evident to Peggy, who took complete control of the finances, that the money they had brought with them, which had seemed so ample in Boston, was dwindling at an alarming rate.

A house in London, Peggy discovered, would cost an astronomical amount – and that would be just a house for the middling sort. Peggy gently indicated to her father that they must move from the lodgings in Mayfair they had found on arrival to somewhere of humbler station.

After many enquiries, Peggy finally found them a suite of cramped, dingy, low-ceilinged rooms let out by a war widow. They were in Southwark, just over the river from Bridewell Prison, which was visible from their parlour window.

At first, Thomas Hutchinson had some contact with everybody he had corresponded with from Boston, including, separately, Thomas and John Pownall.

Thomas Pownall kept open house for Americans visiting London. Hutchinson and Peggy met the American faction there. One of the changes of old age, Hutchinson noted wryly, was that he had grown more tolerant of Thomas Pownall, though his predecessor but one as Governor had not lost his considerable ability to irritate.

Thomas was in the process of offering his personal mediation in Boston to avert a war. Hutchinson struggled to hide his scepticism at that, a scepticism apparently shared by Pownall's formidable wife, Harriet, who Peggy described in her journal as 'as fierce a dragon as I have ever seen'.

The meeting with John Pownall was brief to the point of rudeness on the younger Pownall's part. It did not take place at the American Department, as Hutchinson had hoped, but at Guidon's French Eating House, a dining place for genteel persons in Portland Street. Peggy was specifically excluded in advance by John Pownall, who then, to Peggy's further fury, left Hutchinson with the bill, which they could ill afford.

To make matters even worse, John Pownall treated Hutchinson like an elderly American tourist, giving loud, overly clear and largely unneeded advice on the pleasures to be had in the capital. He did not ask for Hutchinson's view of events in Boston once, and beyond gloomily noting that there would be war soon, as he tucked into his roast fowl, he did not mention the political situation in general, either.

Hutchinson's happiest contact in London, by far, was with Lord Dartmouth, who he had always found congenial. Dartmouth wished with all his might and main to do the right thing, but did not have the foggiest idea what the right thing might be. He listened to Hutchinson's views and experiences at length, nodding wisely, but learning nothing.

Dartmouth, to Peggy's fury, let slip to Hutchinson that the former Governor had been in line for a baronetcy, until his finances were investigated. He would not, Dartmouth informed him sadly and rather tactlessly, be able to support a baronetcy.

Indeed, after a month he could barely support day-to-day living. The London pension arranged by John Pownall had finally materialised. It was far smaller than expected.

Without telling her father, Peggy was scribbling furious letters to Thomas junior demanding that he and Elisha send more money from the family firm than the pittance which had so far arrived. But with the Boston Port Act beginning to bite, as Thomas junior explained in his reply, there was no money in the firm to send.

Outwardly oblivious as poverty turned to penury, Hutchinson tried to recreate his life in New England, especially when the first novelty of London attractions wore off. His aching longing for the sea was fulfilled by taking lodgings in Brighton for weeks at a time – jaunts they could ill afford. Peggy tried hard to point that out, without alarming the old man too much, but he refused to listen, increasingly retreating into a world of his own.

And that is how matters stood when Peggy fell ill. She caught consumption and took to her bed at the Southwark lodging house, staring blankly at the mildew damp patch on the wall. Her constitution had never been strong. The doctors informed Hutchinson, with lugubrious faces, there was to be no escape.

Hutchinson was distraught, beside himself with anguish. Of especially cruel pain to him were the medications he was told to administer by the doctors, which only increased her agony.

The old man woke in the night crying, hearing the sounds of his daughter's agony from the next room, helpless to bring comfort or alleviation. Unwilling to abandon Peggy, even for minutes, he no longer left the meagre stained confines of the lodging house. He had no existence aside from the pain of her being; the constant awareness of her wretched life of hurt in this pit to which he had brought her.

She sat up in bed, fever-bright, and said, 'Must I die? I am not fit or ready to die.'

Hutchinson said she should put her trust in God through Jesus Christ our saviour. He often thought back to his first misery, as a young man – his wife Peggy's death. Now the daughter who had been not only daughter but a second wife to him was leaving him, too. He wished her agony gone, but he wished her with him. He realised he could not have both.

Then Peggy died. She was twenty-three.

CHAPTER 52

John Pownall glared at the reports on his desk. He had summoned the head of the King's Messengers, Nathan Carrington, to discuss them. He had done this most unwillingly. Carrington had witnessed John Pownall's greatest ever shame, as he saw it, his humiliating defeat at the hands of Wilkes over the Foundling Hospital embezzlement. The sight of the portly, gaudily attired, foul-mouthed plebeian brought the sharply painful memories back.

'Sorry I'm late, Mr Pownall,' a breathless Carrington opened. 'The bleedin' streets are blocked solid. Rioters everywhere. I'd string up the whole bloody lot of them by the bollocks, if I 'ad my way. Bleedin' ungrateful monkeys.'

Beneath this show of chummy bravura, Nathan Carrington was nervous of John Pownall. But as he stood before the Under-Secretary's desk, his small eyes widened in his bulbous head: Mr Pownall had a half-empty bottle of red wine and one glass on his desk. It was just after half-past ten in the morning.

'Carrington, do you know anything about arms smuggling from France?'

'No, sir.'

'Neither did I until this morning.' John Pownall paused to pour and sip more red wine. He waved a sheaf of papers at Nathan Carrington. 'These reports were inexplicably sent to Sandwich at the Northern Office. He sat on them, probably literally. I hope it's not too bloody late.'

Carrington blinked. 'Reports ...?'

'Yes, Carrington. Reports. Reports. Reports from our spies at the dockside at Le Havre about munitions stored there, awaiting shipment to Boston. Namely:' Pownall read from the top report of the sheaf in his hand, '"fifty-two brass cannon, with carriages and iron worms and rammers; 20,000 four-pound cannon balls; 9,000 grenades, about 6,500 muskets," then we get tents, tools – like spades and pickaxes – blankets, black stockings for God's sake, handkerchiefs!' He lowered the reports. 'There are no accounts of the French sending the rebels perfume but I'm sure it's only a matter of time.'

'Was that d'Éon, sir? Mr Pownall, with respect, I have fifty men, sir. Just fifty. And with that I'm supposed to maintain the watch on Wilkes, on the likes of …'

John Pownall sighed. 'All right, all right. Stop whining, man. It was not d'Éon. At least not directly.' Pownall gave an ironic mock-smile. 'I am about to contribute to your much-neglected education, Carrington. The gentleman involved in the arms shipment from Le Havre was Pierre-Augustin Caron de Beaumarchais. Playwright and spy. He was sent to England to make contact with d'Éon. D'Éon introduced him to Wilkes.'

Nathan Carrington whistled. 'That ain't good, sir.'

'Indeed not. Beaumarchais became a frequent visitor at the Mansion House, visiting Wilkes as Lord Mayor. He arranged for Wilkes to receive money from the French Ambassador.'

Nathan Carrington went bright red. He spluttered. 'I beg your pardon? Excuse me, sir, but are you telling me the Lord Mayor of London is in the pay of the French?'

John Pownall applauded, ironically. 'Bravo, Carrington. Sharp as a tack, as ever.'

'Can't we stop it?'

'How, you fool? If we arrested Wilkes there would be a revolution. He's the Lord Mayor of bloody London, isn't he? May I continue?'

'Yes, sir. Excuse me, sir.'

'Inevitably, under Wilkes's spell, Beaumarchais became an even more enthusiastic believer in the American rebel cause than he was before. This would matter somewhat less if he had not become an arms dealer of some note.'

Nathan Carrington whistled, fascinated. 'How did he get into that, sir? The arms trade.'

'The usual way. Through a patron. Beaumarchais has set up a company to export arms to Adams and the rebels. Their first purchase is a stroke of genius on Beaumarchais' part. It is a ship appropriately named *Hippopotame*. That means hippopotamus, Carrington. Large animal.'

Carrington gave a smile, albeit a tense one: 'I know, sir.'

'They called it that because there is 900 tons of it. Massive beast. The *Hippopotame* is such a clever idea because it has been fitted out to serve as both battleship and cargo ship.'

Carrington's eyes were wide: 'When are they sailing, sir? Do we know?'

'No, we don't. They will be making a secret arms run from Le Havre. If we can alert the navy and stop that, capture or sink the ship, they will almost certainly give up the idea of supplying the American militia with arms. Policy failed, after a fortune spent on the ship. You see?'

'Yes, sir.'

'But if the *Hippopotame* gets through on this trial run to Boston, then the French will use it to guard future arms flotillas to the American militias and to carry munitions itself. Policy succeeded.'

'We do need that sailing date, sir. So that we can alert …'

'Yes! Yes! And we shall get it, Carrington. Now, listen to me. Beaumarchais' new play is to run at Drury Lane this very evening. It is entitled *The Barber of Seville*, apparently. It has not even opened in France yet. This is a sort of rehearsal, I gather. And that is our good fortune, Carrington, because Beaumarchais is to attend this performance and take notes.'

'Do we know where he is living, sir?'

'No, of course we don't, you bloody fool. Otherwise we could seize him now. Unlike d'Éon, we don't have to worry about diplomatic protection. You and as many men as you think fit will attend this performance at Drury

275

Lane, Carrington. You will seize Beaumarchais, carry him off somewhere and get the sailing date of the *Hippopotame* out of him with rack and screw. Clear?'

'Yes, sir. Very clear sir.'

'Then keep him under lock and key, somewhere, incommunicado until the ship sails. I shall alert the navy as soon as I know the sailing date.'

'Excellent, sir!'

'Well, it should be. My wife and I will be at the performance this evening, Carrington. Cheer you on. My wife tells me the piece is meant to be a comedy. I can hardly wait. Report to me this evening at the theatre with news of your prisoner, when you have taken Beaumarchais.'

'Yes, sir.' Nathan Carrington cleared his throat. 'There is one more thing, Mr Pownall, which might be germane.'

Pownall poured himself more wine. 'All right. Come on, man. Spit it out.'

'We followed d'Éon to a meeting with Wilkes, Mr Pownall.'

'Yes, yes. Interesting. But the universe continues on its serene way, as Mr Newton has described for us. As I said before, they meet from time to time. Quite often, in fact. Was that it?'

'D'Éon's meeting with Wilkes was at the home of your brother, sir. Mr Thomas Pownall.'

John Pownall gave a small gasp but recovered quickly. 'Maintain a watch on my brother's house.'

'Yes, sir.'

CHAPTER 53

In a private box high in the third tier of Drury Lane Theatre, Mary Pownall, née Lillingston, fanned herself vigorously against the heat and the smells. Her thin, angular frame was encased in a green and yellow hooped gown with what her husband thought were over-elaborate lace trimmings, and prissy – again in John's view – green satin slippers.

The style of the dress, John Pownall was thinking, was out of date and made her appear even more provincial than she usually did. The red cardinal cloak clumsily draped over her gilt chair, spilling onto the floor, made the overall impression even more careless.

There was no style to it, no grace. She was still a daughter of Ferriby, in Yorkshire; still impervious to the ways of London society. She was an embarrassment to the London gentleman John felt he had become, his Lincolnshire roots now well buried.

'This is nice,' Mary said to her husband, turning her pointy-nosed, pretty face to him. She sniffed. 'You should escort me out more often, John. Is this the third or the fourth time, since we've been married?'

John Pownall was staring down at the ground floor, far below, trying to catch a glimpse of Carrington, or any of his men, or even of Beaumarchais himself, as he presumably watched from the wings. No luck so far.

He vaguely registered that his wife had spoken, without troubling to hear what she said.

The play was well under way. More for something to do than any real interest he glanced at the stage, where a servant, who apparently went by the name of Figaro, was going through some sort of convoluted machinations on behalf of his master. The whole enterprise appeared to revel in the undermining of authority. What was this foreign balderdash doing on the London stage?

Occasionally, roars of laughter would erupt from the audience, all happily chatting, eating, having mock swordfights on the edge of the stage or calling out ribald remarks to the actors, who as often as not replied in kind.

'So, it's a comedy, is it?' John spoke flatly into the air, unspeakably bored.

He squirmed on his horsehair-padded chair. He had started to put weight back on now the drink had taken hold of him. His plum-coloured velvet coat was too small, his red waistcoat too tight and his yellow cummerbund hardly restrained his rounded stomach. Normally, he would not be seen dead here. He longed to stop wasting his time in this manner.

'Yes, John,' Mary replied, with irony worthy of her husband. 'It is a comedy, which is why you hear people laughing. It's a comedy in four acts, in fact. But there are rumours that Mr Beaumarchais is dissatisfied with it. He intends, so I have heard, to rewrite it for Paris in five acts, making it more serious.'

John blew out his cheeks. God's socks but her bloody Yorkshire accent was irritating. He hoped he would have got used to it by now but he never did.

He noticed something on the stage. 'Is that not somewhat reminiscent of *Romeo and Juliet*?'

Mary gave a small smile. 'Yes, John. There is Lindor, you see? He is serenading Rosine beneath her window. It is a satire on *Romeo and Juliet*.'

'He's got a bloody nerve. Satirising our own bloody Bard. Our swan of bloody Avon …'

'How much have you had to drink?'

'Not nearly enough. This piece of stinking fish should be taken off and sent back to France where they can presumably eat it.'

'Beaumarchais wrote this play out of indignation at the Boston Massacre. Does that help?' Her dark eyes were dancing.

'Whaat!' He suddenly wished he had had fewer

brandies before coming out.

Mary continued, eyes innocently wide. 'One of Figaro's lines, directly inspired by Boston's noble resistance to you, John, is "A tiny gust that extinguishes a candle can ignite an inferno."'

'Well, that's typical, isn't it? Woolly confusion. It's the candle that ignites, not the bloody gust. And this candle can't ignite anything because the gust just extinguished it.'

She laughed like a bell. 'Oh, just now and again I can remember why I married you.'

John smiled, then laughed, briefly. 'No, Mary. Seriously. What I want to know is what happens *after* the servants have become the masters? When Figaro and Sam Adams are running the bloody show. Who deals with the mess caused by people having the power to make decisions they have neither the knowledge nor the judgement to make? Like Adams's bloody Town Meetings.'

Mary rolled her eyes in open boredom, then fanned herself, giving a quick glance at a beau who was smiling at her from the adjoining box.

'John, dear, why don't you try reading the play? Mr Beaumarchais has published the text in English, as it currently stands. We have it in the drawing room at home, as a matter of fact. On that little round mahogany table. There is one line that rather struck me. Figaro says "I always laugh at everything for fear I might cry."'

John Pownall snorted. 'These days, I never laugh at anything for fear I might look happy.'

Mary smiled at him. 'That was rather good, John. You should try writing plays.'

John leaned towards her and kissed her on the lips. 'And you should stop looking at that young man.'

They both laughed.

'See, you do laugh. You should do that more often, you know,' she said.

'What? Laugh? Or kiss you?'

'Both.'

'Fair enough.'

But he still could not see Carrington, however hard he looked.

Nathan Carrington appeared at their box in the interval. 'May I have a word, Mr Pownall? Perhaps outside?'

Pownall left the box without a word to Mary. In the corridor outside he gripped Carrington by both arms. 'Well? Speak, man.'

'Bad news, I'm afraid. That French ship, the *Hippo* ... It has already sailed.'

'What? What are you telling me, man? Have you apprehended Beaumarchais? Have you got that out of him on the rack? Or what?'

Carrington shook his large head. 'We found Monsieur Beaumarchais. He laughed in our faces. He said the ship sailed ten days ago.'

'And you just believed him?'

'He was telling the truth, Mr Pownall.'

Nathan Carrington drew himself up to his full height, a head taller than Pownall. Here, outside the American Department and in charge of his own men, he felt more confident.

Pownall, too, was conscious of his loss of authority. 'The whole damn war could depend on this,' he muttered.

But there was a defeated air about him.

'I 'ad other reasons to believe Beaumarchais, Mr Pownall. One of my men – a reliable chap – his brother was one of the spies at Le Havre, reporting to the Earl of Sandwich. He is newly returned, the brother that is. He saw the ship sail with his own eyes. I have the pair of them with me, if you want to question them.'

Pownall was silent for a moment. Even if the Admiralty would listen to him, which was doubtful, they could not stop a ship at sea in time. Adams would get his munitions. And a plentiful supply there was too.

Ignoring Nathan Carrington, John Pownall returned to

his box. Down below on the stage, Figaro was involved in a complex scene involving his master's desire to possess Figaro's wife.

Mary had gone. Her red cardinal was no longer draped over the chair. The young man from the adjoining box had gone too. Some of his young friends were laughing at him.

CHAPTER 54

Back at his desk at the American Department the next day, John Pownall believed he was thinking with pellucid clearness, despite the drink. The one hope of stopping a war the Americans might well win was to arrest the ringleaders and bring them back to London.

As Gage had failed to act on the warrants sent to him, he, John Pownall, would have to travel to Boston with fresh warrants to get the job done. He knew from Lord North that the King himself was still in favour of arresting the patriot leaders. But he wanted something stronger than the Henry VIII Act the clerks had dug out before. The Henry VIII Act enabled extradition warrants only, not arrest warrants.

John Pownall did the research himself this time, not entrusting it to the clerks. He located a copy of the 1351 Treason Act, which was stronger than the Henry VIII statute. Under its terms, the destruction of the tea in Boston harbour could certainly be construed as an act of war against the Crown. He applied for warrants under that statute for the arrest of Samuel Adams, Thomas Young and John Hancock.

Lord North continued to back Pownall to the hilt, promptly furnishing him with a *laissez-passer* confirming that he was about the King's business and should not face let or hindrance but should be aided in his every request.

The Chief Clerk, William Pollock, booked him on the next sailing to Boston, aboard the sloop *Falcon*, a mail-packet leaving from Falmouth. He was to carry money for the army and sealed orders for General Gage – or Governor-General Gage as he was to be addressed.

Nathan Carrington furnished him with the latest in personal armaments – a pistol which primed itself.

Only one matter remained to be resolved before he left London for Boston: a reckoning with his older brother, Thomas. John felt Thomas plotting with Wilkes, of all people, and with the French, to be in some ill-defined sense a personal betrayal of him. 'How could you?' he said over and over again in his mind to his brother.

A Pandora's Box of resentment opened in John. It was unworthy, he knew that. But why did Thomas have a mansion designed by James Vardy, so much more splendid than his own, admittedly handsome house?

He, John, was a significant figure in English colonial administration, was he not? And what was Thomas? He was an ever-plumper figure of fun nobody listened to. Yet Thomas did better and always had done. The butterfly Thomas had gone to Cambridge and he, with all his industry and application, had not.

John thought of the Hogarth engraving series *Industry and Idleness*. The series told the story of two brothers, the Idle and the Industrious Apprentice. The Idle Apprentice is executed at Tyburn, while his brother, the Industrious Apprentice, becomes Lord Mayor of London.

But in the Pownall family, John reflected sourly, it is the Idle Apprentice who prevails. He may not quite become Lord Mayor of London himself, but he hobnobs with him in traitorous liaison. The Industrious Apprentice is a cuckold who is becoming over-fond of red wine and whose life's work now faces ruin.

John forbade himself any further dwelling on life's misfortunes and the fickleness of fate.

Thomas Pownall still desperately wished to return to Boston. Deep in his soul, he had wanted nothing else since he was forced to leave. But now, after the Boston Port Act and the other measures against the American colonies, he was seized by a desperate yearning to live among Bostonians, to help them, to serve them, to become one of them again.

He had shyly, almost timidly mentioned his desire over dinner, served, as ever, by a dozen liveried footmen. With a glacial smile, Lady Fawkener – his wife, Harriet

283

– reminded him that he had severely limited wealth in his own right. Most of his money was in fact her money. The home he currently dwelled in belonged to her, she pointed out. Her annuity from an endowment was sealed. It was hers. He had no access to it.

'If you leave here for Boston, you abandon your responsibilities to me as your wife and to our children. In that case, Thomas, you will leave this house a very poor man and a very poor man you shall remain, I and my family will see to that. Now ring the bell for the fish course, there's a good boy, and don't ever mention this matter again.'

Being poor at his age was not something Thomas Pownall could encompass. And in any case he loved his stepsons. He loved Harriet, too, in a placid sort of way. He obediently rang the bell to let the butler know they were ready for the next course.

But he had heard his younger brother was to set sail for Boston and he determined then and there on a reckoning before John left.

A meeting in either brother's house, in front of one or other of their wives, was inconceivable to both of them. And Thomas was not to be fobbed off, as he saw it, by a meeting in public, in one of the hostelries John was so fond of, though John briefly toyed with the idea.

They met at the American Department. William Pollock did not even try to stop the clerks listening from the next room.

John got in first, as soon as Thomas walked into the office.

'You are a traitor, Thomas. I could have you arrested for treason.'

'Traitor? What on earth …?'

'You consort with the King's enemies; you encourage and abet them. Wilkes, Beaumarchais, d'Éon. I have the reports, Thomas.'

From behind his desk, John waved the reports at him.

'I consort with the French, as you put it, to arrange arms for the Boston militia.'

'Agh! So you admit …'

'Yes, I most certainly do! I help send arms to the Boston militia so they have a fighting chance. If they take on the might of the British Empire with the weapons they have they will be slaughtered. Every last man Jack of them.'

'The answer, perhaps, Thomas, is not to take on the British Empire at all but to conduct themselves as loyal subjects in gratitude for all that has been done for them.'

'Gratitude? People like you and North …' Thomas hesitated. He was about to say 'and the King' but thought better of it. 'People like you and North have left them in a state of vassaldom, unable to prosper or progress as a society.'

Thomas was standing in front of John's desk like a supplicant, so he was at a disadvantage. But he snarled in a way John had never seen before. It twisted his face. All the older brother's good nature was gone.

'You are a fool, Thomas. You are a naive simpleton. You always were. Gullible to a fault.'

'And you are a murderer. Your Port Act will destroy Boston. People will die there, people I have loved, and their blood will be on your hands.'

'On my hands? On my hands?'

'You make misery, John. With your every action. You always did. Only misery and stink and rancour. You are not a good man. Indeed, you are evil. You are creating death and destruction. You have become a destroyer of worlds.'

'You blame me? That is rich! Even for someone with your woolly grasp of logic that is rich. Blame your beloved Bostonians for letting themselves be led like sheep over a cliff by the likes of Adams. I am restoring order. I am restoring the *natural* order or there will be chaos.'

'You talk of chaos, John. You, the harbinger of war. The

whole town of Concord has been turned into a munitions base. The militia are drilling on Boston Common. When I left, in my last days as Governor, these were the most loyal of the King's subjects on this earth, bar none. What have you done to them?'

'Yes. Blame me for everything. You always did. It can't be fat Thomas's fault. Fat Thomas is perfect. Mummy's boy!'

There were tears in John's eyes; he was sounding more and more childish even to himself. He stood, came round to the front of the desk and pushed Thomas in the chest. Thomas growled and pushed him back. Then Thomas slapped John round the face. They were both breathing heavily.

John dropped his hands to his sides. 'We are no longer brothers, Thomas.'

'I concur most heartily and thankfully. We are no longer brothers.'

And with that, Thomas left.

CHAPTER 55

Margaret Gage and Thomas Young were again meeting at the Crown Coffee House. As soon as the drinks came, she spoke.

'John Pownall is on his way here.'

Thomas Young nodded, thoughtfully. John Pownall had joined Boston's pantheon of infamy. He had been hanged in effigy at the Liberty Tree. He was a figure to strike fear in the heart of man.

'Are you sure?' Young said.

Margaret tossed her head, impatiently. 'I've seen letters from him. He is on the high seas on a ship called the *Falcon*. He has warrants for the arrest for treason of you, Adams and Hancock. My husband is instructed to give him every assistance in the execution of the warrants. This time. You, Adams and Hancock are to be brought back to London in chains on a warship. They want to hang you.'

Young whistled softly, then sipped at his ale. 'So they really mean it?'

'In deadly earnest.'

Young shrugged. 'Let them try.'

Margaret's blue eyes flashed in a way Thomas had not seen before. 'Thomas, are you stupid, or do you think I am?'

Thomas gave a grim smile. 'All right. What do you think I should do?'

'Run, Thomas. Now. Pownall will be landing any day.'

'But my family …'

'Thomas, your family will be fine if you are not there. If you run with them and they catch you they will not be fine. And they will slow you down. Take this evening to say goodbye to your folks and go tomorrow. Adams and Hancock need to do the same.'

'I must warn them.'

'I already have. I sent a runner with a message.'

Young shut his eyes for a moment. 'You are right, aren't you?'

'I tend to be.'

'I'll just finish my ale, then.'

'No, don't. Go now. Go. Kiss Mary. Leave in the morning.'

Thomas and Mary Young held each other tight.

'I don't want to do this,' Thomas said.

'You have to, Thomas. John Pownall is one dirty scoundrel. I won't have him take you. I'll scratch his eyes out first. When we can, the children and I will follow you. Like we did from New York.'

'Yes. Then it was just heresy. The water is even hotter this time.'

'That's my Thomas! My fisher in troubled waters. And I love you for it.'

'Mary!'

Thomas squeezed her until she gasped. Both of them were crying. The children were supposed to be at school but they were still there and joined in the hug.

'Give 'em hell, Daddy!' Rosmond said.

'I will do my level best,' Thomas said, laughter replacing his tears. 'I thought I would never leave here.'

'You fought and you fought well,' Mary said.

'I'll send for you all, just as soon as I can.'

'I know you will. I know. And you will head for Newport, yes? To my folks there? You got that? You won't get distracted and end up in China or somewhere?'

'No. I promise most solemnly, Mary. Newport, not China. And don't worry, Gage's Lobster Backs won't get me, either. I've come this far. I'm damned if I'm gonna let him nab me now.'

'I packed you a bag. A shirt and drawers. A spare blue jerkin. And your Richard Mead *Short Discourse* book. And John Locke. And there's some pie. Some apples …'

Thomas broke down, weeping his heart out. All the

288

children started crying.

'Go now, my darling,' Mary said. 'Go or you will miss the coach. We will see you very soon.'

Mary and the children never saw Thomas Young again. He headed for Newport, as he told Mary he would, but Mary's people there were too poor to help him. So he travelled on to Vermont. There, Thomas Young caught yellow fever which he was not able to cure.

He died quickly, with Mary's name on his lips and her image before him.

CHAPTER 56

As soon as he arrived in Boston, John Pownall plunged into meetings with Governor-General Thomas Gage and his staff. He found Colonel Francis Smith the most congenial of Gage's staff, and the Scottish Major, John Pitcairn, the most pleasingly anti-Bostonian. But he viewed Major John Kemble's American background with suspicion. It had to be tolerated, however, as he was Gage's brother-in-law.

Gage himself was a worry. The Governor-General had that dead-behind-the-eyes look of a man paralysed by fear. Action would have to be wrung from him unwillingly, and with the support of the officers under him, especially Colonel Smith and Major Pitcairn, the ones with the most influence over him.

At the very first meeting at Castle William, Pownall was informed that Young, Adams and Hancock had fled Boston, so his warrants could not be served. Pownall exploded with rage, thumping the oak table at the planning room where they were gathered.

'I have come three thousand miles. Could they not have been held to await my arrival? Is that too much to ask?'

'I'm afraid it is, Mr Pownall,' Major Kemble said, calmly. 'Even here in the wilds we have to abide by the rule of law. No arrest before a warrant is served.'

'And do they obey the rule of law in their dealings with us?' Pownall muttered it beneath his breath. The officers pretended they had not heard.

Colonel Smith, who understood Pownall's anger and sympathised with it, evenly informed him that George Hayley had also fled, taking Anne Hayley with him. As Smith had guessed, Pownall was intending to arrest Wilkes's sister and her husband, even though he had no warrant to do so.

However, one of Pownall's plans did come to fruition.

John Pownall produced the last two reports written to him by William Molineux, the Mohuck leader. The most recent was eighteen months ago. Pownall had suspected the hand of Adams in the reports well before that.

'I would like these reports taken to Mr Molineux by a uniformed officer and returned to him with requests for clarification as per the accompanying note.'

'Presented to him at home?' said Major Kemble, impishly.

The other officers had understood as well; there was laughter round the table.

'Leave it with me,' Major Pitcairn said, in his rolling Fife accent. He held out his hands for the documents.

William Molineux's reports to Pownall were presented to him in the middle of a Mohuck caucus meeting at the Long Room Club. In Adams's absence, Molineux was chairing the meeting when it was interrupted by two Redcoats, led by Major Pitcairn.

The caucus meeting fell silent. Enjoying himself hugely, Major Pitcairn placed Molineux's reports on the table in front of him.

'Under-Secretary John Pownall of the American Department in London presents his compliments and requests clarification of one or two items in your reports to him, as indicated, at your earliest convenience, sir.'

Major Pitcairn and the two Redcoats then saluted and left.

There was silence at the meeting. The visit from the Lobster Backs was obviously a staged event. But it was equally obvious, not least from Molineux's ashen-faced look of guilty dread, that the reports were genuine. The London-born present even recognised his writing.

William Molineux took up the reports. He dearly wished he knew where Adams was – far away, he supposed. Adams would have spoken for him. But one glance at the faces round the table told him any explanation from Molineux himself would be useless, including what he

291

knew to be the truth about the reports, that they had been planned to confuse the British.

'Excuse me, gentlemen,' he said, and quietly left the room, taking the reports with him.

He walked slowly back to his home in Middle Street where he secreted a loaded musket under his jerkin. He then walked to the Ann Street Bridge, over Mill Creek, where he put the musket to his temple and blew the top of his head off.

CHAPTER 57

Under-Secretary John Pownall saw first-hand how life was lived in Boston after his Boston Port Act had begun to bite. For the first time in Boston's history, there was not a topsail vessel in sight in the harbour, except for warships and transport vessels bringing fresh troops, who were housed in tent towns on the Common or on the Neck.

With the British sea blockade tightly in place, the food shortage was felt almost immediately. The farmers from outlying areas of Massachusetts sent in what food they could; olive oil, fish, rye and Indian corn came in by ox-cart. But the Massachusetts farmers and homesteaders were hungry themselves and could not send food they did not have.

The people of Charlestown, just over the Charles River, managed to get a sloop across under the eyes of the British navy. It was loaded to the gunwales with barrels of rice. After that, the British used Nantucket whaleboats, far smaller than their warships, to patrol the inland waterways to stop any supplies getting in that way and stop fishermen bringing their catches into Boston.

Sam Adams, in exile, was in touch with many of the other American colonies and most of them sent what money they could, or they sent flour, fish, beef cattle, pork, grain, rice and provisions of all kinds on laborious journeys overland.

The patriots organised pledges not to buy British goods. These were held in the centre of Boston as publicly as possible every day. A statement from the absent Adams was read aloud, distributed on handbills and published in the *Boston Gazette* and the *Massachusetts Spy*.

'Fourteen regiments are now assembled in this capital and reinforcements are expected to put this barbarous Boston Port Act into execution. The People are determined that this shall not be done.'

Nevertheless, the citizenry with enough money to leave Boston left in droves; the roads were clogged with carriages and carts. Those who stayed, stayed to an increasingly lawless town. There were robberies and assaults on every street. Street gangs formed, stealing money and food wherever they could find it.

Clashes with patrols of British troops increased. One patrol, looking for hidden arms, was stopped by a spontaneous crowd of men, women and children, many of whom were armed. Women were beginning to take the lead in confronting British patrols.

The only enterprises still thriving were brothels and liquor stores, all protected by armed guards. A renewed outbreak of smallpox punished the population further. But the most visible and public sign of the change wrought by the Boston Port Act was on the inn names and inn signs of Boston.

On every street in the town, down came every reference to a king so loved in Governor Pownall's time and so utterly hated now: The Crown Coffee House was renamed the Boston Coffee House. Its sign with a representation of the royal crown was burned for fuel and replaced by a sign with a tricorn hat with a Wilkes cockade on it. Every crown and sceptre, every lion and unicorn went up in flames to be replaced by Wilkes's symbols.

Public buildings were draped in black. The church bells rang out a mournful tocsin incessantly.

The Sons of Liberty, shorn of their main leadership, still issued a Solemn League and Covenant, forbidding all aid and succour to British troops. Officers' bills were not accepted in stores. Contractors refused to supply fresh meat to the army.

Gage gave orders to fortify the Neck. The old fortifications were strengthened, and new fortifications were built. Two 24-pounders and eight 9-pounders were placed in front of Castle William, facing Boston.

The building of the new fortifications offered just about the only work to be had in Boston, especially as the British also set up new brickyards to make the bricks. Any American working there risked incurring the wrath of the Mohucks. But in the absence of Adams and now Molineux, many Bostonians on the edge of starvation took the risk.

Then the patriots relented before the poor starved to death in front of their eyes. They held a Town Meeting. It was called and led, in Adams's absence, by the Mohuck silversmith Paul Revere. At the meeting, they agreed to allow Bostonians to work building wharves and houses on town land, though still not the barracks for the British army. Cleaning docks was also allowed, or digging wells, or working in the brickyards.

Colonel Francis Smith increasingly took charge of war preparations, from the British side. Virtually none of the inexperienced British troops had had gunnery training. Smith took the men in groups of twenty to be taught and practise gunnery on the slopes above Black Bay. He also set up baggage stores to hold equipment too heavy to be carried, as it was clear to all the British military leadership that they would have to march out of Boston and fight soon.

The patriots carried out their own war preparations, armed militia drilling openly on the Common under Captain Parker under the noses of British troops newly arrived from Quebec and New York, quartered in tents on the edge of the Common. The militia were being readied to fight at a minute's notice. The new rapid reaction forces were called Minutemen and there were thousands of them.

There were also less public acts of war. Gunsmiths were the only legitimate trade still flourishing, as muskets were sold under the counter. A 15-pound Brown Bess could be had for four dollars. Women in the countryside were melting pewter plates to make bullets for the muskets.

The British powder store was at Quarry Hill, in Charlestown, six miles north of Boston, up near the cornfields of the Mystic River. It was left completely unguarded, as it was thought to be safe out there, on the far side of the Charles River. The militia under Captain Parker raided it and took as much of the powder as they could carry.

A humiliated Governor-General Gage was left justifying the theft in a letter to Dartmouth. Gage did not mention in the letter that until more powder was obtained, a war could not be fought against the Boston militia.

The theft of the gunpowder made the deployment of troops outside Castle William inevitable, as the British had to recapture enough gunpowder to fight with. Gage, expecting an attack on Castle William at any minute, dashed off a panic-laden letter to North requesting as many men as had been deployed to conquer Canada. There was no reply. North and the cabinet expected Gage to lead a force from Castle William and engage the enemy with the troops he had.

But before Gage could mobilise the few men at his disposal, an even more daring raid and theft than the one on the gunpowder store was inflicted on the suffering Governor-General. Now the Mohucks had lost Molineux, Henry Bass led the raid. It was on the British gun house at Tremont Street.

In broad daylight, in fact on the stroke of noon, Bass and four other Mohucks distracted the sentinel, then unlimbered three 6-inch cannon, under the noses of the guards. In a considerable feat of strength the five men hauled the guns one by one through a nearby garden, then attached them to waiting ox-carts.

The ox-carts pulled them to Concord, where they were added to a huge cache of cannon, muskets – now transferred from Faneuil Hall – ball-powder, foodstuffs, even tents, axes and shoes, all stolen from British troops the length and breadth of Massachusetts.

The stolen cannon were three of the five brought in when the mass of British troops arrived. The other two cannon were still outside the now empty Assembly building, where the British had first put them. The three stolen cannon were the ones Colonel Smith had been using to give the British troops artillery training.

At that point, news reached Castle William of a massive French arms shipment landed at Braintree from Le Havre. The arms had been rapidly transferred by night to the already mighty arms store at Concord.

General Gage's inaction was no longer a viable option. Under pressure from North and Dartmouth in London and Colonel Smith and Major Pitcairn from his own staff, Gage reluctantly agreed to mount an attack on the Quarry Hill powder store to recover at least some of his stolen powder, as a prelude to attacking Concord. A force of 200 British troops overcame the militia guard that had been left on the powder store. The raid was successful.

Attention then turned to the patriot arms store at Concord. Gage attempted to delay an attack until reinforcements arrived. Then he delayed for fear of antagonising the other colonies. Finally, no further prevarication was possible.

Governor-General Gage prepared to move against the rebel arms store at Concord.

CHAPTER 58

Soldiers under Major Pitcairn had visited Young's house in Wing's Lane the day after he left. Mary Young, surrounded by the children, told Pitcairn her husband had returned to New York.

'He is long gone, out of your clutches,' she said to the Major.

'That is as may be, ma'am, but by your leave, we'll search the house.'

'Go ahead.'

Major Pitcairn reported to Gage that Young had left Boston. As visits to the houses of Adams, Hancock and Hayley also showed the men gone and clothes and possessions gone with them, Gage and his staff assumed they had all fled Boston, too.

The British were correct about Adams, Hancock and the Hayleys having left Boston, but their assumption that, like Young, they had left Massachusetts was wrong. They had gone only as far as Lexington, a modest town ten miles from Boston and six miles from the arms and munitions store at Concord.

Adams, Hancock and the Hayleys were staying at Buckman's Tavern, an inn overlooking the Green at the centre of Lexington. The Mohuck silversmith Paul Revere sought out Adams alone there, to share the latest intelligence from Boston, most of it gleaned from footmen at the Province House where Gage was living and where he frequently left military plans open on his desk.

Over wine and cakes, Paul Revere indicated that a well-armed raid on the Concord munitions base was imminent. The entire shipment delivered by the *Hippopotame*, not to mention all those muskets kept and cleaned and cherished at Faneuil Hall over all those years, was at risk, as was the revolution itself.

'We fight, don't we, Sam?' said the silversmith, not

really asking.

'Yes, we fight,' Adams said, his head and hands shaking badly from the palsy.

Revere let out a windy sigh of relief, his plain round face, not unlike an uncut cheese, dividing with relief.

'I'll tell Parker you authorised a defence of Concord.'

'No. Tell Parker to come and see me, himself. Right now, please, Paul.'

Adams made sure he spoke to Captain John Parker in private, walking in the nearby burial ground in the weak spring sunshine.

John Parker looked the part of a military leader. He was well over six feet tall and broadly framed. He had a classically handsome face with unruly, long, curly chestnut-brown hair. As he strode through the burial ground, taking one step to every two of Samuel Adams, he waited for the man he regarded as his commander to speak.

As Adams showed no sign of doing so, eventually, as they reached the newest of the gravestones at the outer perimeter of the burial ground, Parker spoke himself.

'If you order a defence of Concord, I am confident we can hold the munitions store until reinforcements come from the countryside. We will prevail, I believe.'

Adams cleared his throat, a little out of breath from even this short walk. 'Captain Parker, I do not wish a defensive operation to be mounted at Concord. You are to mount an offensive operation instead, attacking the British force as it passes through Lexington, on the Green here, before they get to Concord.'

Parker's normally impassive face looked stunned. 'Sir, in an exposed position out on the Green, we would take casualties. We would take far more than if we dug in at Concord.'

'I know,' Adams said. 'John, our business is to make Britain share in the miseries which she has unrighteously brought upon us.'

'I see.'

'I wonder if you do. John, America herself under God must finally work out her own salvation.'

Parker's fair clear complexion coloured. 'And we do that by taking more casualties than we would at Concord?'

'Yes. Because the tumult will help John Wilkes swing enough of London behind us to bring North down. It will help bring the French into the war on our side, something we must achieve to have any hope of success. Our deaths will not have been in vain, but for the greater good.'

'Did you know I hail from Lexington, Mr Adams?'

Adams looked taken aback, but only for a second. 'No, I didn't.'

'My father, Josiah, and my mother, Anna, were born in Lexington, too. I was brought up among the people who have houses on the Green. Some of them will likely be killed.'

John Parker suddenly doubled over with a coughing fit.

'Are you ill, John?'

'It will pass. I need a direct order to muster the troops at Lexington Green, not Concord.'

'I give you that direct order.'

Captain Parker came to attention, saluting as smartly as he had during his brave and distinguished service fighting for the British against the French and the Mohawk Indians.

'Yes, sir,' he said. 'Order received and understood.'

Then he doubled up with coughing again.

CHAPTER 59

Back in Boston, the bells of Christ Church, between Charter and Tilleston Streets, rang out in warning of a coming British attack. They were the first church bells ever to arrive in Boston. They had once called the faithful to prayer in Chagford, Devon, where John Rowe had spent his boyhood.

In further warnings, the sexton of Christ Church hung two lanterns in the steeple, signalling a land attack. It would have been one lantern for a sea attack over the Charles River. The same signal was shown from the Old North Church, in Market Square.

There was also intelligence that the *Somerset* man-of-war had newly moved into position, blocking the river. Runners hastened to the Mohuck leaders with this intelligence.

As soon as they saw and heard all these signs, many patriots took it upon themselves to ride the short distance to Lexington with a message: 'The British are coming.'

The first man to arrive at Buckman's Tavern with a warning to the patriots was William Dawes junior, a tanner, but more importantly an accomplished actor who had no trouble bluffing his way past the guards at the Neck. Dawes took the best route, via Roxbury. Edward Proctor arrived second, then Paul Revere, who had gone via Charlestown, then a whole group more.

Seven hundred British infantrymen had been placed under the command of Colonel Francis Smith. Second-in-command was Major John Pitcairn.

The force was ferried over the Charles River, landing at Phipps Farm in Cambridge, from where they set off on the road past Lexington to Concord. By now, Adams's and Hancock's hiding place in Lexington had become known, so John Pownall rode with the soldiers to serve the arrest warrants. He was armed with the self-priming pistol Nathan Carrington had supplied.

Under-Secretary Pownall was elated. He was certain Adams and Hancock would be in chains by this evening, and George and Anne Hayley, too, even though there was no warrant for them. They would all be his prisoners aboard a man-of-war sailing for England within the week. Eventually, they would find Young in New York and arrest him, too.

Around him, the British troops showed every sign of low morale. Some of them were drunk. None of them were comfortable. They were wet – they had slogged through a marsh and waded through a long ford up to their middles.

Many of these soldiers had joined the army because they had no other choice, but they also dreamed of derring-do, brave deeds in faraway places. Being part of a detested army of occupation, loathed day and night, week after week, sapped their spirits. The scornful glances of pretty women in the street or in the inns were especially painful.

When Smith and Pitcairn ordered the seizure of civilians they met on the march to act as hostages, the soldiers disliked doing that. These civilians were no different from the farmers the Redcoats knew from back home. One of the hostages they seized, Simon Winship, was from Lexington and knew Captain John Parker and his family well.

There were more military reasons for low morale: the Boston militia was already running rings round them, stealing cannon from under their noses. A milksop operation to steal back some of their own powder, which was protected only by sentries, made their humiliation worse, if anything.

Also lowering to morale, the soldiers had only one day's provisions, no knapsacks and only thirty-six rounds of ammunition per man. The few seasoned veterans among the troops knew this was nowhere near enough. If the militia gave battle they would quickly run out of ammunition. Those same veterans knew Gage should have resupplied them from carts on the far side of the Charles River, once they had crossed. The carts had been expected but did not appear, which sent morale down even further.

Major Pitcairn's advance party of nearly 300 marines reached the Common at Lexington, to find the Americans assembled and ready at the Bedford Road, near the tip of the Green.

Captain Parker had drawn up seventy of his militia in three ranks, as he had been trained to do and as the militia had practised for months, if not years. Parker turned to his drummer and ordered him to beat to arms. The Americans walked forward in single file.

Some of the drunken element of the Redcoats started yelling out the 'Yankee Doodle' song, mocking the Americans. A loose bunch of Redcoats charged without an order and began firing on the run, though their muskets were charged only with powder.

Major Pitcairn felt he had no option but to order an attack, to protect these now exposed men. He yelled out 'Lay down your arms, you damned rebels, or you are all dead men. Fire!'

Captain Parker was standing to the side of the first row of his troops. Adams and Hancock stood next to him. Hancock was armed with a cutlass, which he was brandishing, and a pistol in his left hand. Adams was unarmed.

Hancock was peering into the early dusk, trying to calculate how many men the British had. Adams's palsy had mysteriously cleared for the first time in twenty years. He felt like a young man again, with carmine blood coursing through his veins. He knew the Boston militia were armed with the most modern muskets, good powder and fine munitions from the *Hippopotame* shipment.

Adams shouted 'Fire!'

Captain Parker echoed the command.

The first row of Americans fired their newly landed French ammunition at the British Redcoats, then passed through to the rear to reload while the second rank opened fire.

As the British returned fire, at near-point blank range, eight Bostonians fell dead and ten were wounded. Simon Winship, the captured friend of Captain Parker's family, was shot in the back. John Parker watched him die, as he was racked by the coughing which presaged his own death from consumption just two months later.

John Pownall was riding next to Colonel Smith, when the bulky commander arrived with the 10th Regiment of Foot in support of Pitcairn. He saw Smith get a flesh wound in the arm from a fusillade from the third rank of the American militia.

But all his attention, all his being, was concentrated on Samuel Adams. He pictured Samuel Adams in his mind, quite accurately; he had an etching of Adams in his study. He used to stare at it while he was working.

As the battle raged, he called out 'Adams, I have a warrant for your arrest.' But nobody heard him.

The warrant was never served.

In later years, John Wilkes claimed he sat bolt upright in an armchair at the Lord Mayor of London's residence, the Mansion House, having heard a shot at the precise moment the firing started at Lexington. A smile of delight crossed his face. He was quick to spread the good news in the *London Evening Post*.

Lord North sent an offer of conciliation: backed by the cabinet, he offered to end taxation of the colonies if the colonies agreed to pay the costs of their own civil governments, courts of law and defence. As paying the costs amounted to handing back control of these areas to the colonies, this offer was everything the colonists had ever asked for.

It reached Boston just after the war between England and America had started.

AUTHOR'S NOTE

This is a novel, a work of fiction. It follows the main outline of events in sources classified as non-fiction, but where the demands of drama clash with accounts in the historical record, I have followed the demands of drama.

Author

Michael Dean has a history degree from Worcester College, Oxford, an MSc in Applied Linguistics from Edinburgh University and a translator's qualification (AIL) in German.

He has published several novels. *The Darkness into Light* omnibus (Sharpe Books, 2017): *The Rise and Fall of the Nazis* comprises five titles: *Before the Darkness* – about the German Jewish Foreign Minister Walther Rathenau, assassinated in 1922; *The Crooked Cross* – about Hitler and art; *The Enemy Within* – about Dutch resistance during the Nazi occupation; *Hour Zero* – about Germany in 1946; Magic City – a novel of Jewish identity set in Germany in the early 1970s.

He also published some stand-alone novels: *Thorn*, (Bluemoose Books, 2011) about Spinoza and Rembrandt; *I, Hogarth* (Duckworth-Overlook, 2012), which sets out to unify Hogarth's life with his art; *The White Crucifixion*, a novel about Marc Chagall, was published by Holland Park Press in February 2018.

His non-fiction includes a book about Chomsky and many educational publications.

Holland Park Press is a privately-owned independent company publishing literary fiction: novels, novellas, short stories; and poetry. It was founded in 2009. It is run by brother and sister, Arnold and Bernadette Jansen op de Haar, who publish an author not just a book. Holland Park Press specialises in finding new literary talent by accepting unsolicited manuscripts from authors all year round and by running competitions. It has been successful in giving older authors a chance to make their debut and in raising the profile of Dutch authors in translation.

To

Learn more about Michael Dean
Discover other interesting books
Read our unique Anglo-Dutch magazine
Find out how to submit your manuscript
Take part in one of our competitions

Visit www.hollandparkpress.co.uk

Bookshop: http://www.hollandparkpress.co.uk/category/all/

Holland Park Press in the social media:

http://www.twitter.com/HollandParkPres
http://www.facebook.com/HollandParkPress
http://www.linkedin.com/company/holland-park-press
http://www.youtube.com/user/HollandParkPress